Praise for

James A. Moore and *Serenity Falls*

Coming in July

The Pack: Serenity Falls, Book II

Coming August

Dark Carnival: Serenity Falls, Book III

continued...

WRIT IN BLOOD

Serenity Falls, Book I

JAMES A. MOORE

JOVE BOOKS, NEW YORK

THE BERKLEY PUBLISHING GROUP
Published by the Penguin Group
Penguin Group (USA) Inc.
375 Hudson Street, New York, New York 10014, USA
Penguin Group (Canada), 10 Alcorn Avenue, Toronto, Ontario M4V 3B2, Canada
(a division of Pearson Penguin Canada Inc.)
Penguin Books Ltd., 80 Strand, London WC2R 0RL, England
Penguin Group Ireland, 25 St. Stephen's Green, Dublin 2, Ireland (a division of Penguin Books Ltd.)
Penguin Group (Australia), 250 Camberwell Road, Camberwell, Victoria 3124, Australia
(a division of Pearson Australia Group Pty. Ltd.)
Penguin Books India Pvt. Ltd., 11 Community Centre, Panchsheel Park, New Delhi—110 017, India
Penguin Group (NZ) Cnr. Airborne and Rosedale Roads, Albany, Auckland 1310, New Zealand
(a division of Pearson New Zealand Ltd.)
Penguin Books (South Africa) (Pty.) Ltd., 24 Sturdee Avenue, Rosebank, Johannesburg 2196, South

Penguin Books Ltd., Registered Offices: 80 Strand, London WC2R 0RL, England

This is a work of fiction. Names, characters, places, and incidents either are the product of the author's imagination or are used fictitiously, and any resemblance to actual persons, living or dead, business establishments, events, or locales is entirely coincidental.

WRIT IN BLOOD

A Jove Book / published by arrangement with the author.

PRINTING HISTORY
Jove mass-market edition / June 2005

Copyright © 2003 by James A. Moore.
Book design by Stacy Irwin.

For information address: The Berkley Publishing Group,
a division of Penguin Group (USA) Inc.,
375 Hudson Street, New York, New York 10014.

ISBN: 0-515-13968-8

JOVE®
Jove Books are published by The Berkley Publishing Group,
a division of Penguin Group (USA) Inc.,
375 Hudson Street, New York, New York 10014.
JOVE is a registered trademark of Penguin Group (USA) Inc.
The "J" design is a trademark belonging to Penguin Group (USA) Inc.

PRINTED IN THE UNITED STATES OF AMERICA

10 9 8 7 6 5 4 3 2 1

the man had walked on, forgotten all about him. He did his best to stay conscious through the waves of torturous suffering, did his best to make certain that he did nothing to promote any actions from the man he once trusted. Tommy finally tried counting to one hundred, and then, in a near frenzy by the end of the count, he opened his eyes.

For the briefest of moments hope launched an assault on his soul, fooling him into believing that Mr. Donnelley was gone. Then his eyes focused on the hand that blocked his view. From this perspective he could see the blood that had crusted in the wrinkles and lines of the wide palm; he could see the blisters that had formed on soft hands put to serious labor. He was still studying the patterns of ruin when he first smelled the smoke.

Then Donnelley moved his hand away, revealed for Tommy the devastation that had previously been behind him. The entire view was similar to what he had looked at throughout the night: buildings with shattered windows, the bodies of old friends and familiar faces lying strewn carelessly across the asphalt and on the sidewalks, crimson stains running into the gutters. But there was one major difference: looking from his new perspective, Tommy could see the flames that were growing to consume the remains of both buildings and people.

"See? Just like I told you. The pain will be gone soon." Tommy had believed himself to be fairly grown-up, certainly more mature than his brother John, and John was fourteen—would have been fourteen. But it was simply too much. He was tired, he hurt, and everyone he knew was dead. Even as he watched, the fire grew closer, made blurry temporarily by the silent tears that fell from his blood-crusted eyes.

The fire stopped the tears only a few minutes later. The screams lasted a great deal longer.

The figure of Frederick Donnelley walked slowly, casually away from the center of town, confident that the flames would not touch him. Twenty minutes later, he reached the sign that led into the town proper. It read:

Welcome to Silver Springs
The prettiest little town in Arizona
Population 7,384

Below the dark blue sign were several other smaller signs, legends that proudly called attention to the Rotary, the Lions Club, and a few other similar organizations. The figure of Frederick Donnelley ignored them all, pausing only to chuckle softly at the population count.

Behind him the sun shone down on *the "prettiest little town in Arizona"* as brightly as it ever did, apparently oblivious to the devastation that lay in the fires started by Donnelley. The flames fought against the glory of the sun, struggled to be seen by anyone near, but the only person who could have noticed no longer cared.

Frederick Donnelley lit a cigarette and stared at the desert that stretched in all directions, broken only by the road that led to Silver Springs. The smoke from his cigarette blew toward the south, and Donnelley decided that was as good a direction as any. "Well, that was fun. I needed that." He spoke to no one, and no one answered his comment.

As he walked, he let his mind drift, let himself get reacquainted with senses that had been dormant for far too long. He sniffed the air and caught the pleasing scents of burning flesh and boiling blood. They made his mouth water. They were also a distraction, so he blocked off the aromas and spread his senses farther. His awareness rippled slowly away, drifting across the borderlines placed on countless maps. To the north and the east, he found what he was seeking and let a slow, gradually building smile stretch the corners of his mouth until his teeth were bared, and his lips were threatening to split. "Hunter . . . How very nice. I've been looking forward to seeing you again."

He had only walked for a few minutes, just long enough to finish his cigarette, when the winds started blowing hard enough to stagger him. The gale-force winds lifted desert sand into the air, aiming at Donnelley's back as he walked. The only objects of size that moved other than Donnelley were the tumbleweeds that rolled past as if trying to escape the remains of Silver Springs. Anyone watching would have thought Donnelley was being carried at three times his previous speed. His figure dwindled rapidly as he walked slowly toward the distant horizon.

Donnelley's physical essence was reduced to a fine, silvery ash as the wind struck against him. The ash was carried along with the sands, floating long past the point where the heavier sands were forced back to earth. The winds started moving to the northeast instead of south, and the ash floated along for the ride. And unseen by the life-forms that skittered across the desert, something else went along with the ashes and sand, something that hissed as it lifted into the air.

CHAPTER 1

I

Simon MacGruder walked wherever he went, with amazingly few exceptions. He had a car; he just preferred to use his feet. Seventy-three years of walking on planet Earth had not changed that. He doubted anything would ever change his mind on the idea of a good, brisk walk.

The winter was over, and spring was stretching into full bloom. What better time to start his project? For years he'd promised himself that he would write a book, and he'd always found a dozen or more reasons not to get around to it, but today just felt right. After all, in good health or not, he wasn't getting any younger, and in order to write the particular piece he had in mind, he was going to need to do a little research. Serenity Falls was a small town, but there was still a lot of history in the area and a lot of people he needed to talk to before he actually tried to put that history in a legible order.

Simon loved the town. He had been in love with it for decades, in all honesty. But he wasn't really a part of it as far as a lot of people were concerned. He lived in the woods not far from the town proper and had never seen much of a reason to move closer. He had always been a loner, by choice, thank you very much. It wasn't that he didn't like people, but rather that he seemed only able to tolerate them in very small doses.

Simon MacGruder was fascinated by people, but not to the point where he normally went out of his way to see them.

So instead he had decided to write about them. Though, in all honesty, he never expected anyone to see his history of Serenity Falls, or to even find anyone who would be remotely interested.

The road into Serenity was hardly straight. It took a lot of strange curves as it moved through the foothills of upstate New York. For that reason, Simon walked through the woods around the road, often cutting off a substantial part of his walking time.

And as he walked, he pulled out his tape recorder and spoke to himself, reciting a few of the facts that he knew about the townsfolk.

"Well, it's easy to say there's a lot of people I don't know well in Serenity Falls, but it's also true that I know more of them than most folks do. I'm not talking about the muckety-mucks in office or even the constables who try to keep everything properly taken care of, mind you. I'm just talking about people. Those I don't know well are probably fifty years younger than me, and most of the ones closing in on my own age are either dead or decrepit.

"That's all right. I probably ain't long for the world myself. So let's get her done, as my daddy used to say. There's a lot of families in Serenity that have been around these parts for damned near forever. Most of them aren't worth a cup of tobacco juice, but they have a big part of the history around here stuck to their butts, so I'll be visiting with most of them.

"Of course there are a few I can't visit with anymore. Near as I can figure, almost every family of the original settlers around here died out. But I'll get to them when the time is right, and not a minute sooner."

He took his time with the walk and took advantage of the peace and quiet to cover a lot of the basics for his introductory chapter.

II

Serenity Falls Part One:
From a Bird's-Eye View

Seen from a bird's-eye view, Serenity Falls is a pretty little town. To the west lies a series of foothills and even mountains in the far distance. Running from the mountains through the hills and almost all the way to the town itself is a crystal-clear flow of water. There is no name for the river, as in fact it spends most of its time under-ground, gurgling placidly in places where no human be-ing has ever set foot.

Just at the edge of the foothills, before the town comes into view, the waters break out of the ground at the site of the Blackwell Granite Quarry, or what used to be the quarry before the business went belly-up. The deep cuts made by man are mostly hidden these days beneath the waters that flow quietly through the crust of the earth. The pumps that stopped them from filling the quarry are long silent, dead and forgotten by most. Chil-dren like to use the quarry as their swimming pool, a lit-tle oasis from the heat of the late spring and early summer. It's been that way for over a decade.

Just past the quarry proper, on the road that moves lazily toward the town of Serenity Falls, is the house the quarry owner used to live in with his family. Its founda-tion was cut from the very same granite deposits. Even after fifteen years of abandonment, the house stands strong and proud, if a little neglected by the people who built it. Its grandeur is hidden in a grove of trees, many of which are older than the town itself.

Beyond that is Serenity Falls proper. Serenity isn't a big town, but neither is it small. The population is just over five thousand people, down a bit from what it was only a few years earlier. The death of the man who owned the quarry left many people without work for a while, and the town suffered for the loss on many levels. Many people left the area, searching for greener pastures, as it were. Some may have even found them. For the people who remained behind, times were—and in some cases still are—lean, but they endured. Commuting to the city became a way of life, but living in Serenity Falls—often called Serenity, or even just The Falls—was what they wanted, and they endured.

Just lately Serenity has been getting a face-lift of sorts, reaching back into the ideals of the past and refurbishing many of the main roads to look more like they might have in Colonial times—or at least the way Hollywood has often portrayed the era when European settlers made their homes in the New World. Several of the buildings at the heart of the town are still standing from when the town was settled. They have been preserved as a reminder of the roots of the country, and the county pays to keep them as historical landmarks. Given another year or two, most of the locals figure the rest of the shopping areas will finally look like they belong with the new, improved, old-fashioned facade. There's a little enthusiasm for the notion, too, as a few more tourists showed up this year than in the previous few.

Of course, Serenity Falls has a few strange notions about it. The cemetery where most every family has buried their dead over the years since the town was founded rests almost smack in the middle of Serenity. It's just a fluke, a side effect of the way in which the town was built, but more than a few of the people who've passed through the area have noticed it. There are two churches and a synagogue facing the burial grounds, on the other side of the low stone wall around the entire lawn covered with an endless array of stone sculptures and memorials to those who have shed the mortal coil. Dunhaven Street surrounds the graveyard, and to the north the three houses of God all sit close to each other, rather like triplets that have nothing whatsoever in common. Off to the west are the municipal buildings, the emergency center, and a few small businesses, mostly restaurants like Frannie's Donut Hut—a favorite with the constables and a place that sells far more than merely donuts—and convenience stores. To the east you'll find a collection of streets that spreads out in a leisurely fan, moving off to become varying subdivisions that have sprouted over the years. They might not have grown in this odd fashion, but the lay of the land almost demanded it. There are four grocery stores in the town, and each and every one of them is down one of the roads leading to the different neighborhoods. To the south of the cemetery is what the children refer to as Prison Row, the elementary school, standing alone, and next to it the combination junior high school and high school proper. There were plans to build another building once upon a time, but the money has never really been there. The two buildings are actually separated only by a small breezeway that stretches from one to the other like an umbilical cord made of bricks and glass. Just as with the houses of God, they seem to have little in common from the outside. Inside, they have even less in common. Oh, to be sure, they are all institutes of learning, but let's not kid ourselves; the children who dwell in each of these buildings are as different from each other as snowflakes are from charcoal ash. Age and experience have divided them. That doesn't mean they don't meet from time to time—many of them are related to one another, after all—but when they run across each other, it is seldom on equal footing. That's hardly unique to the town of Serenity Falls, however.

There's enough going on to keep most people there from getting bored. The YMCA often has a few activities planned, and the football, basketball, and baseball teams, while not always winners, are certainly energetic enough to devour most weekend nights. Even when they aren't playing at home, a lot of people cheer on the locals, making an event of the long journeys to the next town over. There're plenty of places to eat, and the drive-in is easily accessed in the comfortable months. And there are books, television complete with cable, and social gatherings to take away the worst chances of boredom.

Serenity Falls used to be one of the stops for the trains, many years ago. That's how the town got on the map, as a weigh station of sorts. But the trains don't work the way they did before the invention of tractor trailers, and the need for people to stop by faded long ago. These days, most people who don't commute to the city content themselves by running one of a dozen or more shops and restaurants or working the farms to the east of town. Not just wheat or cattle in The Falls, there are also several small vineyards that produce fine grapes for a few wineries. Mostly the kids stay away from the vineyards; they know that many of the farmers out that way carry shotguns loaded with salt to remind trespassers that the produce they grow is not for free. Also, almost universally, the farmers have dogs, and the dogs are known for having attitude problems as sincere and mean as those of the farmers when it comes to the uninvited masses.

To the north of Serenity Falls is civilization. There are other towns, some as lazy but not many as pretty as far as the citizens of The Falls are concerned. And beyond them, not far away but still an eternity from the peace and quiet of the little town, is the city. Business, crime, and more noise than most want to think about. Serenity could possibly be called a suburb of the city, but in fact it is a little far away to be an extension in any real sense of the word.

Like all places, from time to time Serenity has bad weather. There was a storm, and while it was hardly the worst storm ever, it carried something dark within its bowels . . .

III

The phone's bell cut through the darkness of the very early morning for exactly three rings. Before the fourth could shrill its way through his skull, he'd answered the damned contraption.

"Hi. If you're trying to sell me something this early in the morning, be prepared to run and hide, because I will kill you."

"Mr. Crowley?" The voice on the other end sounded puzzled.

"Right the first time, cupcake. Who's this?"

The voice was familiar, but then most of the ones who called him were. Almost no one called Jonathan Crowley without knowing exactly who they were reaching.

"It's Kristen Rainer. I don't know if you remember me . . ."

"Of course I do, Kristen. I never forget a good student. They're hard to come by."

He could practically hear her blush through the phone, though they had not run across each other in over twenty years.

"I was just thinking about you the other day and talking to Dan, my husband. I just got stuck on the idea of saying hello."

Crowley put on his glasses and looked around his darkened bedroom, ignoring the idle chatter but paying just enough attention to make sure he could answer any comments that needed a response. She wasn't just thinking about him. That wasn't the way it worked. She was responding to the simple enchantment he'd used on her two decades earlier, when her sorority sister at the university had tried to sell her soul for better grades. Lois Parker had a great body and a good brain and just enough stupidity in her to think she could sell her soul and somehow get it back later, after she's gotten a perfect score on all of her tests for four years.

It never worked out that way. Not for the amateurs. He caught wind of the problem when her grades wound up being perfect, even on the tests she didn't show up for. Happily for the damned fool, he'd managed to remove the source of her perfect scores before it tore her soul into little shreds. Kristen Rainer had been one of the witnesses to his actions. He'd made her forget but had given her a way to contact him if she ever ran across another problem.

And that was the only reason he could imagine that she would have for calling him. "So what's been happening lately in your neck of the woods, Kristen?"

"Oh not much that isn't the usual. You know, a body here, a body there." She laughed, trying to make light of the deaths. If he remembered correctly, Kristen was majoring in criminology back in the day. Gallows humor wasn't really all that unusual in that field. "But there's one case that's really got me a little freaked out, you know? There's someone going around killing girls, and from what the police are saying, which isn't much, it looks like it's ritualistic."

"Really? Well, you know me, the parapsychologist. What's been going on?"

Crowley walked around the room in the darkness, listening to every word the girl spoke. She was a good student back then, and that much hadn't changed. She had all the details that had been given to the public down pat. He grabbed his bags as he listened, making all the right noises to get her to say as much as she knew.

And when she was done, and he was finished gathering his supplies for the trip, he asked her a simple question.

"Are you asking for my help, Kristen?"

"Well, yes, Mr. Crowley. I guess I am."

"That's all I needed to hear, Kristen. I'll be there as soon as I can."

She hung up her phone, and if he'd set it up the right

way, she went back to her bed and her husband Dan and went immediately back to sleep. She wouldn't remember the call. They never did.

That was for the best, really. Few people like to remember the bad things in their world.

CHAPTER 2

I

Simon MacGruder blinked his eyes and looked around the musty room. Most of his day had already been spent looking over the oldest documents that the town had of its history, and now he was looking through stacks of ancient letters and notes from the Hall of Records for Serenity Falls. It sounded so austere: Hall of Records. It was a closet in the library, and he'd been carefully looking over the cartons of paperwork while he took meticulous notes.

Most of what the papers said was beyond boring. Most of it was notes on what happened in the town over the span of 300 years and about as exciting to read as it was to watch the stubble grow on his own chin. Somebody somewhere might find it fascinating, if there was a certain twist of the skull in reading what the price of feed was like 170 years ago, but it was not exactly the sort of thing that was significant.

But there were nuggets there. Little things, really. Notes made in the ledgers of town meetings and letters from one loved one to another. They told a story, if you were careful and tried not to read too much into them. It was easy to read too much. You just had to consider the source of the writings and understand that not every sentence was guaranteed to have a double entendre.

But even then, after a good deal of looking, certain patterns began to show. It was in what was said and what was not. It was the fine lines between the written words that held the best secrets.

Simon took meticulous notes and then set them aside, accepting that there might be something to notice. And then he found the mother lode, as it were, the actual notes on the first trial ever held in Serenity. The trial took place the first year the settlement was established, and the notes he found written in what was left of an old family Bible convinced him that he was onto something.

His eyes ached by the time he was done for the day, and his head pounded with a pulse all its own. He'd done it, though; collected the information he needed for the first part of the book. It was interesting stuff when you got past the amazingly dry details of life back in Colonial times.

He stopped by Frannie's Donut Hut on his way back to the cabin he called home. Frannie was there as always, and so were a few of the people in town who thought he was extra-special eccentric. He nodded to

Frannie and indicated that coffee would be nice. She told him the specials, and he decided to go with a New York strip steak, medium rare, with home fries and a piece of apple pie. The lady who owned the place was brown-haired, with brown eyes, and as tired-looking as he'd ever seen her. She was also in one of her don't-ask-and-I-won't-tell moods. He knew when to leave well enough alone.

At the table next to his, Mike Blake was sipping coffee and counting change. Mike was the local bum, a shame considering what he had once been in his life, and he was likely counting up the money for another bottle of cheap, sweet oblivion. He was too busy counting change to bother Simon, and the old man was happy for that. Whenever the man asked for change, Simon felt obligated to give it to him, even knowing what the money would likely go for. The way the man's wife had been slaughtered was enough to make anyone turn to drinking, and Simon already knew that turning him down would do no good anyway. He'd been down that path himself a long time ago.

He ate quickly and left a decent tip for Frannie. Then he slipped two dollars to Mike as he left the diner. Mike smiled his thanks, and Simon regretted giving him the money. Once upon a time Mike had been a handsome enough lad and prosperous. These days, well, his looks hadn't completely left him. That was something.

He walked home in the warm spring air as the sun was setting. His legs ached, and his head was still throbbing from all of the eyestrain. But he felt good. It was nice to get off his ass and actually do something. He savored the walk home and ignored the pain in his hips and knees.

And still, after all of that, when he got to his cabin, he sat at his desk and started writing, checking his notes often for details.

II

Serenity Falls Part Two:
The Burning of Sarah Hopkins Miles

Sarah Hopkins Miles was not well thought of by the community of Serenity. She was far too independent for that to ever be the case. Her husband had left for England not long after Niles Wilcox first decided the area was perfect for settling. Someone had to go back for supplies, and he was one of the most trusted of the lot brought to the area. The trust Wilcox showed in her husband, however, did not necessarily mean that Sarah herself was above reproach. Sarah worked hard on finishing the tasks her husband had begun. She cut wood and laid the stones that were the foundation for their home in the New World. She tended to their meager farm, tilling the earth and planting the crops, while her husband was doing the work of making certain there were enough supplies for everyone and reporting on exactly where the settlement was located for the purposes of being acknowledged by the Crown.

Sarah was not alone in her duties. There were other women in similar situations, and a few of them were just as independent and determined to eke out a living as she was. Though the men left in the settlement did what they could, these good wives were left to their own devices far more often than not.

It's been said that Niles Wilcox was a stern man, and that much is true. He was not the sort of community leader who felt that anyone should be at ease when they were all dependent on each other for surviving in the colonies. For that reason if no other, the people of Serenity were responsible for tending to the women left behind when their husbands were required to make the long journey back to England. And in order to make certain that the duties were handled properly, he often visited each and every one of the small homes in the area to make certain that everyone was doing what they could.

From time to time he was reported to make extra visits to the home of Sarah Hopkins Miles. It's possible that he was merely being neighborly, merely taking care of seeing that the wife of one of his followers was well and her house sturdy enough to fend off the elements. Certainly no one in the settlement would have considered it likely that the dour man was doing anything he shouldn't have been doing while making his visitations. Wilcox was a devout man, and he was not known to let his eyes stray from his own wife.

But the possibility was there, even if no one spoke of it.

Sarah was, by all accounts, a woman of striking beauty. Though she dressed plainly and was never seen to use her good looks to lure men from the proper course of action, she was the cause of more than one quiet argument behind closed doors between husband and wife. Contrary to many of the beliefs held about the Puritans, they were rather open about certain sorts of matters, infidelity among them. Husbands and wives each had their duties to perform and each had a say in how well the other was performing those tasks, be they pleasant or not. They might not have spoken of such matters to others—save as a last recourse—but they did speak. Sarah Hopkins Miles was one of the subjects that several married couples discussed. There were accusations—apparently unfounded—and there were fights. It was almost inevitable when one considered the situation.

Sarah herself was not privy to the conversations and would have quickly scolded anyone who dared mention improprieties to her. She was a married woman, after all, and doing her best to survive in a bleak situation. That, and she was too busy to even consider the notion of doing anything out of place.

There was a farm to tend and a house to build. She managed both tasks with almost no help from others, save the occasional assistance in the planing of lumber. By the time her days were done, the last thing on Earth that Sarah would have considered was any sort of extra-marital affair. Exhaustion and near starvation were far more likely her companions than any of the men in the area. Sarah had a hard time that first year in the Colonies. She managed to grow enough to survive, but only by eating sparingly and working herself harder than anyone would have thought her capable of.

She was not alone in her ethics. Most of the people in Serenity found little time for relaxing that first year. The winter was quick to let everyone know that there would be no rest for the weary. The weather was bitterly cold, and the snows were deep. Aside from taking care of the occasional town business, most people stayed in their homes, prepared to weather the worst of the season. Niles Wilcox was the exception. The dour man made it a point to check on the wives left behind by the husbands away on town business, and he did so almost every day.

Perhaps it was the frustration of waiting out the cold days and nights; perhaps there was more to the story. Whatever the case, by the time winter was finally ending, the people of Serenity were changed. They were bitter and disillusioned, and many feared that there was simply no way they could hope to withstand another winter as fierce as their first in the New World.

Fear can make people do strange things. When spring finally made its way to Serenity, it brought occasional visitors and they, in turn, brought news. Much of what they had to say was common and mundane, but there were a few who brought tales of witchery and devil worship to the north. There were trials and hangings and burnings going on in Massachusetts and in other places as well. The tales almost always involved women, females who were lonely and easily corrupted by Lucifer to do his dark bidding.

It was said that he rewarded his servants with favors and with pleasure. And around Serenity it soon became easy to believe that some just might actually be in league with the devil. Some, like Sarah Hopkins Miles.

There was talk that Sarah had placed Niles Wilcox under a spell in an effort to seduce him away from the righteous path. It wasn't so great a leap for many of the people, especially after hearing that he went to her house so often. And from that idle rumor—started by the wife of Niles Wilcox—others soon blossomed. Sarah had been seen by no less than three of the women in Serenity dancing naked in the woods after midnight; the fact that none of the three should have been out after midnight and roaming through the woods was not found significant. One woman even explained that she had heard a strange noise and seen Sarah in the woods behind her house. According to the woman—a direct ancestor of Becky Glass and her family—Sarah Hopkins Miles had been fornicating with a goat. From that point on, the rumors only grew stranger and more perverse.

While it was true that the winter was over, Sarah was far too busy with tending her farm to pay much attention to the strange stories, even if she had been privy to them. She had made a vow to her husband that she would have the homestead completed by the time he came back from his long journey, and it was a vow she took seriously, even if he'd made it clear he didn't expect her to manage the feat without him. Sarah worked hard to keep that promise, and in the early part of the spring, she was successful.

Two weeks later, the men of the town came to her and accused her of witchcraft. The accusations were strong, made by women who were well-respected and trustworthy. The leader of the band was none other than

Niles Wilcox, who knew his very life depended on making certain she was properly tried and convicted.

Nothing had ever happened between Niles and Sarah. There had never been so much as a stolen kiss. Sarah would have never considered the idea and Niles . . . Niles was far too afraid to pursue the desires he hid in his heart. He was a married, God-fearing man, and no amount of lust would take him from the righteous path. At least in his own mind.

That is, until the time came to make Sarah confess to the sins of which she had been accused. It can be said with great sincerity that Niles Wilcox did indeed get inventive with his tortures and that a good number of them involved carnal acts of lust. By the time he was finished with her, Sarah Hopkins Miles had been used and mistreated in every way imaginable.

Some would even say that death was an acceptable release from the memories of what was done to her by the good and moral leader of the community. Her death sentence was handled quickly and efficiently, shortly after her tongue was burned with coals to keep her from telling anyone of the sins he committed upon her unwilling flesh.

The community of Serenity agreed that her death was necessary and the only proper recourse to the accusations she confessed to. Sarah was wrapped in bands of hot lead, which were folded over her body in an effort to prevent any possible use of witchcraft as an aid to protecting herself. The burns were bad, no doubt about that. They were bad enough that Sarah passed out from the blistering heat. She was taken deep into the woods, not far from where the stone of what would later become the Blackwell Granite Quarry thrust from the ground. Once there, she was placed, barely conscious and trying to talk past her ruined tongue, among several large pieces of granite that rose from the ground, surrounded by wood and leaves and anything combustible. The wood was set afire, and in short order the flames reached Sarah. She screamed, according to the few documents that remain, for almost twenty minutes before the fire and smoke finally killed her. When the fires had cooled sufficiently, her ashes were scatted through the woods to prevent her ever causing any more mischief.

Her husband did not take the news well. He came back after a long trip and found his wife dead, murdered by his neighbors and by the people he'd trusted to take care of her. Niles Wilcox looked at him and dared accuse his wife of treacherous unions with Satan. Wilcox looked away first; he could not hold the gaze of the man he'd sent to do his bidding in England.

Upon hearing of what happened to his wife in his absence, Albert Miles took his belongings and headed for Boston and the very next ship away from the Colonies. Before leaving, however, he made emphatically clear to his neighbors that what they had done was a sin and that they would suffer for their acts. They would suffer, and so would their descendants. His final act before heading away from the settlement was to burn to the ground the house his wife had built, a final way of ensuring that they would take nothing else from her or anything that had been touched by her hands.

Quite naturally, the people of Serenity had been very mistaken. Sarah Hopkins Miles was not a witch. She had no dealings with darker forces nor any desire to copulate with demons.

The same could not be said for her husband. Albert Miles was driven from England some years later for his arrangements with things unchristian. In time he came back to Serenity and laid the plans for his revenge. Albert Miles was a man who always kept his promises.

III

Crowley knew he was, once again and to his perpetual disgust, in the middle of nowhere. The only radio stations he could get included two specializing in country music, a talk radio show where some clown was telling anyone who would listen that guns didn't kill people, people did, and of all things a hard rap station that was pounding out tale of poor, misunderstood gangstas who only wanted their whores, their homies, and their money. If they had to kill a few hundred cops in the process, that was apparently just fine. Not really what he expected to find in Colorado, but then, he didn't really expect to find much of anything in Colorado but snow bunnies and cowboys. Imagine his surprise.

He gave up and put in a Santana CD.

It'd been a few years since he'd come through this part of the state, and he had to look carefully for the side road that broke off from I-70 and led into the small town of Summitville. He wound his way around Lake Overtree and drove slowly and steadily into what he tended to think of as the world's only xenophobic yuppie refuge. Summitville was a collection of working farms, a small, tidy little town of ridiculously nice incomes, and a few stores that had no right to stay in business without a tourist trade, all sitting perched under a lake that could easily drown the entire thing if it ever decided to break through the dirt barrier that held it in check.

He had no real desire to go into the town again, it certainly held no special feelings for him, but he needed to check on a few things. There had been a few problems in Summitville, and in particular there was one troublemaker he needed to make sure was keeping his nose clean.

Phillip James Sanderson was not the brightest man on the planet, but he was successful. Having read the man's stuff, Crowley often wondered why. He wasn't all that original, and his stories always involved the same themes.

Also, he was a whiner. He cringed on the occasions that he dealt with Crowley, and that was one of the things that set his teeth on edge. The other thing was when people like P. J. Sanderson, best-selling author, decided to dabble in magic. The fool had almost cost several people their lives because he played around with a book when he was a teenager. And there were several people who died because of the same stunt.

The man was ever so apologetic when he was confronted, and in his defense he did help make it right. But that didn't get him off the hook in Jonathan Crowley's eyes, because he could tell that the man was still interested. He still wanted to try it again. So he decided to drop by and pay the hack a visit.

He stopped outside of the bookstore the man owned and ran. The doors were locked, and there was no sign of life from inside. Crowley walked up to the darkened windows and stared at his own reflection in the glass. His face was lean and average. His eyes, hidden behind rimless glasses, were brown, the same as his hair. It was not a remarkable face. He liked it that way.

The dial on his watch said it was noon. He walked away from the Basilisk Bookstore and wandered into the woods. Off a short distance was a subdivision where several kids had been caught up in the problems created by Sanderson. He moved in that general direction, stepping into the heavy foliage and sliding effortlessly between the trees. The sounds of birds and small animals moving through the area came to his ears, and he smiled. That was a good sign. Nature provided its inhabitants with more common sense than most humans would ever experience. Unlike people, animals tended to get the hell out of Dodge when things went sour. The wildlife hanging around wasn't a guarantee of things going smoothly, but it didn't hurt, either.

He did not enter the subdivision. He merely watched for a while. There were people down there, some of them good and some of them bad. He resisted the temptation to check on them.

"They're just fine living their lives. Why cause them any grief?" He spoke the words softly and only to himself. Despite the temptation to check on a few of them, like Tyler Wilson, a kid with the worst manners he'd ever run across and enough testosterone to guarantee he'd get his skinny body waffle stomped, he chose to leave them in peace. Not that they would remember him. Not unless he wanted them to.

Best not to get attached; it always caused trouble later.

He'd had enough of that sort of insanity a long time ago.

There was something out here. Something in the woods that most definitely did not want to be seen by him. The thought brought a smile to his face. Most people upon seeing that smile would have left the area as quickly and quietly as possible.

Jonathan Crowley moved toward the Basilisk Bookstore with a spring in his step. He wanted to know where his little buddy Philly was, and he intended to find out. Business to take care of and all of that.

Getting into the building was child's play. The security system was a joke. Crowley slid through a second-story window into the old house and looked around Sanderson's bedroom. Not much had changed. It still smelled like the crappy cologne the author wore, and his bed was as messy as could be expected from any life-long bachelor. There was a large stack of books next to the bed, easily a hundred or so, most of them waiting to be read. They were mostly horror novels and a few advance reader copies by authors Crowley had never heard of. There were always likely to be a few newer writers hoping for a blurb or two.

He left the bedroom after making sure the books were fiction and not the sort of stuff that Sanderson should be staying away from. The man was in good shape so far. Crowley didn't feel the need to hunt him down and kill him.

He checked the rest of the house and then went down into the bookstore that made up most of the first floor. The lights were off, and there were easily a dozen messages waiting in the answering machine. Tempting though it was, Crowley decided not to listen to them. Instead, he made a quick search through the books lining the shelves and then turned on the computer set above everything else on an island in the center of the store. If he remembered correctly, the man wrote most of his novels while working down in the store. It probably kept him from going stir crazy. Summitville wasn't a booming metropolis, and the bookstore was almost more of a showcase for his own books from what Crowley could see.

He opened several files that were supposed to be secure and looked over the contents. Mostly it was chapters for novels.

He opened a new file and wrote a short letter.

Dear Philly, so sorry I missed you. It's been too long, and I haven't had a chance to check up on you. I want to make sure that you're keeping up with your good behavior.

How's tricks? How's your little friend, Mark? How's the nephew and niece? I hope you haven't gotten them in any more trouble. Make sure to call me if you need me. You know the number.

Keep behaving,
Jonathan Crowley

PS, read the first few chapters of Night's Prayer. Not bad. Not the best I've read, but better than I've seen you write before.

He saved the file and turned off the computer. He was done here.

Crowley left the building a few minutes later. Missing his chance to terrify Philly had put him in a sour mood. Still, much as he wanted a chance to wreak a little havoc, he didn't really have the time. Someone was committing murders in New York, and he wanted to see what he could find out.

He left Summitville a little while later, convinced that he would have to visit again soon.

Something was out in the woods, and it was hiding. Whatever it was, he suspected he wouldn't like it much. And Jonathan Crowley tended to like little as much as he liked killing what offended his sensibilities.

CHAPTER 3

I

There was a lot of history in Serenity Falls, and unfortunately that meant looking at a lot of musty old books and files. He'd have preferred just talking to the local people and remembering the stories that his grandmother had told him, but Simon MacGruder intended to be thorough in his research.

And what the hell, at least it got him out of the house. He hadn't walked this much in years, it seemed. It wasn't long before he started running into people. The first of them was Mike Blake, though the man was in no shape to notice. Blake was passed out at the edge of the cemetery. He was sleeping in the shadow of his wife's headstone. Amy Blake had been a good woman. Simon remembered her fondly. He still couldn't believe that anyone would have murdered such a sweet young lady in that fashion. Oh, the police had tried to keep it quiet, but there was no hiding the nature of the crime in a town the size of Serenity Falls.

Thinking about it gave him the creeps, so he walked on, looking at some of the spectacular markers he found toward the center of the massive graveyard, in the heart of the beast as it were, after making sure that Mikey was still breathing. There were pieces of art in that cemetery, something he felt that a lot of people failed to appreciate. In addition to the numerous traditional markers, there were statues that had been carved in loving memory of some of the people whose families had been interred in these very grounds for almost three centuries. Niles Wilcox's headstone was plain, but there were several descendants of the town founder who had what could only properly be called mansions laid out for them. Their crypts were elaborate affairs with carved angels surrounding them and stained glass windows to shine down the light from Heaven onto their final resting places. Even after more than a hundred years, the crypts were still nearly perfect, if a bit weather worn. On the few occasions when the elements had taken their toll on the heavy, leaded glass, someone or other had come along and paid to have the pieces replaced by real artisans, using traditional methods from decades gone by. Not many people spoke of such affairs in Serenity Falls—it was almost like a dirty little secret—but the cemetery in the heart of the town was a point of pride. Occasionally someone had managed to leave a piece of trash on the well-groomed lawn, but aside from poor old Mike, there was nothing else that was amiss in the area. Vandalism just didn't happen. There was more of a sense of propriety for the cemetery than there was for the houses of God, as far as Simon could tell. And that was a bit of all right in his book, too. His own family was among the headstones.

The bells at the high school were ringing out into the morning air, and he could see the last few stragglers hurrying their pace as they got their five-minute warning. The only exception was one of the Pageant kids, a stocky boy with wheat-colored hair and glasses, who walked on at the exact same pace. If Simon didn't know that Dave Pageant wasn't deaf, he might have had doubts. The boy saw him, blinked twice in surprise, and then plodded on, smiling as if he'd seen a rare bird. Simon thought maybe he had at that. He was well aware of his own reputation among the children in town as a hermit. It had been brought to his attention years ago, and he still found it humorous.

Simon spent the majority of the day reading the few journals he could locate that dated back to the very beginning of Serenity, before the name was changed to Serenity Falls. Long before, as in before the United States existed. He did so with incredible care in the one case where he was allowed to read the original book, as the pages were ancient and threatened to crumble with the lightest pressure. Had he not been on good terms with Marshall Williams, the town's head librarian and the man who actually owned the book he kept at the library in a small safe, he would never have been allowed to look at the piece. Happily, Marshall was an old family friend, and they'd grown up together. The man knew he would never do anything to harm the document. The rest of the papers were photocopies, and he much preferred handling them.

There was the same run of absolutely insanely dry writing to sort through, but for the first time since Sarah Hopkins Miles was burned at the stake as a witch, he found something interesting to look over. It was a case where four of the women in town took sick, all within a few months of a man disappearing. The most unusual aspect was who the women were and the timing of the maladies. He found several references to their illnesses, which when he considered the size of Serenity at the time was not strange.

Still, that little tidbit wouldn't leave him alone. It stuck in the back of his head and, he was certain, flavored everything else he read. There was nothing else remotely spectacular to be found in the early days of the town, and again he wondered what might have been said instead of written down.

When he was finished with his research—and the creation of another epic headache, thanks very much—Simon unsettled the locals at Frannie's Donut Hut by picking up a dinner for the second time in one week. That was almost a record for the number of times he showed his face in The Falls in one month, let alone in a seven-day span.

Amused but still not offended by the looks he received, he finally went home and then settled in to write his accounts.

II

Serenity Falls Part Three:
Planting a Bitter Harvest

He came into the town almost seventy years after it had been settled originally. By then Serenity was prospering, the people living well, and the community growing past the first stages of building. It was a town, a real town, as opposed to a scattering of buildings that were geographically close together.

Niles Wilcox died of old age, content with his lot in life and with few regrets to haunt him in his final days. His wife bore him three strong sons and a lovely daughter, all of whom had children of their own. Many of their progeny had children as well by the time he came to Serenity.

By that point the name Wilcox was synonymous with success in the area. The Wilcox family owned the mercantile and all of the finest homes in the region. They were wealthy beyond most people's imaginings, and they were powerful within the community. Most people would have gleefully joined the ranks of the family in any way they could manage. Naturally, there were exceptions.

The stranger came into Serenity with little more than a wagonload of supplies. He set himself up in a field near the edge of the town and made camp there. Though his tent was built near the edge of the road, he did not offer greetings to the townsfolk who passed by his makeshift home. Nor did he acknowledge the offered welcomes of any that tried to approach him.

He merely rested for a few days, and then he got to work. Every day for a fortnight, the stranger rose with the sun and walked the woods and hills surrounding Serenity. From time to time he was seen climbing high into trees or wading through the river where it came closest to the area. He was often spotted up in the hills where, years later, the quarry would crop up. The people in the town, simple farmers by and large, paid him little heed, though when he came up in conversations in the marketplace, those who were present could all tell stories of where they had seen the man.

He was handsome enough, by all accounts, and if his clothes were an indication, he was well off. On several occasions he was seen carrying a small black pouch and fondling the contents. It was almost inevitable that someone in the area would decide that pouch must hold his wealth. It was just as inevitable that sooner or later someone would covet what he had. Though the area had prospered, there were always a few who felt they could be better off than they were. If the wealth came quickly, all the better still.

Lud Hardwick was the one who felt he could take the black pouch from the stranger. He waited until well after the sun had set on a night when the moon was hidden by clouds and crept into the camp where the odd man slept. The knife he carried with him was sharp enough to slice through the bindings that held the tent sealed from the outside world with ease. He found the stranger lying on a bed made of furs and silken fabrics, holding the pouch close to him, its drawstrings wrapped around his left wrist and balled into his hand.

With the skill of a natural predator, he crept close

enough to the man to see his sleeping face and placed
the blade to the man's neck. His plan was simply to
grab the small bundle and make off with it. The knife
was mostly for show, though he'd use it if he absolutely
had to.

He needn't have worried. The stranger's hand almost
blurred as it lashed out, grabbing his knife hand by the
wrist and twisting hard enough to bring Lud to his knees.
Lud wanted to scream, tried to in fact, but the stranger
clapped a hand over his mouth faster than he would have
thought possible, and pushed him to the ground. The
stranger hit him seven times in his head before he fell into
unconsciousness, each blow feeling like a sledgehammer
crashing into the side of his skull.

When his attacker was motionless, the stranger bound
him quickly, placing a coarse fabric gag into his jaw and
strapping it in place. He then opened the pouch the man
had earlier sought, extracting a long paddle with a thick
needle at its end. Working with a level of expertise that
would have shamed most artists, he used the needle,
dipped in a thick, foul-smelling ink, to make marks on
the flesh of his prey. The ritual was very involved and
extremely time consuming. Long before he'd finished,
the man was obliged to carry his victim deep into the
woods. Almost two days passed before the designs were
completed. A third day and night were needed to then
hide them.

Lud awoke with no recollection of what had happened to him and a very powerful fear of the stranger.
Even thinking about the man left him queasy. He made
a point of being far from the stranger's campsite from
that moment on. Beyond that new phobia, little changed

in his life. He was still far more interested in gaining wealth than in working for it, a trait that remains prevalent in his family through to the modern day.

Lud Hardwick never spoke of his encounter with the stranger. But others spoke of the stranger. A few saw him wandering through the woods late at night—and as is almost always the case in these situations, they really never bothered to explain just why they were out in the woods late in the wee hours, merely telling what they saw—often doing nothing more than looking at the ground, but in some cases meticulously scraping away the topsoil, as if searching for something.

At some point, before the end of the spring, he found what he was looking for. He dug into the soil and pulled forth several misshapen lumps of metal. They were black with age, and though it was doubtful they could have any noticeable value, the stranger took them back to his camp as if they were the most amazing treasures he had ever found. It's said that the day he discovered his prizes, the stranger's face bore a smile that chilled the locals to their very souls.

The next day he left town, taking with him one grandchild from each branch of the Wilcox family. He took Sarah Hensford, Laurel Goodfellow, Gertrude Wilcox, and Emily Wilcox. All four were found later, disheveled and pale. None of them could recall exactly what had happened to them, but all of the girls suffered nightmares for years afterwards.

And all four later gave birth to children within the year. The pregnancies were hidden, which when one considered that the girls were unmarried, isn't really very surprising. The infants were born into the family on the same day, all delivered by Gertrude's mother, a practicing midwife. They were all taken from their mothers and carried away from the house. Gertrude's father claimed to know a family in the next valley that would take them in and care for them. Perhaps that was really what he meant to do, but it certainly isn't what finally happened.

Gertrude's father carried the bundled newborns into the woods, walking for almost a full night and half of the next day before handing the children over to the stranger he'd seen only in passing nine months earlier. He gave no sign that he recognized the stranger, nor did he dare make any pretense about the care of the children. The stranger merely nodded and took them.

The stranger left immediately, headed to the north of town. Gertrude's father wandered over to the next valley, walking as if in a dream. In time he came back and proclaimed that all was well with the children. They would be happier where they were, and none would know the shame that had befallen the family. He was right about half of what he said. No one ever learned of the family's illegitimate progeny. The stranger took them to each of the four corners of the town and used them as he needed to. They were sacrificed in the name of vengeance, their bodies torn asunder and their blood spilled in the fertile soil of Serenity.

Summoning a spirit of sufficient power takes sacrifices. In this case it took the lives of his firstborn by four different women, all of whom were blood of the blood he sought to make suffer most. Niles Wilcox had destroyed his wife when he was away. Albert Miles had sworn he'd have his revenge upon the town. On the day he killed the children of the girls he'd submitted to violent rape, he finally planted the seeds of that revenge.

"Serenity shall know no peace. Serenity shall know no prosperity that isn't tainted with sorrow. Serenity shall pay me back for my grief a thousand times over, and in the end, every soul will scream." Those were the last words spoken by Albert Miles on the subject. He moved on from there to other places, with other plans and dark intent.

III

Answering the phone was almost always an adventure. That was what Crowley loved and hated about the damned things. Oh, there were exceptions, to be sure, but even those could be fun. On the rare occasions when he got a phone solicitation, he made it a point to spend as much time as he could getting inventive with his insults, and if he'd had any friends to talk about it, they could have explained that Crowley was very, very creative when he set himself to that task.

Most times, however, the calls were from people he knew and had prepared for keeping him abreast of unusual situations. This time the call came from a man he'd long since taken for granted was dead.

Professor Irving Weissmuller—Irv to his friends—was an anthropologist and amateur xenobiologist. He and Crowley had spent many a lunch together back when the latter was still teaching. Irv liked to talk about the possible realities of Bigfoot and Nessie. Jonathan liked to shoot down most of his theories and from time to time encourage a few new ways of looking at old possibilities. Far be it from him to stop someone from seeking enlightenment, unless their methods involved dabbling where they shouldn't.

The call came just as he was heading into Ohio, of all places. Irv just wanted to shoot the breeze. They always wanted to shoot the breeze. Irv sounded like he'd been sucking water into his lungs for a few hours. He was wheezing and pausing constantly, even when John was doing the talking. Crowley found it painful to listen to the man who had been so damned vivacious when they worked together.

He kept it short and sweet because he couldn't stand the noises. He got Irving's address, jotted it down, and paid him a visit. Irving Weissmuller had retired to Dalrymple, Ohio, a spot that barely made it to the map. The town had a population of around seventeen thousand, and finding the retirement home where Irv resided was easy.

Getting out of the car, a bright red '76 Sunbird, to see the old boy was a lot harder. But he did it. He managed to leave his sprawling old Cadillac and walk up the narrow concrete path that led to the front door of the Sunset Retirement Community without turning tail and running all the way back. A very large and rotund man with immaculate clothes and hideous dandruff showing in his red hair walked Crowley back to the room where Weissmuller was resting.

"Irv? How the hell are you, old son?" Crowley didn't smile. He almost wanted to, but normally his smiles caused people to panic a bit, and he wanted Irving to stay as calm as possible. The man was sitting up in his bed and doing crossword puzzles. Doubtless every page before the one he was working on had been filled in completely, and Crowley had every reason to believe they were done without the man ever looking at the cheat sheets in the back. Irving had a mind like a steel trap.

The eyes were the same. They were a pale blue and clear as the sky on a perfect day. Otherwise, there was little to remind Crowley of the man he'd been friends with in the past. Irving's body was ravaged by the years between them, withered and wrinkled and shrunken to the point where he was a mockery of himself. Old age and emphysema did that. The thick, dark hair that had always been there was gone, and the hands that held pen to book were palsied and liver spotted. If his smile was the same, it was hidden well by the oxygen mask. And his normal slacks and sweater combination had been replaced by a massive, fuzzy yellow bathrobe that practically swallowed his body. Somehow, that part fit him anyway.

"Jonathan Crowley . . . sonovawhore . . ." He smiled, and his eyes flashed with the same impish humor he'd always shown.

Crowley walked over to the edge of the bed and sat down. "What's the big idea, Irv? Giving me a call and then sitting in bed when you know I'm on the way. Aren't we supposed to be checking out the ladies somewhere instead?"

The old man chuckled and shook his head. "You could be your own son, Johnny."

"You're still the only person I let call me that, you know?"

"Good to know some things don't change." Irv paused to suck down a little extra oxygen, and Crowley waited patiently. "I thought all that crap you told me was just crap, John." His smile was gone, but the look of astonishment in his eyes was almost enough to make Crowley want to look away. "I thought you were just kidding a dreamer."

"Bullshit, Weissmuller. You wouldn't have called me if you believed that." The words were harsh, but his tone was friendly. He had very fond memories of the man in the bed.

"Tell me what's going on, Irving. Tell me why you called." He spoke softly, barely above a whisper.

"I was right, John. There are real monsters."

"I know." Crowley took off his glasses and wiped the lenses on his crew neck. "I've always known."

"So." Irving leaned back in the bed and folded his hands over his robe. "Several deaths so far. None of them reported as deaths, per se, Professor Crowley. Just several disappearances."

"Talk to me, or if you still keep notes on all of these things, just show me the pertinent ones." He slipped his glasses back in place and then crossed his arms. If he left them at his sides, he'd be tempted to do things he wasn't allowed to do, and that would come back to haunt him later. There were rules he followed, and breaking them normally had unpleasant side effects.

Irving pulled out a small sheet of papers and handed

them over. Crowley scanned them quickly, catching the unpleasant trend that ran through the dates and times. "Always at night?"

Irving nodded in response.

Crowley handed the pages back to his onetime coworker. "So, what would you like me to do, Irving?"

"I'd like you to help, John. For old times' sake." Irving stared hard at him, and Crowley could tell he was having trouble accepting what he was seeing. It was a little disconcerting, he guessed. Frankly, he'd long since gotten used to the way he looked. "That third name on the list? That was my granddaughter."

Irving closed his eyes, and Jonathan Crowley placed his hand over both the withered paws of the bedridden man. The pulse he felt against his fingers was weak and erratic.

"All you ever have to do is ask, Irv. You know that." The man he spoke to had drifted into a troubled sleep. Crowley would have known if he was just faking it. He left the room quietly and left the building the same way.

He really couldn't spare the time to do a thorough investigation, so instead he broke down and read the articles that the local rag had about the disappearances. All of them had taken place at night, and in every single case, the person who vanished was walking the streets. Hell, looking around the hole-in-the-wall town, he didn't figure it would be too hard to find a solitary person walking at night. You'd just have to listen to the echoed footsteps ringing off the sidewalks. Dalrymple didn't look like the sort of area where you'd find too much going on after the sun called it a day and went to sleep. That was being as kind as he allowed himself to be. He guessed the only thing open after hours in town was one of the three bars he'd spotted. Coincidentally, one of those very establishments was in the area where the disappearances had all occurred, and it looked, according to the articles he found, like the Backburner Grill and Tavern was the last place several of the people had been seen.

He didn't have information on each and every one of the people who'd left the area, but most of the names indicated younger women. Crowley resigned himself to a night at the local pub.

He walked around town first, seeing what little there was to see. Several houses were impressive, but mostly the place looked like a hundred other small towns he'd been in. It was poor, it was crumbling, and most of the people looked blissfully ignorant of anything amiss. People had that ability, that special talent for ignoring what they didn't want to see. It pissed him off when he let himself think about it.

The Backburner was a well-kept place and busier than he would have expected, especially for a weeknight. The clientele ranged from the twenties all the way up into octogenarian, but mostly on the younger side of fifty. Most of the people in the place looked well off. It wasn't exactly a yuppie bar, but it was definitely upper middle class. As a good number of the missing had been seen last in the vicinity, Crowley was a little surprised not to see more written in the newspaper about the disappearances. Had the place been a true dive, he would have expected that sort of response from the local press.

He entered the bar a little after ten at night to order a beer. The bartender, a kid who should have been in college but instead was slinging drinks for a living, looked at him as if he were a particularly unpleasant sort of insect. "Help you?" The man's voice was nasal and designed for whining.

Crowley smiled broadly and watched the man's face go a few shades paler than it already was. "Yes, you can. I'd like a bottle of Sam Adams." When the little snot nose reached for a mug and the tap of beer, Crowley cleared his throat. "Hard of hearing, princess? I said a bottle."

The look of superiority vanished, replaced in record time by a slightly terrified nod. The twerp's hands shook as he reached into the cooler to pull out a bottle and pop the cap. Crowley paid and left a two dollar tip. Best not to piss in the wrong spots before he had what he needed.

The bar stayed fairly busy, with couples coming and going, several groups playing billiards and spilling beers as they laughed and snorted. Crowley sat in his little corner and watched them all, saying nothing and seldom responding to the curious looks shot his way. There were a few he was almost tempted to respond to, of course, attractive women who looked him over and made all the right moves to get his attention, but he ignored them anyway.

There was something he needed to do in town, and then he had other things to take care of in other places. There wasn't enough time in his days as it was. The last thing he wanted or needed was any sort of relationship. So he sipped his beer instead and tried to remember what it was like to actually not push away from him everyone he ran across. It was a brief moment of introspection, and he didn't let it last.

Happily, there was always someone willing to come along and distract him from his need to analyze his own existence. In this case, it was a rather statuesque young woman around twenty years of age. She had dark brown hair, amazing blue eyes, and the sort of body that was normally reserved for the interiors of gentlemen's magazines. Most of the men and a few of the women watched her as she walked into the bar. Not only because she was attractive but because she was alone.

Crowley ordered another beer to nurse and waited while the woman met up with a few of the local stallions and shot them down, one after the next. He was both amused and—he had to admit it—a little fascinated. Normally bars seemed like meat markets. Maybe the lady just wanted to window shop. While he watched and studied the situation, he took a few small packets from his jeans pocket and mixed their contents with his beer. He had a notion about what he was up against and decided to prepare for the worst. Simple magic, really, but decidedly effective in the right circumstances.

He watched and waited until it was almost closing time, and then Crowley slipped outside the bar and found a comfortable spot to wait. The bar was situated at the corner of two streets, with a small parking lot and one streetlight in the entire area for illumination. The Backburner was closed, and two neon beer signs were the only light left in the place. Crowley watched from the shadows as the last few cars left the parking lot, and ten people went on their way, hoofing it toward their destinations. The brunette was among the pedestrians leaving the place.

She thought she left alone. Crowley noticed otherwise.

There was a darkness moving in the shadows. It was black against the dark gray of the night, and even from a distance he could almost feel the cold emanating from it. Crowley slid off the low brick wall he was sitting on and started following.

Whatever was following her was good enough to avoid detection from most people, but not so great at paying attention to what was right behind it. Jonathan Crowley watched it as it stalked the girl, his ears and eyes open to every nuance. Adrenaline was already thrumming through his muscles, preparing him for whatever might come his way.

It was a fault of his, the annoying tendency to get cocky from time to time. He got so busy watching that patch of shadows stalking after the homecoming queen that he forgot to pay attention to where he was stepping. The cat let out a howl worthy of a saber-toothed tiger when he stepped on its tail. He jumped one way, the cat jumped another, and the girl let out a shriek that was positively epic.

The cat was gone in an instant, a calico flash that vanished around a corner even as Crowley spotted it again. The girl didn't run. Instead, she reached into her painted-on jeans and whipped out a canister of pepper spray, which she promptly aimed at the afterimage of the cat.

Crowley slid back away into the shadow of the closest building and tried to find the dark figure that had been following the girl. For her part, the girl was doing her best to look everywhere at once, still not convinced that she was safe. It might be one thing to bravely leave the bar alone, but it was quite another to walk down the dark streets by herself, fully aware that several other people had disappeared recently.

He gritted his teeth, baring them in a feral smile that had nothing to do with being cheerful. Whatever had been following the girl was missing, and that meant it could be anywhere. Also, like as not if it stalked at night, it could well have spotted him, too.

That wasn't really a comforting thought. Then again, the scraping sound from above didn't do much for him, either. He stepped back just as something hurtled at him from the roof of the building. Even in free fall it was good. It almost nailed his head into the ground, but he blocked with his arms and threw it to the side. The impact on his arms felt like he'd tried to catch a truck, but he was alive. That was always a plus.

The dark thing rolled and came up flawlessly. Then it let loose a hiss and came at Crowley, eyes blazing a dark red as it approached. Crowley crouched low and slid forward on the balls of his feet, his shoes sending a small flurry of papers and garbage sliding before him. The thing in front of him backed up a step, eyes narrowing. The eyes were humanoid, at least. That was also a plus.

After a half second of looking at each other, the two of them moved forward. Crowley swung a hard left that rammed into a rib cage. His opponent never made a sound but instead brought its hand around and slapped Crowley across the face, sending his glasses flying and opening four lacerations across his cheek. The pain was sharp and hot and pissed him off. He felt the skin wounds start itching furiously as the flesh began to knit itself back together.

He also felt the rib cage of whatever was fighting

him crack with a deeply satisfying sound when he side kicked it. The figure was muscular, lighter than he expected, and very annoyed by the broken bones in its chest. Unfortunately, the damage didn't slow it down in the least. It came back at him in a blur, swinging just wildly enough to make it impossible to block every blow. Several cuts appeared on his arms and chest as he tried to fend the thing off.

Crowley returned the favor, swinging fast and hard, his lips peeled back in a smile as the fighting continued. He was rapidly getting frustrated, because whatever it was he was fighting—not human, that was a damned certainty—was putting up a better struggle than he'd expected. It wasn't that he didn't like a good fight. He just liked to be prepared for the conflicts when they came his way.

Frustrated with fighting in the enclosed area of the alley—and really, really not thrilled with the slimy stuff that coated his back when the thing knocked him on his ass for the third time, Crowley braced against the wall and kicked the dark thing with both of his heels, knocking it out into the street. He followed after it a second later, spitting the taste of his blood from his mouth.

And looked at his opponent in the light for the first time. The man was maybe twenty-five and looked to be in fairly good shape. His hair was a dark, curly mess, and his face was relatively handsome, give or take the red eyes and the bared fangs.

"Oh, shit." Crowley shook his head as he spoke and rolled his eyes toward the heavens. "Are you a vampire?" Crowley walked toward the man, scowling. He'd been hoping for something a little more exotic.

"Yeah? What's it to you?"

Oh, and he was a witty verbalist, too. This was just getting better.

"I was really wanting you to be something better than just another bloodsucker, is all. I mean, if I'm going to invest my time into looking for a monster, I'd prefer something a little more original, okay?"

The undead man looked at him as if he were crazy and then graduated up to looking offended. "Hey! You ruined my meal, asshole. I don't need you insulting me, too."

Crowley made mock-sympathy noises and kept coming closer. "Listen, precious, I don't know if you're aware of this, but you aren't supposed to feed on the nice, half-drunk girls you see on the street. You're supposed to offer them a ride home and hope for a kiss on the cheek."

"Larry?" The voice was clear and sweet and just a wee bit slurred. Crowley looked over to see the brunette he'd been trying to protect heading straight for the vampire who'd been wanting to snack on her.

"Hi, Dora." Crowley was pretty much forgotten as the man headed over toward the young lady. "How've you been?" The voice was calm and pleasant, and Crowley shook his head with disgust. If the damned fool girl had been listening, she might have caught on to the fact that her buddy Larry was a dangerous thing to be playing with.

"Screw that, Larry! I was waiting at the bar for almost three hours." The tone of her voice dropped about half of the attractive away from Crowley's assessment of the girl. She sounded righteously pissed off, and he was briefly tempted to let her walk into the vampire's reach.

"Hey, I said I'd try to make it. You know I have a busy schedule." Apparently he hadn't been a vampire for long. Crowley moved along side the walking corpse, shaking his head in amazement.

"You didn't say any such thing, you prick! You were going to meet me for drinks, and we were supposed to go see a movie." She walked closer, her bright blue eyes narrowed to angry slits.

Her expression changed when Larry hissed and bared his fangs. She didn't have a chance to scream before he was moving across the street in her direction, his eyes blazing and his hands hooked into claws.

Crowley broke the vampire's spine before he could reach his target. The vampire went down hard and got up almost immediately. He wasn't standing up straight, but he was standing. Dora took the time to let loose a good, loud bloodcurdler of a scream, and then she opened up on Dracula's dumber cousin with her pepper spray.

Larry did the only sensible thing he could have and started screaming himself, clawing at the red coating that was burning all hell out of his eyes. Crowley didn't feel too suicidal, so he looked around for a weapon. As a rule, if it gets back up after having its back broken, it's probably not ready to call it quits, and the wounds he'd already suffered were still healing.

Dora looked torn between apologizing to the crying, hissing Larry and running away to hide. Crowley made it easier on her. "Listen, Dora?"

"Yes?" her voice trembled.

"Do yourself a favor, and go home. Forget all about Larry here, because he's already dead, okay?"

Dora's pretty face crumpled, and she nodded her head. Despite himself, Crowley felt for her. He walked over and looked in her eyes. Then he spoke softly, taking the time to do it right. "Larry was a good man, and unfortunately he got in with the wrong crowd. Make sure you take precautions not to do the same thing, okay?" He watched with satisfaction as her eyes got a distant look. "Now, I'm going to give you my card. If you have any problems, don't hesitate to call me. Maybe I'll be able to help."

He handed her a card and watched her walk away. Then and only then did he bother with Larry. Larry, the undead broken boy, was exactly where he had been a moment before. He was also still rubbing furiously at his eyes and trying to get rid of the concentrated hell that was trying to burn them out of his skull.

Crowley smiled and walked over. "Hey, Larry. I'm going to put your body to rest. You understand me?"

Larry nodded and managed to stand up. His eyes were even redder than before, though of course a lot of that was now irritation. "I'll kill you if you come close to me."

"Larry, you can barely walk, and I know you're healing up nicely, but I will kill you." To illustrate his point, he knocked the vampire's feet out from under him and watched in satisfaction as the walking cadaver fell down and groaned in pain. "The only question here is whether or not it's a fast death."

"You won't get away with shit. I've already called the others . . ."

"I'm sure you have, precious." Crowley nodded and placed a foot against the vampire's knee. Then with one savage stomp, he shattered the kneecap and tore the cartilage around it. The vampire couldn't actually get paler, but he tried. He also let out a few moans, screams, and foul words at roughly three decibels above the norm.

Crowley let him holler away and then grabbed him by the bad leg, hauling him back into the alley. The vampire hissed and moaned and kicked at his arm and leg, but the strength wasn't really what it should have been, what with a ruined spine and all. Crowley finally dragged him off the main strip and settled down near a Dumpster. He found a broken pallet and pulled a long shard of wood away, fingering the jagged tip.

"How many people did you kill, cupcake?" Crowley made sure to smile as he approached. The vampire growled in a way that was decidedly not human, and crawled backward as best it could. It didn't growl so much as whimper when it pushed off with the ruined leg. Still, considering the broken spine, Crowley was suitably impressed.

He waited for half a minute and then shattered the other kneecap. Larry was making a lot of noises now, but as quiet as everything was, Crowley wasn't overly worried. He had doubts about the police interrupting his fun.

"Listen. I can break bones all over your little body until the sun rises." Crowley crouched near his prey. "I really don't mind. But you might, because, really, undead or not, I know this shit hurts. So why don't you make it easy on yourself and tell me how many you've killed and where the rest of your little group is hiding?"

"Well, that part's easy enough to answer . . ." The voice came from above him, and Crowley shook his head. He knew this wasn't going to be any fun at all. With that knowledge in mind, he leaned back a bit and looked up at the edges of the buildings that made up the alleyway.

He'd counted seven figures up there before they dropped down from above.

CHAPTER 4

I

More books. Simon MacGruder was beginning to regret his decision to actually do research for his history of his hometown. The damned thing was never going to be published either way, and here he was acting like he was a real writer. Still, aside from the eyestrain and the dust, it was rather a nice way to pass the time. It beat the hell out of rereading all of his Zane Grey novels, anyway.

He jotted occasional notes but again found little that was truly fascinating. Learning from the local accounts about some of the punishments the townsfolk inflicted back in the day made him wonder if there would be anywhere near as much crime in modern times if the penalties were still as harsh. "Probably," he mused. "Most people who do the crimes never bother to consider the punishments, I suspect."

There had been an incident with a revenuer when the

town was just settling into itself, and if that was an example of old-school discipline, he was glad he'd never been caught the few times he let himself slide to the wrong side of the law. He made a lot of notes about that one and decided to see if he could locate where the man's remains might have been located in the woods. It would make for a change of pace and maybe even an interesting place to take a few pictures. You never could tell.

When he'd had enough of the stuffy closet-cum-office, he decided to walk around town for a bit and stretch out his tired old legs. Growing old still sucked, and it still beat the alternative.

He'd walked most of the streets around the town's center within an hour, nodding to a few familiar faces and smiling to himself whenever someone came by and was surprised to see him. There were probably a few people in the area who thought that seeing him this many times in only a few weeks was a sign that the end times were near. Being a hermit apparently meant he wasn't allowed more than a few visits a year before tongues would start wagging.

Simon was getting ready to head for home when he heard the voices. They were not unusual, certainly not unnatural, but they caught his attention because there was something strained about them. Not far from the conjoined brick-and-steel mess that was the high school and middle school combined, Simon saw a group of five boys standing in a tight circle. They were in the shadow of the school building, and he could see them clearly enough, but they weren't exactly out in the open. Anyone in a car would surely have missed them entirely. He wasn't sure why at first, but the gathering did for him exactly what the voices coming from the group had done. It gave him a fluttery feeling in his stomach.

As nonchalantly as possible, he walked in that direction. The boys failed to take any notice of him. They were too busy with their latest prize, a girl a few years younger, maybe ten or eleven if he had to guess, who was surrounded by them all and crying. She had long brown hair and bright, tear-streaked eyes that hid behind round glasses. At the moment, one of the boys had a hand on her leg, and another was lifting her skirt.

Simon MacGruder didn't even bother looking any further. The boys were in their later teens and had broad smiles on their cruel faces, but he only acknowledged that fact as he moved in closer and grabbed one of them—short, with long, dark, curly hair—by the back of his neck and hauled him backwards with a rough hand. The kid let out a squawk and stumbled. MacGruder helped him along with a hiking shoe to the back of his knee.

There was a fat kid with pants too small and a belt that practically cut into his stomach. He'd been busy with his hand on the girl's thigh, and turned a vapid face in MacGruder's direction just in time to get an open-handed slap across his pudgy cheek. He let out a yelp and jumped back as if the old man had thrown a blazing fire at his face.

"What the hell are you boys doing?" He didn't speak; he roared, the world going red for him in that moment. There was no concern about whether or not the parents of these delinquents might want to press charges for assaulting their precious angels, nor the least worry about lawsuits. That would come later, if at all. Right now he was too furious, too shocked by what he was seeing. Five boys practically ready to rape a little girl who wasn't close enough to the age of puberty for anyone to notice.

There were two boys who looked right at him, their mouths twisted in an unusual blend of fear—being busted by an adult was sure to still generate that, at least—and anger—because, of course, they could no longer play with their newest toy. He recognized them immediately.

"Well, and I'm sure your mother will be glad to hear of this, won't she, Perry Hamilton?" The boy's hair was bleached almost white, which only made the rash of pimples on his lean face stand out even more. At the mention of his mother, however, he flinched back and dropped his eyes. "Andy? What do you suppose your father will find for you to do when I tell him about this?"

Andy was the one who broke first, just as Simon expected. Murray Hamilton was not exactly the sort of man anyone wanted to piss off. He pointed over to the first boy he'd grabbed, who was just starting to stand back up. "That goes for you, too, Marco DeMillio!" He glowered at the kid and watched with a certain amount of satisfaction as the local tough cringed. That was one of the advantages of being a hermit that he tried not to exploit: most of the people in town thought he was crazy to begin with. "Don't think I don't know who you are. I suggest you get your little ass home before I get to my phone, boys, and maybe start thinking of a few chores you can do before your folks think of other ways to punish you." That got all of them but the fat kid nodding their heads. Pudgy was far too busy reeling from the shock of anyone actually striking him. Simon took a menacing step in the round-faced boy's direction and watched him run off, still holding his cheek as if it might break.

"FREEZE!" Every last one of them stopped where they were. "You get your little asses over here and apologize to this girl, or so help me, I'll make every last one of you regret it." All of them came back, none of them thrilled by the notion and none of them quite bold enough to speak out against the old man who, as Simon well knew, every kid in town was a little scared of.

Marco was first. He shoved his hands into his too-tight jeans and looked right in the girl's eyes. He was a handsome boy, and there was maybe even a little bit of a crush from the girl, but if so, Simon suspected it would fade away when she really gave thought to where things might have gone. They were only kids playing around, but Simon could remember a few times when harmless little games had gone wrong in Serenity Falls, and he felt in his heart that this one almost certainly would have gone way too far.

"I'm sorry, Jessie. We didn't mean to scare you. We were just goofing."

"That's what they call it these days?" Simon shot him a dark look. Maybe they were just goofing as the punk had said, but he wanted to make good and damned sure the boys knew he understood what was on their minds.

Marco looked away and headed toward the dump his family called a home. Even in good times the DeMillio house was not exactly neat and clean. His mother worked too hard, and his father had been dead for years. That wasn't an excuse for rape, especially since DeMillio himself was just at the age where he'd be doing hard time for anything stupid he might pull.

Simon watched while the rest of them apologized, even the fat kid. When he tried to shake hands with the little girl, she shook her head and moved closer to Simon. "That'll do, boy. Get your ass home. I see you anywhere near this girl again, and I promise you, you'll have a reason to wear your own skirt instead of jeans." The kid got the hint and raced his shadow as the sun started setting.

He looked at the little girl, who had managed to compose herself. She was busily picking up the books that DeMillio and his boys had thrown around. Her face was still wet, and her bottom lip was pushed out a bit in a pout, but she wasn't crying anymore.

"Are you okay, sweetie?"

"Un-hunh. I mean. Yes, thank you, sir." She was looking at him sheepishly, her eyes flicking around for an escape route.

"You're Walter Grant's little girl, aren't you?"

"You know my daddy?" She seemed shocked.

"Course I do. Isn't a family in this town I don't know. Let's get you on home, before one of those damned fool boys gets any more notions." There were places in the world and even in the state of New York where a girl of her age would have told him to shove it or simply run away. That wasn't the way it worked in Serenity Falls. Not too many kids would dare disobey the average adult unless they had reason to feel threatened. Apparently the girl had decided he wasn't the worst of the people she could run across on the street. She followed meekly and was a little surprised when he took her books from her hands.

They spoke for a while as they walked. Her name was Jessie Grant—he'd known that but couldn't for the life of him drag it back into his head—and she lived only a little over a mile from where he had his cabin in the woods.

"Jessie. I want you to watch for those boys. I think they're the sort that will cause you no end of troubles if you let them." She nodded her head, barely speaking at all except to answer direct questions, her eyes warring between looking at the sidewalk at her feet and sneaking looks at MacGruder as he walked with her.

The silence was maybe uncomfortable for her but didn't bother him very much. He was used to it. He gave her back her books at the edge of her driveway and waved amiably as he went on his way.

Behind him, Jessica Grant stared at her unexpected savior for a long moment before bolting for her front door. When she got inside, she kept the encounter to herself. Best not to scare her parents. They had enough troubles lately.

II

Serenity Falls Part Four: Corn Whiskey, Taxation, and the Revenuers

There have been times when a farmer's livelihood often depended on the ability to make a decent batch of whiskey. Just after the Revolutionary War was one of those times.

The farmers in Serenity understood the need for taxes, just as they'd understood the reasons for gathering their rifles and waging war on the British government that insisted on trying to make them less than full citizens. By and large, they had no problem with paying their fair share of the monies needed to run a new country.

But the Whiskey Tax, they all agreed, was going a little too far. Under the new government the farmers were supposed to pay a fairly heavy tax on all of the whiskey they produced, not just what was sold. It wasn't an idea that sat well with most of the people in Serenity—even those who merely drank the stuff could see that the price would go up—and it smacked of a certain tea tax that was still in the memories of many.

The good farmers of Serenity and several of their regular customers agreed that the tax shouldn't be paid. They also agreed to give warning to anyone should the revenuers come, as they most surely would.

And several of the farmers made sure they were properly prepared for any unwanted visitors. It took time, but eventually the revenuers came, just as predicted, and they came wanting money. The farmers of Serenity sent them on their way with a firm reminder that they should never come back. Most of the revenuers were warned off with a gesture from a rifle, but there were exceptions. Those who decided that they would perform their duties regardless of threats, or who were foolish enough to say they'd be back with reinforcements met up with the painful process known as "tarring." Considered the ultimate insult of the time, the victim of a tarring had hot pitch poured over clothes and skin alike, and then was liberally coated with feathers afterwards. While a few have found humor in the idea, none of those who suffered the burns caused by the hot tar or the ruined flesh from peeling the substance from their bodies were among those who laughed about the punishment.

Allan Chadwick, a revenue man sent after the first three were driven away, did not follow the normal rules. The man had served under General Washington during the war, and he was picked by the president himself for the job of revenuer. The two men had similar philosophies when it came to handling unpleasant matters: they found the source of the trouble, and then they removed it. He brought his own rifle to the show, and when one of the local farmers—Darren Pace, who never had children that were his in any legitimate fashion, but who was known to have slept around with several married women—had the nerve to fire a warning shot, Chadwick returned the favor by landing a bullet in the farmer's midsection. Pace died a few minutes later, but not before half the people in the area heard his screams.

It could be argued that Chadwick had his punishment coming to him, but there would certainly be a few who disagreed. Chadwick, as with two of the previous revenuers to come into the area, was tarred for his troubles. The difference in his case was that the responsible parties decided to tar his whole head and his shoulders. Chadwick screamed at least as loudly as the man he'd killed, but his cries of pain lasted far longer. He was blinded and deafened in the process of being coated with hot pitch, and there's every likelihood that his mouth and nose were filled with the substance as he struggled to catch his breath. The farmers held his head under the stream of hot tar for no less than a full minute. When they were finished, they covered him with feathers and pushed him into the woods, leaving it to the Lord Almighty to save the man if the Lord did see fit.

Chadwick and the Lord failed to come to an understanding. The revenuer stumbled through the woods in an agony the likes of which he'd never imagined possible. He fell over obstacles that wouldn't have tripped an infant, and he soon found crawling easier than walking. On three separate occasions he tried to remove the cooled tar from his face but was forced to stop when the pain proved too fierce to ignore.

Allan Chadwick had time to reflect on his life as he lay in the woods and prepared to die. Blinded and deafened by the punishment meted out to him, he knew it was only a matter of time before he succumbed to the elements. In time his mind broke. He saw visions of a world not at all like his own, and he lost himself in the explorations of that strange and frightening place. He had nothing to write with, no way to communicate his last thoughts to the world, but he felt the need to tell his tale just the same. In the end, as dehydration and fever brought on by infection took hold of him, he ran his right index finger over the coarse granite where he rested again and again, marking the ground with his flesh and blood and never even feeling it.

His body was taken by the wild, scavenged for edible flesh, and left to the elements and insects. In time there was nothing left of the man save twelve buttons from his coat and the stain on the ground where he had written his last comments. Human eyes have never seen whatever he may have written. But it's still there, in the ground, a pale, rusty stain; the final testament of a man who died trying to perform his duties.

Incidents in Pennsylvania ended the Whiskey Tax before there were any more attempts by revenuers to collect their due from the local farmers of Serenity. The murder of a local farmer and the resulting murder of a revenuer isn't even a footnote in the history books, and the only record of the deaths rests in a moldering document held in the root cellar of a church building that is part of the Serenity Falls Historical Society's property. There is also the headstone of Darren Pace, but the only words on the monument that can be made out merely claim that he died defending his beliefs from tyranny.

III

Well, torturing his prey was really not going to get him anywhere, so Crowley leaned in fast and rammed the makeshift dagger deep into Larry's heart. Larry obliged him by dying. One less vampire to deal with suited him just fine.

The rest of them were in the process of slithering down the walls into the alley. They were all female, all attractive, and if he had to guess, all the victims that had been killed by Larry in the recent past. It was a little weird watching the rejects from the morgue as they climbed down the wall, their hair falling ahead of them. He'd seen it before, of course, but it was strange just the same.

"Ladies . . . don't expect this to go the way you want it to."

"You killed him . . ." A girl who looked far too young to be one of the bar-hopping crowd was looking at Crowley with pure hatred in her eyes.

"Yeah. It's what I do. He killed you, right?"

"No. He made me better."

"Oh, listen, I am not going to argue with you about this."

The girl was all of five feet tall, blond with hazel eyes and a load of makeup to hide how pale she was. He looked down at her as she approached, swinging hips that had barely developed and doing her best to look seductive. They were all so young, and now they believed they would stay that way forever. She grabbed at the front of his shirt as she got close enough. He broke three of her fingers to let her know that wasn't a very good idea.

And when she let loose a grunt of pain, the rest of the merry band moved in, determined to rip Jonathan Crowley to pieces. There are times for fun and games and times to play nasty. This situation warranted the latter of the two. Crowley backed away, heading for the street again. The last thing he needed was a lack of space for cutting loose properly.

"I have to tell you girls something. I'm not a nice man, and I don't pull punches when it comes to fighting with the fairer sex, especially when they're already dead." They came anyway, the short one still waving her hand as her body tried to regenerate the damage he'd done.

One of the older girls let out a whooping battle cry of a scream and charged. The others closed in, too, in hot pursuit. The bad news was that there were seven blood-sucking monsters trying to kill him. The good news was that they had not, contrary to Hollywood's more recent depictions of vampires, suddenly developed martial arts skills or the ability to move like Olympic-level gymnasts. They were faster than human, to be sure, but not exactly overflowing with combat skills they hadn't had before they were changed.

He broke the neck of the first vampire as she reached for him, twisting out of her way and grabbing her head as she slipped past. The cold, dead flesh kept moving, and the creature let out a soft sigh as she fell to the ground. The second one managed to hit him in the stomach, just above his privates, and Crowley fell to the ground himself, wishing desperately that he could make the pain fade completely before the rest of them dog piled on top of him.

A heavyset brunette planted both of her heels on his chest and reached out with her hands for his face. He was far too busy worrying about the long nails of a badly dyed redhead to even think about her. The copper-haired one was doing her best to tear his testicles away even as she sank her fangs into his calf.

The two vampires bit into his flesh at almost the same time. The one on his leg bit flesh away, and the one squatting on his chest managed to contort herself until she sank her teeth into his neck. He felt their tongues moving across the wounds, felt the lips of the one on his neck press tightly as she started sucking. There was, he had to admit, something very erotic about it, even through the pain.

But he bet the girls didn't see it that way at all. Both of them pulled back from him, their mouths stained with his blood, their teeth bared, and their faces puzzled. The brunette shook her head, and the redhead started spitting. And then both of them jumped away from him as the flesh of their mouths started to smoke and steam. The redhead tried to speak, but the words were garbled and strained, and the situation only got worse for her when her mouth caught fire.

Crowley kicked her in the jaw and sent her rolling off of him as her entire head started burning. The brunette he shoved with all of his strength just before he rolled to his hands and knees.

Crowley was smiling as he stood up. The remaining vampires were looking absolutely terrified as the brunette joined her friend in the unexpected combustion. Everything from her torso to her scalp was blazing, the flames bright enough to light the entire alley. She had the good courtesy to fall on the one with the broken neck, leaving both of them burning in no time at all.

"Neat trick, hunh?" Crowley smiled as he walked toward the remaining vampires, all of whom where huddled together, justifiably freaked out by what had just happened. "I learned that one a long time ago." He moved closer still, and as the little one with the broken wrist tried to run past him and back into the deeper recesses of the alley, he grabbed her long hair, hauling her back like a fisherman with a nice-sized catfish. She clawed at his arm, her fingers digging deep into his flesh. A few seconds later she was thrashing and screaming as her fingertips caught ablaze. There was a very brief flash of guilt in his stomach over that one, but he killed it quickly. She wasn't a little girl anymore; she just managed to look like one. Thinking about the child that had been killed made him hold her tighter as she struggled.

The others were separating, getting ready to run as the flames started up the struggling vampire's hands and arms. He finally let her go, and she ran hard, howling her pain into the early morning darkness.

He didn't bother watching. He knew for a fact that she would continue to burn until she was completely gone.

The other three were moving fast, hauling their asses away at high speed. Crowley went after one that reminded him of a girl he'd known a few lifetimes ago and tackled her hard, sending her to the ground. He pinned her there as she groaned and writhed and tried to slither out from under him.

"Shhhh . . . Here's the deal. Tell me where your master is, and you get to go free."

"Unnn . . . Get offa me!" she whimpered, struggling and puzzled by the fact that she couldn't toss him aside with ease. In only a short time she'd become used to knocking grown men aside like a dirty dishrag. He reached into his left front pocket for the collection of dust he'd taken from a cemetery near his home. The powdery substance was dark gray and stank of corpses long dead. He set the small envelope aside and pinned the girl to the ground.

"I'm going to tell you one more time. If you let me know where your master is, I'll set you free." She bucked and groaned in a twisted parody of sex, her rear end pushing against him as she tried to rise to her hands and knees. "It's not gonna work, cupcake. I'm not excited by necrophilia."

"Please, mister . . . I'll do anything you say." She kept trying. He had to give her credit for that. "Just tell me what you want . . ."

"I already told you how you can get free."

"I can't tell you. He left . . . I don't think he's in town anymore." She licked her lips and tried her best to look excited by the compromising positions of their bodies. He imagined it wouldn't be hard for her to find victims. He thought about how many more of her kind she could make if given the opportunity. It made it easier for him to end her existence.

"Now, see, that was the wrong answer, sweet pea." His hand slid up her back until his fingers touched the base of her skull lightly. He leaned down close to her ear and whispered softly. The words were ancient and powerful and tore the vampiric spirit free from the body it inhabited. She never even had a chance to scream.

Five more words, and the entity that had inhabited her corpse was torn asunder. Her body slumped down immediately, and Crowley pushed away from the remains. Without the demonic force to keep it looking lively, the decay that had taken place since her death quickly took over. At a guess, she'd been dead a little over ten days.

Crowley stood up after grabbing his little envelope of powder. He poured two small piles of the dust into his palm and blew on them. The resulting clouds moved in different directions, one to the north and one to the west. Both of them left a trail in the air. He followed the one to the west first. He did not speak nor did he move quickly.

He had to finish what he'd started, and he had to do it soon. There were other places he needed to be. In the end, he found the two vampires in their hiding places.

The first one fought hard and managed to break a few of his ribs, which really didn't leave him very forgiving. He killed her and made it hurt.

The second one groveled very nicely and told him what he wanted to know after he broke both of her legs. Crowley left her dead a few minutes later and headed for the house where the one who started the entire mess tended to sleep off the days.

The building was an old three-story monster, but it was well kept. The walls were solid brick and stone, with little wood, and the windows had heavy-duty bars over them, the better to keep out unwanted intruders. Jonathan Crowley, as a few unfortunate souls could have told you, was not known for letting a little thing like steel bars stop him.

He scoped out the building carefully, his eyes looking for flaws in the foundation, the security of the windows, and anything else that might be considered a weakness. He was far more meticulous than the average real estate examiner. The bricks were solid and well grouted. The bars over the windows were cast iron and bolted directly into the brick in most cases. There was one exception: a spot where the only way to place the deeply imbedded bolts required that they be driven into the grout. It only took Crowley a few minutes to pry the thing loose. Happily, he managed it with minimal effort and was even able to place the metal frame back into the same holes.

He moved through the darkened interior of the house with ease, his eyes rapidly adjusting to the absence of light. Most of the rooms were simply furnished, with spartan use of the space provided. That didn't surprise him overly much. Like as not most of the areas inside were only for window dressing. At least on the first floor.

The doors were all locked, but Crowley didn't have trouble using a little logic to figure out the way to the basement. There was no guarantee that the cellar of the house would be the place where the vampire chose to sleep, but logic dictated it. Brick walls and iron bars would certainly help keep the place standing—fires normally didn't do as much damage to baked clay as they did to well-seasoned wood, and very few people could easily get past iron bars—but if Crowley somehow wound up as a vampire, he sure as hell wouldn't want to be where the sun might reach him, and he'd already discovered that there were no windows to the cellar.

Not every vampire would be killed by the touch of the sun, but the younger ones were. So he tried the cellar first. It was completely empty, not a sign of anything having been in there for a while, either. The floor was solid concrete, and the walls were well-mortared brick. It was possible that the vampire had his haven under the cement floor, but not likely. Of course, not every idea works out as planned. He had figured to check for signs of the undead and maybe make their lives miserable for them. He hadn't counted on the cellar door being slammed shut behind him, and he most definitely hadn't been expecting the wooden door he'd passed through to be a fake.

Crowley ran up the stairs as quickly as he could and grabbed at the door handle. It came off in his grip. He stared at the doorknob for several seconds as a deep chill crawled up his spine.

"Oh, shit."

"Indeed, Mr. Crowley." The voice came from the other side of the barrier, and it was as cold and dead as the grave. Masculine and deep, but not in a friendly way. There was a faint accent, but he couldn't place it, and that was never a good sign. It meant that whatever he was dealing with on the other side of the door was either from a place he had never visited—not very likely as he'd traveled the globe very extensively—or it was old enough that the accent was no longer familiar. Either way, that probably meant an ancient vampire, and the simple fact of the matter was that if it was as old as he suspected, it was also very likely to be extremely powerful.

"Who are you?"

"Oh, please, do not feel the need to insult my intelligence. I have no desire to give you my name." If he'd expected a gloating challenge to his abilities, he was disappointed. The words were spoken solemnly, and the deep tones were hardly happy about the current situation. "You've killed my offspring with ease, and I have heard rumors of you. Do not expect me to make it easy for you to find me or to kill me. I am leaving this town, and I am leaving behind nothing of importance."

Crowley cursed under his breath and was rewarded by the voice on the other side starting up again. "Mr. Crowley, I have no particular dislike for you, despite the inconvenience of having you destroy my children. I suggest you leave well enough alone. Do not attempt to follow me."

"What? You plan on leaving me alive?" He couldn't help the laugh that came out of his mouth as he spoke.

"I have no reason to kill you. Not yet, at least. You have your missions in this world, and I have mine. Besides, I believe that you are . . . not powerless, but less able to do things against me if I am not attacking, isn't that so?"

He didn't bother to answer, but it irked him that the vampire understood his limitations. That was happening more often these days, and it was damned inconvenient.

Crowley threw himself against the door and felt his shoulder bruise itself against the thick metal hiding behind the wooden sheath. The wood cracked, but other than that, the door was undamaged by his efforts.

"I have no doubt you'll get through the door, eventually. In the meantime I leave you. If you attempt to follow me, I will not be as kind a second time."

Crowley looked the door over, surprised to see that the hinges were on the other side. No doorknob, no hinges, and the only way he could get through was to batter a heavy steel door until either it or the doorjamb gave way.

With no other choice, he started ramming himself against the metal, furious that he'd been set up.

CHAPTER 5

I

Simon MacGruder sat at the table and tried not to stare at the man across from him. Barry LeMarrs was a massive man, weighing in at an easy three hundred–plus pounds, with a waistline that probably came close to epic. He had an appetite to match it, and no hesitation to devour the food put in front of him. He ate almost constantly, with a neat, precise methodology that didn't quite jibe with his obvious gusto for epicurean pleasures. It was like watching a madman have a perfectly logical discussion in even tones: a paradox that almost hurt the old man's head when he thought about it. In plain English, he'd never met a prissier lard ass.

But despite what the meal was going to cost him, he was glad to spend the money. LeMarrs was a font of knowledge, to be blunt. The man knew damned near everything that went on in town with the same sort of easy confidence that MacGruder normally associated with the upper echelons of the ladies' quilting bee club and the Daughters of the American Revolution—both of which had been less forthcoming than the eating machine sitting across from him in the Imperial Diner at the edge of town. Barry had insisted, because as with everything else, he seemed to like to keep his gossiping nature off to the sidelines. People might talk, after all.

When he'd finished the strip steak he'd been slowly consuming, Barry smiled and ordered a piece of blueberry pie with two scoops of ice cream. While he waited, he finished up the story he'd been telling.

"So, it was a mess. My great-great-grandfather willingly let the slaves come through his home, but my great-great-granduncle decided it was best to send the escapees back to their rightful owners." That was the other thing about Barry LeMarrs: he sounded like a news reporter on helium. Big as he was—and he was tall and well as wide—his voice was better suited to a ten-year-old boy. Simon had to stop himself from chuckling whenever the teacher started talking again. He knew better, of course. At least one kid a year got himself in trouble for making fun of the man's unusual vocal attributes.

"Well, I looked as far as I could, but I never did find out what happened to your great-great-granduncle. I know he died, but I have no idea how. Can you enlighten me?"

LeMarrs eyed him suspiciously for a moment. "And why did you say you wanted all of this dirty laundry again?"

"It's not dirty, Barry, it's history."

The teacher nodded and then smiled as the girl he'd probably taught only a few years earlier sauntered over with his pie and a pot of coffee. The teacher's eyes traveled over her form quickly, and Simon would have felt a bit of disgust at the notion, but he'd been eyeballing her earlier himself. She was a cute thing. He just had to remind himself that she was also young enough to be his granddaughter if he'd had any kids. It didn't seem right, somehow, that his libido still looked when he knew better. It seemed worse that the man across from him looked. After teaching the girl through her formative years, it seemed . . . vile to watch the man react to her presence.

Of course there was also the mental image of the poor girl crushed under LeMarr's considerable bulk to consider.

"What I don't get is why you're writing all of this." Barry nodded his thanks and attacked the pie with his fork, making sure to scoop up a decent lump of melting ice cream at the same time. "It's been done before, you know."

"Well, Barry, I gotta say, I've read the histories that have been done of Serenity Falls, and every last one of them is lacking."

"How so?"

"They don't tell you anything. Seems a shame to me to write a history book and not actually say what's happened in the past, don't you think?"

Barry nodded and laughed around a mouthful of pie. He had the decency to cover his mouth with his napkin as he chuckled. "Fair enough. You trying to write the sort of history that doesn't always get published?"

Simon nodded. "Yeah, I guess I am." He frowned for a moment and slurped a bit of his tepid coffee as he tried to put it into words. That was the problem he'd run into more often than any other in his writing endeavors: he wasn't a writer. Words did not come easily to him. "I want to try to put the whole town into perspective, Barry. I want, just once in my life, to be able to see the big picture."

"Sounds like a noble enough cause to me, Mr. Mac-Gruder. So I'll answer that question." Barry took a sip of his own coffee and added three packs of sugar. "Glenn LeMarrs was killed by some slaves he tried to turn over to a bounty hunter. It isn't common knowledge, but my family's Bible has the information penned into it. I like looking at that old book from time to time. Lets me see a bit more of that big picture you were talking about." The man smiled, and his face looked as young as his voice for a moment. Simon wondered how miserable LeMarrs might be with his lot in life. Forty-five years old and never married. There had been a big run of rumors for a while that he was homosexual, but if he was, he managed to be incredibly discreet in a town where discretion was sometimes a lacking element.

Simon MacGruder didn't think Barry LeMarrs was gay—not that he much cared one way or the other what the man did with his sex life, thanks just the same—he just figured the middle school teacher was lonely and sad. Why else would a man let himself get that large?

They chatted for a few minutes more, and then LeMarrs excused himself with a proper thanks for the snack and a promise to let Simon look at the family

Bible as long as he came over for dinner in exchange. Simon agreed gladly and then paid the substantial tab for the meal.

He was still trying to work out how best to write down his notes for the night when he almost tripped over Mike Blake. It wasn't unusual for Simon to mosey through the cemetery on his way home, even after the sun had set. He had no fear of the dead, and he sometimes paid his respects to his folks or to the one girl who'd stolen his heart away before she died. Elizabeth Glass had been a beauty, and he'd have probably married her, but there had been some sort of trouble when he'd been away in Korea, and by the time he got back, Liz had been buried for almost two years. Half a lifetime later, and he still missed her.

Mike apparently had the same problem. He'd passed out near his wife's grave again. Simon sighed and squatted next to the man. Even from three feet away he could smell the bourbon on the ex-banker's breath. He was a little sad and a little disgusting, but he was still a good man under the dirty clothes and the booze.

"Get up, Mike." Simon shook the man's shoulder roughly.

"Huhnn . . . What?" The man's voice was slurred by drink and stupor. His breath alone would have been enough to cause inebriation.

"I said get up. Let's get you over to my place for a night. Your clothes are ripe enough to stand on their own."

Mike's face went from a deep pout of confusion to a bright smile as he saw MacGruder. "Oh, hey, Simon. How are you today?"

"Sober." He snapped the word and almost immediately regretted it. Mike was a sad sack, but he didn't deserve anger. He deserved to have his wife back. "Sorry, Mike. That was mean."

Mike shook his head and managed a weak half smile. "No, Simon. That was fair. I'm drunk, and I know it."

"Damn, Mike. This is twice in one week I found you this way, and I don't even come into town that much." He helped the man stand up, which wasn't much of an effort. Mike was pretty damned good at being drunk and walking at the same time.

Mike just nodded as they headed out of the cemetery.

"You gotta stop this shit, Mike. Amy wouldn't approve."

"You're right, Simon. I know that." Mike lowered his head and looked at the ground as Simon moved them both in the direction of his house.

"I can't make you stop, Mike. I wish I could, Lord knows . . ."

They walked the rest of the way in near silence, and Simon helped the man strip down to his skivvies and dropped his clothes in the washing machine after emptying the pockets. He made Mike take a shower and then poured him into the guest bedroom's double bed.

After a while, Mike started snoring loudly. Simon did his best to ignore the noise and wrote down his notes for the day.

II

Serenity Falls Part Five:
The Underground

There was a time, just before the Civil War came around and turned the nation on its collective ear, when good people living far above the Mason-Dixon Line did what they could for the slaves trying to escape from the Southern states. There was a series of places throughout the Northern states that took in the escaped slaves and helped them find their way to different places where slavery was not considered a decent way to treat a human being. Some people referred to this loose conglomeration of hiding places as the Underground Railroad, though no trains were actually involved in the procedure, unless a daring escapee managed to hide on one to get part of their traveling done.

Serenity was not exactly a place with high traffic. It never had been. For that reason it was almost ideal as a location for a hideaway. Worth LeMarrs and his family were sympathetic to the cause, and they had room to spare. Though they hardly took in hundreds of escaped slaves, they did manage to care for a few dozen over the years.

Worth believed in the basic tenet that all people should have the freedom to live out their lives as they saw fit, so long as no one else was hurt in the process. The farm the family owned was large, and the crops were normally good enough to keep them in comfort through the year. He was a good man who felt the need to help out in a dire situation, and he saw the Underground as a test of his faith in the Lord above. He did not like to fail tests.

Worth managed to keep his secrets from his neighbors, though it was sometimes a bit of a challenge. People in Serenity tended to be friendly with each other, and a few of them liked to gossip a bit. Still, none of the escaped slaves he took in were ever found or hurt.

Things changed a bit when Worth died and his brother took over the farm. Glenn LeMarrs was an energetic lad with a long list of tasks he set up for himself and the belief that he could achieve anything. Sadly, his beliefs did not jibe with his abilities.

He tended to the farm with the same passion as his brother before him, looking after his widowed sister-in-law, Rachel, who was both kind and a hard worker, and the children as well. He was good at farming, and he loved his family. Most importantly, he didn't want to disappoint the memory of his brother. But Glenn was not very good with numbers, and he was often distracted by the notion of women. Rachel was completely off limits to his mind. She was his sister-in-law, and it wasn't even a notion he would allow himself to play with, at least when the lights were on.

But for all his altruistic dreams, he was still a man, and he still had urges. The farm suffered from his distraction and from his general lack of experience with monetary matters. There was a while when he was certain he would lose the farm and ruin all that his brother and his father before them had built.

He needed a way to save what he was in danger of losing. He found it when he contacted a bounty hunter named Marcus Solomon, who was perfectly willing to buy back the slaves who came to the farm seeking freedom. Capturing the poor wretches was easy; they came seeking solace, and he provided it. He gave them a place to stay and fed them fruit and sometimes even meat. He merely failed to mention that the food was laced with mild poisons that left those who consumed it paralyzed. Marcus Solomon provided the drug for a nominal fee.

Glenn and Solomon had met before, had become if not friends then certainly friendly associates through mutual connections in the gambling arenas. Unlike his brother, Glenn had spent a bit of time traveling and seeing the country when he was younger. While he always managed to look respectable on the home front, he was not exactly associating with the finer elements of society while on the road.

Any good farmer knows that at least a few chickens must be kept alive if there are to be eggs. As has already been stated, Glenn LeMarrs was not a good farmer. He was a greedy and desperate farmer; the two should never be confused. Marcus Solomon was more than eager to take every escaped slave that came his way, and he was also the first to make the suggestion that Glenn could relax a bit by taking advantage of any female slaves who came along. To that point the idea had never truly occurred to the young man. He considered slaves little better than animals, and thought of them the same way when it came to sex.

But after the hunter's offhand comment, that changed. Glenn learned to like sampling the wares that came his way and derived extra pleasure from the ones who fought back. Taking them by force made it easier for him to believe that he still had control of his own destiny. And if he sometimes thought of his sister-in-law while he did it, he made sure never to cry out her name.

What guilt he might have felt he salved with the forced conviction that they were only animals, that they deserved the punishment. And, really, they were little better than animals. They were mere savages that managed to look human.

Any last shred of guilt was taken away by the money that came in. It wasn't enough to make a fortune, but it was enough to pay off the debts that he'd accrued. The debts came fast, but at that time, the slaves were doing all they could to escape from what their lives had become. And there was also very little by way of communication between the houses where the slaves hid.

He kept up the practice for almost two years, making sure that Rachel and her children knew nothing about it. He could justify his actions to himself but knew better than to think he could do so with her.

All good things must come to an end. His financial salvation became his ruin. Somewhere along the route to freedom, someone got wise to what was happening.

The knowledge did not sit well.

And Glenn LeMarrs never realized when he was being set up.

Almost two years to the day after he'd started his little entrepreneurial exercise, the runaway slaves retaliated. Marcus Solomon got careless, it seemed, and wound up screaming for hours before he died. He'd had a full seven runaway slaves in his possession when one of them, a lean man named Willie McWhirter, managed to slip free of his manacles, sacrificing several layers of skin and a few ounces of blood to manage the task.

Willie was not a violent man. Though he'd lived on the plantation and worked hard for the masters, there were rumors that he was the bastard child of Rodney McWhirter, who owned the land and the slaves as well. If there was special treatment for his possible lineage, no one ever told him about it. He'd spent too many years being whipped and worked hard to have enough spirit left in him to be violent. But he'd been a witness to Glenn LeMarrs's attack on one of the girls, a young thing named Ellie Mae, who happened to also be one of the four slaves who'd run away from the plantation in Alabama with him. Ellie Mae fought back against LeMarrs, just the way he liked a girl to struggle. That gave him all the excuse he needed to be as violent as he wanted. Solomon, the only nonescaped slave to know his dirty little secret, laughed when he saw one of the girls violated and battered. He called it "breaking their spirit."

Willie McWhirter called it an abomination, though he barely understood what the word meant. It was enough to make Willie hunger for more than freedom. After he'd finished getting out of his chains, he slunk over to where the bounty hunter lay sleeping and moved as carefully, as quietly as he ever had. He hit the man in the head with a rock that was roughly the size of a grapefruit, just to make sure he stayed asleep. Then he found the keys to open the rest of the manacles and made short work of freeing everyone else.

Willie did not have the stomach to be truly violent. Others in the band of escapees didn't have any problem taking care of matters themselves. How many details are needed to explain that Marcus Solomon suffered greatly for his sins? Is it enough to hear that the skin was peeled from his arms? Enough to know that the two women he'd forced himself on made sure that he would never have the desire again? Perhaps, perhaps not. It should be enough, however, to know that his death was many hours in coming, and that long before Solomon left this mortal plane he had told all of his secrets to the ex-slaves who decided to question him.

And perhaps it will help with perspective to know that Willie McWhirter never slept easily again. He'd known that plantation life was hard, that it could steal away the innocence of any soul made to suffer. He just never really understood that the void filled after innocence is lost is sometimes filled with madness.

Willie went with the rest of the escapees to find Glenn LeMarrs. He was afraid not to. More afraid even than when he ran from the world he'd known in search of a myth called freedom. At that time he still didn't know if it really existed and was actually a little scared to find out.

Still, he went back to the LeMarrs place with his gathering of runaways, and while they looked to him for advice many times in the months to follow, for the next few days he was basically excess baggage. His arms were too badly ravaged by his escape for him to do more than walk along with the group. Ellie Mae was kind to him and tended him as best she could, though she was almost as badly battered as he. Sometimes he could almost forget what she'd done to the bounty hunter.

Almost.

They spent three days near the LeMarrs farm before

they decided it was time to get their revenge. They watched, they studied, and they learned. Three days to know their enemy and his actions. And then they were ready.

They waited until the sun had set, until the lights in the house were turned down and only a single lantern burned. And then they waited a little longer, until that lantern was taken from the house, carried by LeMarrs himself as he moved toward the two-story barn where the escaped slaves could stay in what they believed would be safety.

When the light from his lantern reached the second level of the structure, the escapees moved as quietly as they could and followed. They had only been away from the farm for five days, and already the man had found new fodder for his appetites. The woman wept as she was violated, and her agonies seemed to drive LeMarrs to work harder to create more screams. He'd wrapped a kerchief into her mouth to muffle the worst of the sounds, keeping him safe from discovery by his brother's family.

He never considered the need to be safe from his previous guests. Ellie Mae reached him first, and if her anger had manifested grimly with Solomon, it was a thousand times worse with LeMarrs. She caught him with his pants down, literally and figuratively, and fell upon him with a ferocity that would have shamed a rabid bear. Her teeth broke the skin on his face, and she pulled back with a chunk of flesh that included most of his nose.

Whatever precautions for keeping silence LeMarrs might have made did not include stopping his own screams. He shrieked wildly as the group fell upon him, and he soon discovered that men could be violated in much the same way as women. Ellie Mae exacted her revenge with the handle of a rake. The other woman used a scythe and employed the business end.

That would have been all, it would have been finished, if not for the widow trying to discover the source of the screams. It would be fair to say that Rachel LeMarrs was not overly fond of her brother-in-law. She found him mildly repulsive, and her skin wanted to crawl away whenever he stared at her. It seemed his eyes could almost look through her clothes, and that was not a pleasant idea to her.

Just the same, she had never actually wished him harm. She had certainly never wished to find him dying the way she did. Rachel had never imagined that anyone could lose that much blood or that the human body could actually contain that much of the substance. Her scream upon making the discovery came close to rivaling that of her dying brother-in-law.

She did not die that night, but she was made to suffer the same fate as the women Glenn LeMarrs had drugged and kept for a time. There was no lust in what was done to her, merely rage and a need for revenge that was not sated with the death of the man who'd tortured and violated the runaway slaves.

That knowledge would not have made the crime any less reprehensible had Rachel known. She kept the secret until the day she died and, on the occasions when she let herself consider what had happened, she thanked God that she had no children from the forced union.

The ex-slaves responsible for her suffering were never seen again in the area.

Some weeks later, four runaway slaves attempted to

seek shelter at the safe house they'd been told of. Two of them died from the bullets she fired at them. The other two fled and warned others that there was no safety for their kind in Serenity.

III

Fourteen hours, twenty-seven minutes. That was how long it took Jonathan Crowley to batter down the stainless steel door that blocked his freedom in the house where he'd hunted for an ancient vampire. His shoulder was still bruised and bloodied and would remain that way as long as he encountered nothing of the supernatural. There were rules that he had to follow, and one of those rules required that he heal normally unless there was something otherworldly around him. Unfortunately, his car didn't qualify for aiding in his regeneration. It could change shapes—as evidenced by the fact that he was currently driving a massive Silver Cloud instead of the Sunbird he'd taken into town the day before—but it could not help him repair the damage he'd done to himself.

"I ever find that bastard, I'll make him suffer for as long as I can." He rolled his shoulder, wincing at the tenderness he felt through the muscles. The way the shirt stuck to the bloodiest spots didn't do a thing to make his mood any better. "I can't believe I let that fucking corpse pull a fast one on me. Shit, I'm getting sloppier all the damned time."

He'd paid a visit to Irving on his way out of town. Irv was not looking any better, but he was glad to hear that the local problem had been eliminated. He thanked Crowley before he slipped back into a deep sleep. They'd never meet again, and that bothered Crowley more than he liked to admit. But that was a part of the price he paid for taking back the responsibilities he'd given up for a few decades.

The drive helped. It always did. Hitting the open road and traveling from location to location was one of the few pleasures he allowed himself in the world. That, and killing the stupid idiots who richly deserved to die.

And speaking of idiots, there were a few in front of him on the lonesome stretch of highway he traveled toward the east. He still had to get to New York and find out about who or what was killing people off in ritualistic fashion.

His cell phone rang twice, and he answered it as the SUV in front of him slowed and sped up almost randomly. "Crowley."

"Mr. Crowley? Hi, It's Kristen again." She sounded out of breath.

"What's new, Kristen? Did you find out anything else I should know about?" Hearing his voice, she'd have never expected to see the expression on his face. It was rare that anyone called him back after they'd made their invitations to him. The last thing he ever needed was to hear from someone a second time, unless they had new information.

"Well, I just wanted to let you know there was another death. I know you're coming here as fast as you can, but I thought you might like to hear about it."

"Who died, Kristen?"

The woman's voice cracked when she spoke. "I-I have a friend in New York, from back in college. You might remember her, Denise Winters?" He stayed quiet. Denise Winters had been a vivacious little girl with a reputation for being easy. Last he'd heard, she'd left the school not long after getting hooked on the heavy stuff.

"Yeah. I remember Denise. Did something happen to her?"

"No . . . not to her. To her daughter, Brianna. Oh, Mr. Crowley, Denise is just a wreck . . ."

"Well, I had some unfinished business to take care of, Kristen. I'm very sorry for Denise. Listen, why don't you give me her address? I'll pay her a visit, and we can talk about what happened."

She told him the street name in a little town he'd been to a long time ago. A place called Beldam Woods, New York. "Kristen, if you talk to Denise, you let her know I'm coming, all right? Let her know I'm going to ask her some questions that she might not like, but that I'm going to fix this once and for all."

She promised she would, and he let it go and wished her well. After he hung up, he drove most of the way through Pennsylvania, stopping in Allentown to rest. The EconoLodge was pleasant and inexpensive, but there was a group down the hall that he would have gleefully dismembered. Judging by the number of motorcycles—Harleys, and big ones at that—parked in the lot near where he settled his car, the fight wouldn't be worth it.

He changed his mind a little over two hours later, when the noise from the idiot squad hadn't toned down in the least. He had three options. He could interfere himself, call the manager, or call the police. He tried option two first, and was promptly rewarded by apologetic laughter. "There's no way, dude. I'm just a weekend manager here, and I want to keep my legs. I am NOT interrupting those guys."

"Then why don't you call the damned police, precious?"

"Hey, listen, I'm not paid to risk life and limb. There's no way in hell I'm calling the cops on those guys. You want to do it, you go right ahead."

"I'm coming to your office in about ten minutes. I'm gonna kick your ass myself."

"You don't bug me, mister. Those guys? They bug me. I'll take my chances."

"Bad mistake." Crowley slammed the receiver back into its cradle and pulled back on a pair of jeans.

He noticed the massive bruises on his shoulder from his earlier work as a battering ram and decided he'd try his luck anyway. He also decided he'd try the polite approach first. He knocked, and he waited patiently. Well, as patiently as he ever did for anything. When the sound of hard bass from a screaming heavy metal band drowned out his knocking, he tried a second time with a much harder rap of his knuckles on the door. On the third attempt, he hauled off and kicked the door hard enough to make it rattle in the frame.

That one got somebody's attention. The music died down to a mere whisper of its former self, and the door opened to reveal the grizzled face of either a biker or a

Viking peering through the vast cloud of smoke and the heady perfume of spilled beer and various liquors. He was guessing biker, as the Vikings as a whole were long gone, and most of them probably hadn't worn leather jackets heavily adorned with patches and spikes.

"What ya need, bro?" The man was not smiling. He looked a tad annoyed.

Crowley smiled for him and crossed his arms. "I need sleep. That's why I came here. I want to sleep."

"Yeah? Have a good time with it." The man started to close the door, already bored with the conversation, and Crowley blocked the path of the closing barrier with his foot.

"I will, just as soon as you turn off that fucking music and ease up on the screamfest, Scooter."

"Say what?" Biker boy sucked in a massive breath and squared his shoulders.

"I said turn the fucking music down, you buffoon." He put on his best smile to ease the growing tension. It didn't work. He also tried to dodge the ham hock–sized fist that came for his face and failed miserably in that attempt, too. His nose tried to turn itself inside out as the biker from hell connected. Crowley staggered back and hit the wall on the opposite side of the hallway.

He felt warm blood trickle into his sinuses and grinned properly. "Now that was rude . . ."

The biker didn't agree. He came into the hall and stomped his way over to where Crowley was lying on the ground. Seen in the light of a room not filled to overflowing with marijuana and tobacco smoke, he was even uglier and gray haired as well. His size-twelve boot came up fast, aimed squarely at Crowley's chin.

Jonathan Crowley had the dubious honor of being the cause of many a person's nightmares, and that was for good reason. In addition to going out of his way to hunt down and kill supernatural creatures, he was also adept at most forms of armed and unarmed combat.

Biker boy was just good at kicking the shit out of things. Jonathan Crowley tended to think of hand-to-hand fighting as a source of stress relief.

The biker's foot stopped three inches from Crowley's face, held in place by the two surprisingly strong hands that caught it. He used his own shoe and the foot inside it to punt the man's testicles into the next week. The burly man standing over him let out a deep groan and fell backwards, clutching at his privates even as his eyes went wide and his face went dark red.

"You sonuvabitch . . . I'll kill you."

Crowley stood up, his lips peeled back from large teeth, and his eyes glittering behind his rimless glasses. "Shouldn't make threats you can't keep, Scooter."

"What the hell?" The sound came from higher up than it should have as far as Crowley was concerned. He looked over at the doorway and saw a giant of a man standing in the entrance to the room Scooter had just left. Said giant was every bit the Viking. Crowley could even imagine him with the horned helmet, or maybe a big battle-ax in his hands.

"He got bitchy." Crowley wiped the blood from his nose with the back of his hand. Scooter groaned on the ground, trying without success to stand up and hold his balls at the same time.

The giant—complete with a massive mane of dark red hair and a beard that was just starting to show a few gray hairs to counter the flaming red—looked at his companion on the ground and then back at Crowley. Crowley imagined several scenarios in which the Viking came through the door and tore him into little pieces. He was, without a doubt, one of the biggest human beings Crowley had ever seen. He had to turn sideways to get out of the door and into the hallway.

The man loomed over Crowley, and he wasn't even trying to loom. It just happened. "Yeah, well, we've been drinking a bit . . ." His eyes narrowed slightly, and he looked at Crowley, assessing whether or not he felt the man in front of him was a serious threat. Crowley didn't like that the giant wasn't looking very impressed.

"I noticed. I came over to ask as nicely as I could if you guys could keep it down. I've been trying to sleep."

"Come on, Burt. Let's get you back in the room." The Norse god lifted his companion from his prone position with ease and half carried him through the doorway. When he was done depositing the aching biker on the floor, he turned around. "We'll try to keep it quiet, mister. Sorry about that."

Crowley nodded his thanks and watched until the door was closed. Then and only then he sighed and sagged a bit. The noise levels stayed down. After five minutes, he went back to his room. There was a brief pause to go to the office and verbally rip into the weekend night manager.

Sleep came quickly and brought with it the usual insanity.

CHAPTER 6

I

Simon MacGruder hadn't been inside the Blackwell house in over fifteen years. The last time he'd still been working at the quarry. He circled the place warily, feeling his stomach do a few nervous rolls. There was something about the place that gave him the creeps. Of course, he knew a lot of the history of Havenwood already. He'd been around almost as long as the house, and he remembered the bad things that had taken place there.

He was here mostly just for inspiration. He wanted to remember better times, and he wanted to remember the people who had lived there as clearly as he could before he started writing about their lives and their deaths. Was it three generations or four that had lived in the place? He couldn't remember.

After looking over the aging ruin, he moved past

the rusted gate of the stuccoed wall surrounding the property and walked onto the grounds. The grass inside was thick and wild and half buried under vines and weeds. No one had tended the place in a very long time, and he wondered how it was that nothing had ever been done about maintaining the old house or at least selling it. There had been a time when the parties thrown at the old house were nearly legendary. Old man Blackwell had known how to treat his employees, and he could still remember how the place had looked in its heyday. Of course he'd only been a tyke back then, but he could still see it in his mind's eye. Sometimes he thought having a good memory was a blessing, and other times he felt the weight of his years like an anchor around his neck. Being back at Havenwood was a little of both.

He'd had his first kiss on this very property, from a sweet little girl of fifteen by the name of Erin Lockley. She'd had gorgeous blond hair and the biggest blue eyes and a smile that stole his breath away whenever she cast it in his direction.

Three days after that kiss, Erin had been hit by a car and dragged almost a hundred feet before the driver stopped. She hadn't survived the accident, and that was a blessing. The man who hit her had been Simon's own father, and while there was no proof of foul play and certainly nothing his father said or did to add to his suspicions, Simon had always wondered just how accidental the car's impact had been. It was just a feeling he'd always harbored, brought on in part by the way his father looked at Erin whenever he saw her, as if she were a bug. The dislike had definitely been mutual, if completely silent. Neither ever said a bad word about the other, and it hadn't stopped Erin and Simon from holding hands and taking walks together, but it had been real.

Good memories and bad memories alike flooded his head, and after several minutes of reflecting on both, Simon got up the nerve to head up the short flight of stairs to the porch of the old mansion.

The windows of the old place were mostly intact, a fact that was almost worth puzzling over. Granted, Havenwood was a little out of the way, but that had never stopped kids from being kids in the past. Also, he knew good and damned well that a lot of Serenity's children made use of the closed quarry for swimming and maybe a little make-out session from time to time. He'd fully expected all of the glass to be knocked out of the frames. He was pleasantly surprised to find otherwise.

Simon walked across the time-warped and rotted floorboards of the porch and looked inside the old place. There was actually still furniture inside, rat-eaten and shredded, true, but the furniture was still there. A thick layer of dust had settled over everything a long time ago, and the entire thing was almost surreal. He could hear the ghosts of previous conversations, and the echoes from other times seemed to come from somewhere inside the place, not from his head.

He almost got up the nerve to go inside. He might have actually done it, too, if he hadn't seen a rat scurry past. The damned thing was as big as a dachshund and nowhere near as cute.

When he was done looking around, Simon walked back into the front yard of the place and stood near the tree that had shaded both him and Erin over five decades earlier. A ghost of that first kiss flushed warmly across his lips, and he smiled for a moment.

There were good memories in Serenity Falls. Not each of them as special, but there had been good times. Why else would he have stayed as long as he had so far?

The sun was starting to set, and he had barely stopped on his walking tour of the town and his trek through memories he'd barely let himself remember until now. Simon MacGruder left Havenwood behind and headed back toward his cabin in the woods.

He wasn't there to hear the voices that continued after he left. Even if he had been, he'd have just attributed them to his mind playing tricks on him. Nothing but rats, spiders, and a few mice lived in Havenwood. Of that he was certain. And he was right.

But they were not all that moved through the old house. There were other things as well, and the dead did not rest easily within the walls of the old Blackwell home.

II

Serenity Falls Part Six:
When Johnny Came Marching Home Again

World War I was not kind to Serenity Falls. The town was larger then, with a population that was close to seven thousand people strong, but a good many of the men in the town were taken away by their sense of patriotism, and many of them came back from the European front in pine boxes.

Just to add to the fun, Spanish influenza killed almost a thousand people before it was done visiting the town. The flu was an equal opportunity destroyer, and folks from both sides of the river died at such a speed that many people felt the end of the world had come to them. In some ways, they were right. Serenity was devastated by the epidemic. And so, when he finally made it home, was Johnny Blackwell. Johnny had gone into the army as an optimist, but he came home bitter and disillusioned in not only the war efforts, but in his life as a whole.

Most people agreed that the wheelchair he brought with him in place of his legs probably had a lot to do with that. But just as significantly, he returned to a family home that was empty of family. The whole Blackwell clan had been eliminated by the Spanish flu, which Johnny himself had endured and survived while in Europe. Johnny hadn't known about that little fact when he was recovering from the loss of his legs. Perhaps the doctors thought to spare him any additional pain; perhaps the news was simply never sent. Whatever the case, he came home to find that he'd lost everything.

Johnny had little by way of company. From time to time he would be visited by Doc Parsons, who tended to his legs and gave him exercises to help maintain his strength. He was also visited by Maxwell Deveraux, who delivered groceries for a nominal fee and by Angela Bradenton, who came to Havenwood three times a week to clean up and prepare meals for him. It took almost six months of her conversations with him as she worked and cleaned for Angela to finally get Johnny to actually speak to her instead of merely responding to her comments. Though they had attended school together, they'd never been close enough to really know each other. She came from an entirely different world in many ways. Where Johnny had been born into wealth and privilege, Angela had been the seventh of seven children born to parents who managed to survive at poverty level on their farm.

Eventually, Johnny came to look forward to her visits, if not with a mind toward courtship then at least with a mind that was desperately tired of being alone. She would work on whatever needed mending, make his bed for him, wash the linens, and cook, and he would either fidget with the paperwork for the quarry—having the foreman report to him about production—or work on his hobby of carving figurines out of wood. The first ones he made were of his family. He made one of each member and went to great pains to make them as close to perfect as he could. Angela marveled at his talent with the carving tools he used and often praised him highly. He ate the flattery and attention as greedily as a starving man would devour a Thanksgiving dinner.

It almost became an obsession with him. He strove to make more and more of the figures to impress her, and he did everything he could to make them perfect. When he'd finished with his own family, he started making figures of hers. Using photographs and her careful descriptions, he carved duplicates of each member of her family and placed them beside his own. His only reward for his efforts was her delight as he presented each statue for her approval.

Angela loved to see each work as it progressed and told many of the people in town that he was really quite talented with his skills. Several people came by to see Johnny Blackwell, and when they did, he showed them the carvings and listened to their words of admiration. When he was finished with Angela's family, he took the time to start working on other people in the town of Serenity. Though a few people protested the idea of being duplicated in this fashion, none of them complained too loudly. It wasn't wise to anger the man who was the primary source of income, for one thing, and it was harmless enough, for another.

It took John Blackwell—no longer called Johnny by anyone in town—almost fourteen years to finish the carvings. He made one of each person he knew in town, and made even more of people he'd only heard of or seen on the streets. He spent several hours of every day working on the figures, both before and after he married Angela. One could say that their marriage was almost inevitable; she was his only real companionship, and

despite his often dour attitudes, he could be very charm-
ing when the mood struck him, which it almost always
did when around Angela.

The ceremony was small, with only her immediate
family in attendance. The newlyweds traveled as far as
Colorado for their honeymoon, and came back after almost a month away. If the family of the new bride had
expected special rewards for giving up their daughter,
they were sorely disappointed. John Blackwell was not
a miser, but he did not play favorites with his in-laws,
either. Life went on as it had before in the town.

But at Havenwood life got a little stranger and a little
brighter, too. Angela gave birth to a strong, fine son. His
name was Alexander, and he was the bright point of
both his parents' lives. At least in public. Every Sunday
after Alexander was born the couple took their child to
the Methodist church in town, staying for the sermons
and making generous donations to the church's welfare.
Once a month they even attended the family events that
took place on Saturdays when the weather permitted,
and despite his handicap, John at least cheered on the
teams that played against each other in softball or whatever game they chose.

And every night, after most of the town was asleep,
John continued making his wooden figures. If she was
willing, and most nights she was, he and his wife performed the rituals that are supposed to unite man and
woman as a couple. And if she was bothered by the fact
that he had no legs, she never complained. She made
him feel complete.

Right up until the night when he finished the last
carving. When he showed her the final piece, the one

that completed every single person living in town at that time, Angela rewarded him with a vigorous session in bed that left him drained and satisfied as never before. It was the last time they were together as man and wife, and the last night he breathed.

Angela held her husband under the water of the claw-foot tub until he was dead. Though he struggled, he had no real fight in him at that point. The poison she'd set in his food saw to that. The town doctor declared it a horrible accident and gave all the consolation he could. Angela Blackwell never remarried, and like her husband before her showed no favoritism to her own family, even after his death. The only person she seemed to care about was her son, Alexander.

Alexander grew up in a loving environment and cared for his mother through her autumn years until she died of old age. In time he himself married a young woman from town, who bore him two sons and one daughter. His wife was loving and kind, and he returned the favor until she died of breast cancer a few years after the birth of their daughter. His oldest son, William, died in the Korean War. His youngest son, Joseph, took care of him in his later years and mourned his death when the time came. His daughter left town amid a scandal involving one of the local boys. There were rumors that she was pregnant at the time.

Joseph married Clarisse, a woman of extraordinary beauty, and they had three fine, beautiful children, but that is another tale. In time the figures that John Blackwell had carved were forgotten, which was precisely as Angela wanted it when she boarded them up in the second room that adjoined the master bedroom. They weren't meant to be seen by anyone except for her. And once she had finished her use for them, she felt no need to see them again.

Angela had finished the mission that the voices gave her, and she had done it without remorse. As far as she knew, the duties she performed were sacred. And if the whispered words that soothed her to sleep every night were not sent by her Creator, they were most certainly sent by what she chose to see as her god. The voices stayed with her well after her son took over the family business. And she obeyed them until the day she died.

No one in Serenity ever accused Angela Blackwell of being mad. No one ever knew. She was good at keeping secrets. But then, so were most of the people living in Serenity.

It was almost a tradition.

III

Jonathan Crowley actually managed to relax for two days as he headed for New York City. After that, he was back to being busy in no time. The first order of business was a check at one of the libraries in Manhattan to find out what their archive of papers had to say about the murders. It was remarkably little, save the names, locations, etc. There was no mention of how the deaths occurred, save a note that there were certain "ritualistic aspects that were not being disclosed." He took down notes and then went walking.

Adele Elizabeth Sawhurst, aged sixteen, was the first victim. She'd been found naked in an abandoned apartment almost ten miles from her home. She had been sexually violated and severely mutilated. There was no mention of ritualistic markings, but then again, if she really was the first victim, there would be no similar markings to associate with her. She'd been reported missing almost a full month before her remains were located.

Next in line was a stripper with the dubious name of Montana Lakes. Hardly an innocent by anyone's standards, the girl had done a few amateur porns and was fast building a solid reputation in the field before she disappeared. As she was known to like to party, not too many people were surprised when she disappeared for a few days. Everyone was still shocked when they learned how she died, however. Her body was found only one day after she was last seen. This time the remains were found in Hell's Kitchen. There was brief mention that certain similarities between her murder and another crime under investigation might be an indication that the same perpetrator was responsible for both.

By victim number four, the papers were leaning heavily toward that magical phrase: serial killer. By victim number five, they were all trying to come up with a catchy name to call the latest in a long list of sadistic torturers. No doubt they were stymied by the lack of letters confessing the crimes and giving away juicy tidbits that they could plaster all over their front pages.

That was around the time that Crowley got his phone call. Now he was here, and two more girls were dead and connected with the same series of deaths. Crowley was not amused.

He made it a point to attend the funeral of the latest girl—Maria Delcastos, age fifteen and an honor roll student at a private Catholic school—and stood politely off to the side while the family wept and wailed and howled their grief into the skies. He never got near the services proper, instead moving through the large cemetery and clearing off a few headstones as he gathered supplies for more of his most useful powders. Amazing how much power was contained inside the mold off a dead person's grave. Amazing, too, the number of people who could not sense that power.

Crowley wasn't overly fond of graveyards. Not because the dead gave him the willies—which they didn't, even when they were as chatty as the specters hanging around this one—but because he really didn't much care for human grief. Too many memories he would rather have simply forgotten.

He made himself think about the present instead of the past and collected what he needed even as he did a little community service and cleaned up a few of the worst areas in the cemetery. He also set a few small surprises for anyone else that might decide to desecrate the headstones in the place. Nothing fatal, just scary as all hell. They could all do with learning a little respect for the dead.

Not that he was planning to follow that notion himself. After all, he was here mostly to defile the grave of a little girl who'd already been tortured enough.

He kept himself busy until the sun had set and the security staff had closed and locked the gates. Not being seen was one of his many talents, and he took full advantage of it. He found a branch and pulled the pocketknife from his jeans and whittled for almost three hours in the darkness before he decided it was time to do what he had to do.

With slow, deliberate steps he made his way over to the grave and set down the small wooden carving he'd made. It wasn't much, but it would do as an offering. "Hi, Maria. Want to talk to me?"

There was silence for a moment, and then the wind picked up enough to ruffle his short hair. Crowley leaned back on his haunches and looked at the inscription on the young girl's grave. All around him he heard the sudden silence of the insects and animals that came out at night.

The girl's pain was gone, but the memories lingered. She spoke, and Jonathan Crowley listened.

CHAPTER 7

I

Simon MacGruder spent the first half of his day sitting in the woods and listening to the wildlife around him. He knew for a fact that he wasn't far from where Sarah Hopkins Miles had been burned at the stake. There were only so many places were multiple rocks thrust themselves from the soft soil, and this was definitely the only one that matched the descriptions. Of course he'd known about the place where the witch died long before he read the books. For as long as he could remember people had spoken of the witch of the woods. Local legends told that if you asked her the right way, she would grant wishes. That part he didn't believe, but that had never stopped him from sharing the stories with the occasional kid who came to his place and asked him questions. Somewhere along the way he'd become a bit of an enigma to the local children. He knew that and found

it amusing. It was funny to think of how many of them
equated a crazy old hermit with a great and powerful
sorcerer. Who was he to correct them when they were
obviously having fun?

The weather was still nice, and he took a long stroll
through the woods, wondering what they had seen in the
course of centuries. Had the Indians ever come here?
Had they settled and been driven away by the European
settlers? Had some of the early colonists tried to settle
nearby and been driven away? He had no idea. After all
the time he'd spent in the woods near Serenity Falls, he
still had no understanding of the land that he lived on. It
was the magnitude that stopped him. Even with all of
the headaches and volumes of lore he'd been reading
over, he knew that long before Serenity had been here,
these very woods had been growing and thriving.

It was humbling, really, to realize that all he had
done in his life was nothing compared to what had happened even in these woods where few human beings
had ever set foot. Maybe that was the real reason he
wanted to write the history. He wanted to be remembered for something other than being the town recluse.

And that thought was enough to get his ass back in
gear. He had people to talk to and things to write down
before the day was done. He thought about talking to
the Hardwicks, but they had never been his favorite
family in town. So instead he went to the police station
and asked if he could look at some of the older, closed
case files. Jack Michaels was the chief constable, a
good-looking enough man and pleasant to deal with.
He'd never given Simon the least bit of grief in all the
time they'd known each other. Bill Karstens was his

second in command and had definitely been a bit of an ass from time to time, but never in a serious way. They were in the middle of a shift change when MacGruder got to the dull brick building. Karstens was just getting ready to go home to his wife and family. Michaels, who could have decided he needed his nights off and made his other men cover the late shifts, was just getting ready for another late night shift.

Michaels scratched at his curly hair and shrugged. Karstens looked like he wanted to charge money for it, not because he needed the cash but because it would somehow be more official sounding if he charged for the use of the public records.

After doing that nonverbal communication trick that longtime associates and friends sometimes did—in this case he was doing it with Karstens—Michaels shrugged. "You want to look at a bunch of cases from the 1930s through the 1960s, I won't stop you. You're gonna have a bear of a time sorting though them though, Simon. A lot of those boxes have been shoved in corners since I was a kid."

"Well, since I'm gonna be using them, if I get a chance I'll see about putting those old cases back into proper order if they managed to get messed up, Jack. That sound like a deal?" He directed the question at Michaels but meant it for Karstens. Karstens seemed mollified that MacGruder wouldn't be getting something for nothing after all.

"More than I would have asked, Simon. But it surely can't hurt. You never can tell, maybe we'll start one of those cold case files like they have on Court TV." The chief constable was joking. His assistant, on the other hand, nodded as if this was the best idea he'd heard in weeks.

Simon nodded in Bill's direction—he of the perfectly pressed uniform and neatly trimmed, military-style mustache. If he could have seen through his dark sunglasses inside the old building, he would have probably kept them on. "Might make you guys famous, if you can solve a few of the older ones around here."

Karstens tried not to look too greedy at the idea of being in lights. Simon had a powerful suspicion that Bill Karstens would have loved nothing more than his own cop show. Something where he could tell people the consequences of even the smallest abuse of the legal system. He knew he wasn't being fair, but there was something about the man that just begged to be mocked.

After a few more minutes of chatter, Bill Karstens left for the day, and Simon leaned up against the man's desk while Jack poured them both a cup of coffee. "I heard about what happened the other day at the school, Simon. You should have come in and made a report."

It took him a minute to realize what the constable was talking about. "What? Them boys messing around with that little girl?"

Jack nodded.

"Wasn't much to it. They left it alone when I told them I knew who they were."

"Just the same. You should have reported it. Then I could put it on their files and nail the little shits if they did anything else wrong." Jack shook his head. "What the hell is the world coming to when you have to worry about teenagers molesting little girls?"

"Same thing it's always been up to, Jack. I've lived in

Serenity for a long time, and I've seen a lot of bad things happen here."

"Yeah. I guess you have. You looking at anything special this time around when you go into the files? Or are you just looking for trends of the ages?"

He looked at Jack Michaels for a long moment without speaking. He knew the man would have no objections to what he was doing, but it still felt strange sharing anything after the number of years he'd spent only sharing his opinions on earth-shattering subjects like the weather. "I want to look up what happened to Alexander Halston's crew, and I want to see what the official word was on Darryl McWhirter. Later on, I might want to look up a few more."

Michaels looked at him blankly for a moment and then nodded. "You really are pulling out the old stuff, aren't you?"

"That's what happens when you decide to write a history of the area, Jack. You gotta look at the old stuff, or there isn't much history to the book." He sipped his coffee and tried not to grimace. The man in front if him could have made water taste like crap, but his heart was in the right place.

"Well, I guess there is that." Michaels put on his official face, which had been known to strike terror in a few of the younger miscreants in town but had never been very impressive to Simon. "So, just so we're straight here, Simon. I don't want you actually using any of the official records as parts of your stories about Serenity Falls, okay? If the case isn't solved, you shouldn't even look at it, but I'm trusting you to be discreet."

Simon looked back at him and smiled. "Honestly?

I was there for the ones I want to see the most, Jack. I just want to refresh myself. It's been a lot of years since I thought of Alexander Halston or Darryl McWhirter. I don't think there's much in those files that I don't already know."

"You might be surprised."

"I doubt it. We're talking about Sam Hardwick, here, right? That man couldn't have surprised me on a bet."

"Yeah, I've heard he was a bit more predictable than most." Jack smiled a bit. "Not exactly a man who loved surprises."

Simon nodded and smiled. Old Sam was about as predicable as the tides. He hated surprises. Not that he didn't get a few of them in his day.

After a few more minutes of amiable conversation, Simon MacGruder left the chief constable to get to his work and headed down to the file room. He was on his word that he wouldn't snoop where he didn't belong, and knowing full well that the file room had cameras, he planned to behave just exactly as he should.

The sun had long since gone to bed by the time he found what he was looking for. The files were well buried under what passed for evidence in cases that had come and gone decades ago, and true to his word he'd spent a good deal of his time sorting through the boxes just to set them into some sort of less chaotic order.

He sat, he read, and he remembered a few of the times he would rather have forgotten. Later, he would write them down.

II

Serenity Falls Part Seven: The Murder of Darryl McWhirter

Time eases most memories, makes it easier to forget the mistakes we make. In Serenity Falls, time has even made it possible for people to forget about Darryl McWhirter.

Darryl McWhirter came to Serenity in April 1934 with the clothes on his back, a bottle of cheap red wine clutched in his hand, a drunken song in his heart, and nothing else worth mentioning. That was the first strike against him. The second strike was that he was of mixed heritage. Looking at the man, no one could decide if he was white, black, Latino, or even American Indian, so the automatic assumption was that the man was of mixed heritage. Not a good list of credentials in the early thirties.

Still, Serenity was hardly the sort of town that would turn away people in need. Despite the grumblings of several less tolerant citizens, John and Amanda Glass took the transient in and gave him a place to sleep and food to eat—of course, he had to work for it, but that was only to be expected.

Darryl proved himself to be a fair worker, more than able to handle the minor chores that were assigned him, and soon became a part of the town. While hardly wealthy, the Glasses provided room and board for Darryl McWhirter and gave him a little extra money when they could spare it. Rumors started that McWhirter and

Amanda were having an affair, but they were promptly squashed when McWhirter himself took down Sam Hardwick for making a snide comment that was just loud enough for everyone in the vicinity to hear.

Calm, slightly tipsy, and quiet Darryl McWhirter beat the living tar out of Sam Hardwick then and there, asking no questions and giving no quarter. One little-known fact around town was that McWhirter had spent a good amount of time in the twenties earning his living as a bare-fisted boxer. While most had long forgotten how Darryl passed, many of the older citizens still talked with reverence about how "Ol' Darryl McWhirter whupped the sin out of Sam Hardwick" with three punches to the face and gut. A mean feat at the time, as Hardwick was easily a half foot taller and fifty pounds heavier.

McWhirter then went on to scold all in hearing distance who had maligned Amanda Glass. "As fine a woman as I ever met, and decent enough to take in a mutt like myself. I'm not fit to walk on her floors, but still she and her husband took me in." Darryl then promised the same treatment he had meted out to Hardwick to anyone else that dared to insinuate that "Miss Amanda" was less than a saint, and the same for "Mister John." From that point on, the rumors stopped.

At least until Sandra LeMarrs disappeared. Sandra was only twelve years old, certainly too young to run away. Right around that point, people started wondering where she could have gone. But when they found the body, people started wondering who could have done such a thing. Sam Hardwick was the first to ask the question: "Just what do we know about Darryl McWhirter?"

Well, Darryl was a nice man, at least in the eyes of most of Serenity, and the question remained unanswered.

Until the body of eight-year-old Tobias Henderson was found on the side of the road, stripped and used and discarded not far from where the Glasses had their farm. The second time Sam Hardwick asked what anyone really knew about Darryl McWhirter, a few people started hearing the questions and giving serious thought to what the answers might be. By that point, people cared less about the fact that Sam Hardwick, the man who had lost three teeth to one punch, was the one asking the question and started caring more about the answer.

Darryl McWhirter was a stranger in town, all but a beggar living over with the Glasses, who were less than well off, and maybe a bit strange themselves. Four years they had been married, and not sign one of any children . . . well, it just wasn't natural.

Mind you, those small rumors stayed small, almost dwindled and died over the course of a year when no more deaths came around to claim any children. During that year, Darryl stayed around the farm and helped with the chores and even scrounged together enough money for a few extra shirts and another pair of pants, between the bottles of red wine that he purchased and nursed over a week or two at a time.

But when Eric and Elizabeth Reeves disappeared, the whole town started asking themselves the same questions all over again. John and Amanda Glass considered sending Darryl on his way, mostly for his own sake, because even they heard the questions and rumors that had started going around town. They decided that

Darryl had a hard enough life without being sent down the road to find another place to live.

Rumors started that the Reeves children had been seen talking with Darryl McWhirter near the park not long before they disappeared, that he had been carrying his bottle of wine . . . That maybe he had offered some of the wine to the children. People around town started to recall that McWhirter had been seen a few times with Sandra LeMarrs, and pushing Toby Henderson on the swings, and wasn't it just a little strange that a grown man had been seen telling the children stories in the park from time to time?

People around Serenity started warning their children to stay away from that Darryl McWhirter; no one knew enough about him. Naturally enough, no one considered asking the children what they thought of the man; they were only children after all. Most of the children that were seen with him thought he was a fine man, one capable of telling almost magical stories of the rest of America, and the man certainly had stories to tell. He warned them to stay away from a town called Summitville, any town called Summitville, as he had been to that very town three times and each time in a different part of the country. He told them about California and the weather that was almost perfect all of the time. He told of the time he had actually seen Santa Claus in person, and helped the man with his deliveries, as Santa had a fearsome cold that year. He told the tales of wonder and of dread, and he taught them a few lessons along the way. He explained why it was so important to obey your parents and to never enter a house where animals would not go.

He told tales of Alaska and the gold to be found, and he told tales of Florida and surviving a hurricane that had destroyed most of Miami. Mostly, he told them stories when they were bored and he had the free time.

The children could have told their parents all this and more; could have told of how Darryl McWhirter lost his family—wife, daughter, and two sons—to a train wreck in Mississippi, if only the parents would have listened.

Perhaps they could not hear the children past their own questions and the louder questions asked by Sam Hardwick. When the children were taken away from the park if Darryl came too close, he thought that he understood where things were going for him in Serenity. He was hardly naive, he'd heard the rumors himself, and for a while had simply hoped they would go away.

When the rumors grew stronger instead of fading, Darryl decided that the time had come to leave Serenity, to move on to greener pastures. Fate decided that he could not go. Darryl slipped on a rock while carrying water back from the well. He and the jugs he was carrying went down the deceptively steep hill between the well and the house, and all of them broke against a very solid oak tree. He managed to break his leg in four places. Dr. Martin Parsons examined his leg and set the breaks, placing Darryl in a cast that would keep him still for several weeks.

Martin Parsons was a well-known doctor in the area. He took care of most of the families in Serenity back then and was known for his amiable bedside manner as well as his ability to fix just about anything that wasn't fatal. Parsons was all but a saint in the eyes of most people in town.

So it was no surprise to anyone that Sam Hardwick was ready to rouse up a hanging party when Parsons told him about the strange comments that came from Darryl McWhirter's mouth. Comments about the children that were missing, and the children that had died. Less of a surprise still, that Hardwick was able to gather a substantial group of followers on a hot summer night. If Dr. Parsons said it was so, then surely it was so. Saints do not lie.

Two days after Darryl broke his leg, when John and Amanda Glass were off in town doing their weekly shopping, Sam Hardwick and his group of followers dragged a screaming Darryl McWhirter from his room at the Glass residence. Donna Worthington remembered the sight, remembered the screams as the angry mob pulled him, hollering and swinging, out of the house. She remembered the sound of his cast being shattered and the sight of a leg trying to mend and the odd ways in which the leg moved after being freed.

Mostly, she remembered the screams. Five minutes after pulling him from the house, the gang that was led by Sam Hardwick strapped Darryl McWhirter to the elm tree in front of the Glass house and lit themselves a bonfire. Darryl McWhirter played the part of the fire's fuel. According to Donna's diary, McWhirter thrashed and screamed for fully three minutes after his skin had caught ablaze. She swore, in her diary, that he was still screaming after his tongue had burned away.

Four weeks later, after the police had investigated and discovered that there were no witnesses to the burning—none willing to come forward at least—Martin Parsons was caught in the act of molesting Andy Harrington.

Roberta Harrington came home from a visit with some friends a few hours earlier than was initially anticipated to find her son in tears and the doctor hastily trying to button his own pants and those of the boy. No one believed his claim that what he was doing to the boy was part of his medical examination. Dr. Martin Parsons was arrested and thrown in jail. His lawyer made bail in less than twenty-four hours. Two days after being caught with his pants down, Martin Parsons left town in the wee early morning hours. He was never seen again.

By way of apology, several concerned citizens, Sam Hardwick among them, purchased a very fine marble headstone for Darryl McWhirter. They even moved his remains from the potter's field into the cemetery over at the Methodist church. No one bothered to find out if McWhirter was a Methodist.

Life went on in Serenity. Most people forgot about Darryl McWhirter. The Glasses never did.

III

Jonathan Crowley sat down in the dim gray and institutional green room and waited patiently for his new friend to come out of his holding cell. There was security glass between the chair where he sat and where Tony Marcuso would be sitting, but there was nothing he could do about that.

Marcuso himself meant very little to Crowley. He was just a source of information. Unfortunately, the current incarceration meant he had to treat the little shit like he was worth something. He wasn't, not really. He'd been found guilty of dealing heroin to little kids and of several muggings before he'd been sent to Ryker's Island.

The man looked about like Crowley expected. He looked lean and hard and tough and greasy. There were several tattoos on his arms, mostly words in Italian and one of an inverted pentagram that made Crowley's lip twitch.

"Do I know you?" The man's eyebrows knitted over his falcate nose as he scrutinized Crowley.

"Not yet, but you're about to." Crowley smiled and was happy to see the little shit on the other side of the glass flinch.

"Why do I want to know you?"

"Well, for one thing, I brought two cartons of cigarettes with me." He leaned down and lifted the two boxes of Marlboros. "They may not be your brand, but what the hell, right? I'm sure you can find something to do with them."

The man nodded. Some stereotypes are true. Cigarettes worked just fine as currency when you were locked away. "For another thing, I just want to ask a few questions in exchange for the smokes."

"Like what?" The moron had the good sense to look dubious after hearing that.

"Like why you and your little brother decided to start dealing with the supernatural."

Marcuso shook his head, and his skin got just a little

sweaty. "We were just scamming people, man. No biggie."

"Yeah? So why don't you tell me what happened with the scam? Way I'm hearing it, you had a good thing going, and then it went bad almost overnight."

"I don't want to talk to you." Marcuso looked at him and did his best to appear intimidating. He wasn't exactly gifted in the fearsome appearance department.

"Fine." Crowley put away the cigarettes. "I'm good either way."

"Wait. Why you want to know about this stuff?"

Crowley leaned in closer to the glass and smiled broadly. "Because I think you let something loose, Tony. I think there's something out there, and I have to know what it is if I'm going to stop it."

"I can't help you, man. There's cameras on us."

"They aren't working. I made sure of it."

"Yeah? How?" Marcuso was justifiably dubious.

"Same way I'm going to touch you in around five seconds."

"There's glass here, dude."

Crowley reached forward slowly and placed his hand on the thick acrylic shield between them. He kept smiling at Marcuso as his hand pushed through the barrier as if it weren't even there. Marcuso let out a small squeal, and Crowley smiled even more broadly as he touched the man's skin.

The Italian kid let out a whimper and might have peed himself. He certainly flinched. Crowley gripped his hand and slid his fingers up higher. Marcuso looked like he desperately wanted to run, but Crowley knew good and well that there was no way for him to move.

"Here's the deal, Tony. I'm going to stop whatever you let out. You're going to tell me what it was, and I'm going to stop it. And if I can't, I'll show it where you are and let it handle what it needs to in order to put paid on your account."

"What? What do you mean?" Oh he was good and greasy with sweat, his skin was hot, and his muscles were twitching hard under the illustrations he'd put on his arms.

"I'm going to show you a neat trick. I want you to watch very, very carefully, okay?" His eyes were locked on Marcuso's, but when he looked away from the kid, he stared at the tattoo of a pentagram on the boy's arm. Marcuso let out a louder squeal this time, and Crowley felt the flesh on his fingers start to tingle as they covered the star and circle drawn on the kid. "Feel that? Remember the feeling, Tony. Remember it well, because if I fail, you're going to feel a lot worse."

Marcuso still couldn't move, but his eyes were wide, and his mouth strained open in a silent scream. The muscles in his neck were standing out in thick cords, and his entire body was covered with a heavy sweat.

Crowley pulled his hand back and slid it back through the solid barrier. Marcuso whimpered for several seconds, breathing hard and coming as close to tears as he had probably ever been in his entire adult life. Macho boys didn't like to cry. Marcuso definitely saw himself as macho.

"Look at it, Tony." The convict looked at the marking on his arm, saw the differences that most people would have never noticed. There were fine lines of ink that had moved and shifted and been added to the tattoo. "I know what you're thinking. You're thinking you can just cut it off, and everything will be okay." Crowley smiled at the look of surprise on the kid's face. "You're wrong, but by all means, feel free to slice your arm apart. It'll just move somewhere else. I marked you, Tony. When I'm done doing what I have to do, I might take it off, but not before then. Until I clean up this mess, you are going to be a wanted man. Not wanted by the cops, but by what you summoned here. That, and every thing like it in this world." He smiled wide and happy as the kid realized what he was saying. "You think you have problems being someone's bitch now? You don't know shit about being hurt and humiliated, but you will, Tony. Unless you tell me everything you know."

And did Tony talk? Oh, yes, he talked. He talked for hours about his brother and the things they'd gotten themselves into. He spoke, and Crowley listened. He didn't take notes. He didn't have to.

CHAPTER 8

I

Sometimes it was best to go back to the scene of the crime. Simon MacGruder took the trip to the Pageant farm, walking at a steady pace. Several of the local kids passed him on the way, including the little girl he'd come to the aid of a few days earlier. She waved brightly, no longer afraid of him, and he smiled and nodded. She was a cute little thing and almost made him think of his own days in school, but those were longer gone than he cared to think about, and there was nothing he could do to bring back the times when he was that innocent about the world. *Christ,* he thought, *listen to me. I've grown positively morbid.*

And he supposed that was fair, really. He was about to embark on a trip down parts of good old memory lane that he would rather keep locked in the past.

The Pageant farm was a good ways out of the town

proper. He guessed in a lot of places two miles was
enough to warrant the use of a car, but the kids around
him, including several from the farm itself, were walking, and he supposed he could still do it himself. Hell,
he knew he could and considered that fact a point of
pride. Let the other old farts get too decrepit to walk. He
figured if that ever happened to him, it would be time to
lie down and die.

Dave Pageant walked past him, his glasses perched
on his nose and a heavy book bag strapped to his back.
A kid around his age was walking with him, and it took
Simon a moment to recognize Stan Long. The kid was
growing like a weed. They both cast glances his way but
didn't speak to him. It never hurt to be cautious around
grown-ups. Simon still remembered that rule from
when he was a kid himself. Just like he'd learned that
the opposite became true when you got older: it never
hurt to be cautious around kids. He didn't much bother
with that rule himself, but he saw and knew plenty of
people who eyed the younger generations with a strange
blend of envy, suspicion, and fear. They could have
their whole lives ahead of them as far as Simon was
concerned. He knew what a lot of them would face in
the future and wouldn't have wanted to go back to those
times for anything.

A perfect example was just around the corner. April
Long, older sister to Stan, was having a fight with a boy
he'd seen around but couldn't for the life of him remember the name of. April was pretty enough to be a cheerleader, and the boy was stocky enough to be on the
football team. He didn't know if they were on the teams
or not, but he'd have hardly been surprised. He'd have

bet money that five minutes earlier they'd been holding hands. He'd have won that bet, too. But now they were squabbling at each other, and he suspected both would be brooding about whatever slight had caused their momentary rift for the rest of the night. Being that young meant falling in love almost every day and learning about rejection just as often. Youth meant drama, and he'd had enough of that to last him, thanks just the same.

His knees were aching by the time he made it to the rolling lands that were owned by the Pageant family. Most of the kids had long since broken away and headed for their homes, but Stan Long had continued on with Dave Pageant, and they were now sitting on the split rail fence that surrounded the entire place.

It was a massive farm, and it just about needed to be with the number of people who lived there. The term "nuclear family" had nothing whatsoever to do with the Pageants. There were something like twenty, maybe even twenty-five family members living in three separate houses. Dave and Stan looked at him as he approached the fence and seemed rather surprised to see someone as old as him climb over the top of it. He smiled and nodded, and the two boys waved tentatively.

If Dave had any objections to the stranger entering his family's property, he kept them to himself. Being back on the property brought back memories galore. Seeing the older twin sisters of Dave Pageant as they moved around the house brought back even more ghosts from his past. They looked an awful lot like most of the Pageant girls, which meant they had red hair and figures that caught even the eye of an old man like himself. Probably it was best not to dwell on the times he'd had with one of the Pageant girls when he was younger. She was dead and gone, and her family had likely never heard about their indiscretions. Mary-Elizabeth Pageant had known a lot of tragedy in her life, like the deaths of her younger siblings. She had known happiness, too. But most of that had been with a man other than Simon, and though he sometimes longed to reminisce about her, he knew better than to talk to anyone in town about the things they had done when they were in their early twenties.

Andrew Pageant nodded to Simon when he saw him. Andrew was not a striking figure, but he was solid. Simon nodded and waved. He didn't volunteer any reason for being on the farm, and Andrew didn't ask. Both men knew Simon wouldn't cause a lick of harm to anything on the farm, and both men knew as well that from time to time Simon and several other people felt compelled to come out here and brood. It never got out of hand, and no one felt a need to talk about it.

Some secrets were supposed to remain secret. It benefited the community. Also, there were a few too many people who could still suffer from the consequences of their actions. But there was also something about revisiting the scene of the crime, as it were, that drew people to the farm occasionally. Andrew Pageant tolerated the visits as long as nothing was disturbed.

Simon MacGruder settled down near the place where everything changed for Serenity, and pulled out his pipe. The twins came by and waved, both young enough to be his own grandchildren and both looking as inviting as a glass of cold water in August. He didn't doubt that he could have had one or both of them if he

were inclined. Seemed to run in the family, the willing-
ness to explore forbidden territory.

All he had to do was remember Mary-Elizabeth, and
he was tempted. The very same memories also stopped
him from doing anything about the veiled invitation in
the smiles from the girls. But it was oddly flattering to
be thought of as male by the two of them.

The littlest girl on the farm—*Tina? Antonia? Tasha?
Something like that*—stared at him from nearby, her
eyes wide and her blond hair blowing like corn silk in
the light breeze. He patted his knee, and she came over,
settling against him like he was an old friend. There was
something comforting in the notion that anyone could
be innocent enough in this day and age to trust a
stranger. And there was something scary about it, too.
Because, really, not all strangers should be trusted.

And that was the root of almost everything in Serenity Falls as far as Simon could tell. Strangers could
cause all sorts of problems. They could also have all
sorts of problems caused for them.

Some time later Andrew Pageant's voice rang out for
his kids to get ready for supper. The little girl flashed
him a smile with her baby teeth and waved a sloppy
good-bye before running around the side of the house.

Simon stood up and felt his knees protest his decision to squat for as long as he had. He walked it off on
his way back to the fence. Dave Pageant nodded his
way again, and Stan was already walking toward the
main road. Just to remind the kid that sometimes older
people could do it, too, Simon did a fast walk back to
the road and started walking on the opposite side of the
asphalt. There were no starting bells and there was no

vocal acknowledgment, but he and the little kid started racing somewhere along the way.

He let Stan Long win the race, but he kept it close. As the boy headed off the main road to his own place, he paused and shot another smile at Simon. Simon winked back and waved a farewell as he moved back for his home. He had writing to do and felt, for reasons he didn't understand, that he had best get to it and fast. He felt like time was running out. He just wasn't really sure who it was running out for.

II

Serenity Falls Part Eight: When the Carnival Came to Town

There was a time in this country when the circuses didn't just show up in major cities. They couldn't have possibly survived if they worked that way. In the past—and it's a past that is more distant in some areas than it is in others—the smell of sawdust and the sound of calliope music were common enough in Serenity. Once or twice a year there would be a circus or a carnival moving through the area that would stop for a weekend during the longest part of the summer, and during those occasions it was almost a certainty that the sound of children laughing and the smell of popping corn and candied apples would be prevalent, regardless of the weather. That those days faded away is almost inevitable. A town the size of Serenity Falls is hardly worth the notice of the modern day circuses. The cost of caring for the animals and transporting all of the equipment has long since seen to that. Also, Ticketmaster doesn't often set up in places that small, and almost everyone who performs live deals with one or another of the companies that makes selling tickets easy and relatively painless.

But not that long ago, the circuses still came by, and even after they had faded to distant memories in the town's collective unconscious, there were still carnivals. In the early part of the 1950s, the last circus to visit Serenity had been a faded echo for over a decade, so naturally, everyone was excited when the poorly made posters seemed to almost mysteriously manifest themselves overnight. The garish pictures found on the side of the barbershop and in front of the Merriwether Drugstore proudly told one and all that the Alexander Halston Carnival of the Fantastic would be in town for one full week. It was all the buzz in the small town, and exciting enough news that even the dourest members of the community looked forward to the visit. It had, after all, been a very long time since anything even resembling a circus had come through the area, and everyone looked forward to the diversion.

Alexander Halston himself made the arrangements to use the empty field on the Pageant farm. The money wasn't much, but every member of the Pageant family would have free passes, and there was the promise to clean up the site when the carnival was finished with its business. Earl Pageant was not exactly the friendliest man in town, but neither was he the meanest by any stretch of the imagination. And, many of the locals agreed, even if he were opposed to the idea, it was a certainty that his wife Marie would have convinced him to let the carnies use the lot, just to keep their kids out of trouble for a week. The Pageant family had a long history of causing minor chaos, which was only to be expected really. There were eleven children in the household, three by Earl and his wife and eight they'd taken in when Earl's older brother and his wife died during a barn fire. So it's really not a surprise that many of the folks in town, and normally out of earshot of the Pageants, claimed the two adults on the farm had their hands a little too full for comfort.

All such worries faded away when the carnival came to town. No one had time to consider if anyone was staying out of trouble when there was so much to see and do. Even watching the carnies unpack their train-loads full of supplies was an event in town. Somehow or another they'd managed to get their boxcars onto the private line used by the quarry, and then, using the two elephants with the show, pulled the cars from the tracks and through the woods over to the Pageant field. There were several families that made a day of the event, going so far as to pack their lunches in picnic baskets and settle in for a meal and a show. Almost as if they expected this, the carnival folk took turns giving very small but entertaining displays of their talents. There were clowns to keep the locals amused, and even a few acrobats who managed to get in a little show time by pulling stunts even as they carried supplies. As advertising went, the word of mouth about some of the performers was far superior to the posters that had been plastered throughout Serenity. By the time the Halston Carnival of the Fantastic had set up properly, all but a handful of the people in town had scrounged up the money to attend the festivities.

The third Friday night in June was picture perfect. The temperature was just right, the sky was clear, and a full moon lit the way to the field almost as well as the torches that the carnies had placed for that very purpose. There were several games of chance, where the young men in town could do their best to impress each other and their lady friends. Despite all of the warnings and rumors that the games would be rigged, a lot of young ladies went home with prizes won by their dates. There were rides like the Ferris wheel—it was a small wheel, but bigger than anything in the area, and that was enough to make it seem gigantic—not one but two roller coasters, and the merry-go-round. There was cotton candy enough to make a small army ill, candied apples, hot dogs, caramel corn, and funnel cakes with fruit toppings and powdered sugar. There were animals from around the world, and while they may not have been the healthiest or largest lions and elephants and apes, they were more than most in town had ever seen before. It was, simply put, magical.

And as is all too often the case, a few people had to try to understand the magic better than they should have. One of the attractions that held the most fascination— in the same way that fatal accidents seem to draw the eye and capture the mind—was the freak show. Oh, to be sure there were the usual attractions. There was a bearded lady and a fat woman and a skinny man. There was even a two-headed calf, but there were others there as well, who seemed to defy what anyone expected to see at the carnival. There were real freaks . . . monsters even. There was a man with no legs. He had a serpentine tail from his navel to the ground instead, and he had fangs just like a cobra's. His body was hairless, and there was the faintest hint of a scalelike pattern just under his skin. The snake man did not speak, but he smiled eagerly whenever anyone came near. Not far away from that dark figure was a creature the signs claimed was a succubus. While she seemed perfectly proportioned, most of the women found the wings on the young woman's back unsettling. They were dark and leathery, the same color as the thin, pointed tail that flicked casually behind her. And the horns on her head bore a strong resemblance to those found on a ram. Though the succubus said nothing at all, every man who saw her was enraptured. In private a few of them confessed to having dreams about the girl-woman that night. In public, none of the men could agree on what she looked like. Each, it seemed, had seen something different. Two separate people managed to sneak cameras into the tent where the freaks were housed. Not a single picture taken of the succubus came out clearly. The last of the truly outrageous members of the freakish cavalcade was a creature that couldn't possibly have ever been human. The signs said it was a hellhound, and most upon viewing the thing could readily agree to that title. The animal was enormous, surely as large as a black bear, and covered in a thick black fur. In most ways it truly did resemble a dog, but there were definite discrepancies. Dogs do not, as a rule, have slitted pupils that glow with their own light. Most are not likely to have teeth as black as midnight, or to breathe out flames. And no one has ever been able to claim that a dog could corrode metal with its urine. But the hound held in that freak show managed all of that with little effort. A good number of the people viewing the animal decided it was best not to give thought to what it might eat. The answer likely involved something screaming as it was torn apart.

Whether the oddities on exhibit were real or not is up to interpretation, but those who actually saw them were impressed. And a few of them, five of the Pageant children to be precise, decided to find out for certain if the creatures were real.

Alan Pageant, his cousins Minnie, Joe, and the twins Isabelle and Anita, all left the house after promising a great deal of suffering to anyone who dared tell Earl and Marie about their late night escapades. They waited until almost two in the morning, and they moved very quietly indeed. Their destination was the freak show tent.

The following morning, Earl asked where the children were, annoyed that they had not yet handled their chores. Though having eleven children on the farm could be a burden, it was also very useful for getting a lot of the smaller tasks around the place taken care of without any extra effort.

It took Andrew Pageant—the father of Dave Pageant—all of three seconds to rat out the whole lot of them. Despite being one of the youngest on the farm, there was very little that intimidated him, and his siblings and cousins were not on that short list. Earl went directly to the tent of Alexander Halston for the sole purpose of finding out if he knew anything about what was going on. Halston was pleasant and expressed concern but assured Earl Pageant that he knew nothing at all about where the children might be.

Earl took things the sensible way and went to the town constable, one Martin Hardwick, son of the very same Sam Hardwick who believed in mob rules twenty years earlier. Martin was not prone to the same sort of hysteria as his father—even his father wasn't very prone to that sort of thing since he'd helped murder Daryl McWhirter. Some experiences can actually change a man.

Then again . . . sometimes old habits resurface.

The Pageant kids did not show up for dinner. Martin Hardwick, along with two of his fellow constables, searched every trailer in the carnival with the permission of Halston and the assistance of several of the carnies. They left no tent unchecked. Not surprisingly, they found nothing.

That, of course, didn't stop the rumors from beginning. All it took was one look at the monsters in the freak show to convince most people that something was up. Not the freaks, the monsters. It would be hard to say with any conviction that Sam Hardwick was behind what happened, but there were a few people who wouldn't have been too surprised to find out it had been. Some time after midnight a rather substantial gathering of the locals did their best to reinvestigate the Carnival of the Fantastic. Perhaps it would have gone better if the people in Serenity were the first to ever cast suspicious eyes at the carnival for something that had happened while they were in town. But they weren't, not by a long stretch, and the carnies were prepared for uninvited guests.

Being prepared, however, did not mean they were at all pleased by the notion. Alexander Halston and his clutch of employees stood in the center of the ring made by the tents and waited as the people of Serenity tried to sneak in and do their own investigating.

The townies were surprised, to be sure, but they were not so surprised that they couldn't throw a few accusations. And who do you suppose made the loudest accusations? Why, that would be Sam Hardwick. Sam was certain that the carnies had done something to five innocent children, and for him that was enough reason to provoke a fight if he had to.

Twenty years had not made Sam any less of a sizable man. If anything, he was broader of shoulder—and of belly—than he had been in his youth. And while it can be said that some of the mass he carried was cellulite, most of it was not. He had worked the quarry for many a year, and he had never been the sort to shrink away from physical efforts. Sam Hardwick did not merely ask if the carnival folk knew what had happened to the children. He demanded to know where they had hidden the bodies. One of the clowns and, depending on the crowds, part-time ringmaster, a young and energetic man who answered both to Rufo and his real name of Cecil Phelps, tried to defuse the situation by offering a balloon animal to Hardwick. Sam responded by squeezing the balloon in his hands until it popped loudly and by making several derogatory comments about the heritage of the entertainer. While it is true that Rufo the Clown was a happy, cheerful man by nature, he took offense to the comments, and the fact that Sam managed to crush his hand at the same time as the balloon animal couldn't have made matters any easier on the boy.

Rufo planted a size fifteen clown shoe squarely into Sam's crotch and smiled even more broadly as the man let out a squeak. His smile faded by several degrees when Earl Pageant placed a shotgun against his left nostril with enough force to knock off his clown nose and very calmly asked where his children were.

No one was willing to move or make a comment that would bring around permanent harm. Scott Michaels, one of the local men who had come along almost exclusively to stop the sort of bad incident that had killed a drunken drifter twenty years earlier, begged everyone to stay calm, and the situation slowly spiraled down to a more reasonable and less brutal sort of confrontation. After almost an hour of facing off and chest beating on both sides, the would-be interrogation came to an end.

But no one was happy with the conclusion. The children were still missing, and the carnies were still bitter about taking the brunt of the accusations. It was decided that they would pack up their things the next day and move on. They had enough problems without getting a few of their number thrown in the local county jail for the privilege of being different. Cecil Phelps, the shoe-wielding clown of testicular destruction, went back to his small quarters with visions of a twelve-gage barrel dancing in his head. He never woke up. His train car–cum–house managed to catch fire just before the sun rose. He—and four other members of the carnival's crew who woke up during the fire to discover their doors barred from the outside—died screaming in the conflagration.

Did Sam Hardwick do it? No one living knows for sure, but later that same day, he told his son the constable that he'd gone home and slept after the confrontation. His only witness was his wife, who could be said to live in terror of Sam's temper. Whatever the case, Alexander Halston changed his mind about leaving and demanded a full investigation into the deliberate act of arson. No one attended the carnival that night, and the carnies themselves would have driven away anyone who tried. Rufo the Clown was well loved by his friends and associates.

Perhaps it was unhappy coincidence, perhaps not, but during the long, silent night when the carnival and its performers mourned the loss of their friend, the monstrous dog who made up one of the most frightening acts in the entire Carnival of the Fantastic managed to get loose from its pen. Alexander Halston did not talk about where his freaks came from, nor did he treat them as monsters. He was a good enough man in his way, even if a long life on the road had made him a bit bitter. The animal had never been mistreated, nor did it want for food. Most of the carnies knew it by sight and had long since accepted that its strange appearance had nothing to do with its pleasant demeanor.

What they didn't understand was that the beast was hardly a dog. Deformed or not, it could reason well enough, and it knew how to behave when the public was around. It also understood on an instinctive level that the carnies were kindred spirits. They were above reproach.

The same was not true of the people in Serenity. The

townsfolk had hurt people close to the strange hound, and unlike the rest of the carnies, the dog called a "Hound of Hell" by the signs in front of its cage knew who had done the killing. And all too like the rest of the people who worked at the carnival, it wanted revenge. It wanted to return the favor, and it did so.

The Pageant farm wasn't exactly far away, but the hound moved past it without a second glance, heading toward the town proper. While it traveled across the fields and into the woods, the snake man and the succubus slid from their own places in the carnival and moved to the Pageant place. They had unfinished business to take care of, and the only way to handle it completely was to make sure that everyone knew the truth about the missing children who had caused all of the problems in the first place. The snake man did not talk often, and when he did, the person listening had to know how to translate his muffled speech. The girl called the succubus knew how to understand him and knew what he'd seen. Together the two of them entered the Pageant farm with minimal fuss. Together they pulled Earl and Marie Pageant from their beds and dragged them out of their home, the long blades they carried keeping both of the people from struggling too much.

Together they revealed the bodies of five dead children to the couple, and watched while the two people who had raised them cried and broke into tears. Neither of the freaks from the show had the remotest chance of ever living a normal life. Both accepted that and dealt with it in their own ways. But neither of them was bitter enough in nature to actually let five children die for no reason and not say anything about it. The succubus—a girl whose real name was Doreen Miles—spoke softly and explained that certain members of the carnival were not quite what they appeared. Two of the clowns in the troupe were on the run from the law. Beyond that she could only say that at least one of them had caught the children on the grounds and taken them away at gunpoint. She gave both of the clowns' names, and then the two of them moved away to let the parents have their grief to themselves.

And while the Pageants were learning the final resting place of five of their children, the biggest dog ever to step into the town of Serenity was getting far too much attention for its own good. It howled, it sniffed, it growled, and it moved straight down the streets of Serenity, past the places where the people of the town shopped and in some cases slept and deep into the heart of the town. Martin Hardwick, Percy Grey, and Fred Grant of the town constables very carefully aimed their rifles and watched it come toward them.

If the dog had no concerns about them, it had a funny way of showing it. The animal took one look at the three men, growled a challenge, and charged them like a runaway freight train. All three men fired their rifles and watched in shock as the animal kept coming. They saw the bullets punch into its hide, they saw the blood that spilled from the wounds, and still it came on.

Fred Grant knew he was a dead man when the creature came his way, breathing gouts of flame and baring fangs that had to be as long as his fingers. He fired again and again, his finger slick with sweat and his aim off. The hellhound bit through his rifle in one massive chomp and knocked him on his ass as it went past. He played possum right then and there, silently praying to the Almighty that the damned thing would never look at him again.

He got his wish. Whatever the creature was—be it a true hellhound or a freakish dog—it was not as immune to bullets as it first appeared. The beast got as far as Marty Hardwick and collapsed on the ground, dead from massive trauma. Or mostly dead at any rate. Constable Hardwick lost his right foot when he decided to kick the dog in a fit of bravado. Whether it was merely a muscle response or the animal was still alive, no one will ever know, but it bit through his calf and ankle as easily as it had broken the Remington rifle in Fred Grant's hands.

There was no time for celebrating. The men dragged Hardwick into one of the squad cars and drove like mad to get him to the hospital, Percy Grey clutching his hands around the ruined stump of Martin's ankle the entire way.

And while they were gone, the body of the hellhound vanished. Several people swore it just disappeared in a blast of flames, but there was no proof of that. There was no proof that the beast had ever existed, but that didn't stop news of its demise from spreading through the town and from the town to the carnival.

Sam Hardwick heard about the conflict almost immediately. So did the carnies. Sam called his friends and anyone he could think of, certain that the animal had gone back to the carnival. It was still dark when the villagers stormed the proverbial castle for the second time. That the castle was made of canvas, and the villagers carried rifles and road flares, which probably didn't make the destruction any harder.

Earl Pageant tried his best to calm everyone down. He knew who had killed his children, and he wanted justice done, but he did not want murder committed on his property. He did not get his wish. None of the carnies lived through the confrontation. They'd expected to perhaps have to fight, but they never expected rifles. It just wasn't done that way.

The people of Serenity did not all participate in the massacre. Truly, it was only a handful of people. But they were enough. Sam Hardwick himself killed at least five of the performers. Earl Pageant killed only two. Both were clowns, and they were the right ones, as the succubus gave very detailed descriptions of the both of them to the grieving man.

Road flares work well for burning things. The carnival tents and trailers burned brightly through the night and well into the next day. The apes and elephants were the only known survivors. The Hardwick family sold them to the zoo in Utica on the sly and for a very small amount of money. What little remained by way of evidence managed to get itself buried on the Pageant farm, with a little help from a few of the other local farmers who didn't mind sharing in the effort. Just what exactly happened to the snake man and the succubus remains unknown. No one who was willing to talk about the entire incident could claim to have seen them.

There is a field behind the Pageant farm where nothing is planted and very little aside from weeds will grow. Sometimes, when the wind is right, Dave Pageant goes to sleep with the distant sound of calliope music playing. He has never told his parents of the sounds. They are his secret treasure. If he had told them, they'd have laughed it off as the imaginings of a child, and they would have told each other it was nothing, nothing at all. To the best of their knowledge, they'd have been right, too.

Sometimes ignorance is bliss.

III

Often the old methods are best. When money and polite queries fail, it's sometimes useful to just break a few bones. Crowley worked his way through several sections of the five boroughs with a song in his heart and a desire to get answers.

A few times that came close to costing him his life, but that was part of the fun, really. What was the point if there wasn't risk involved? Though he was the first to admit he had a few unfair advantages over the average person.

The problem with looking for information is that you have to find the people who actually can provide said knowledge to you. That's a whole lot harder than it looks, especially when the ones you're looking for tend to have only nicknames as monikers, and it gets even tougher when some of them seem to have decided to die.

His little snitch in Ryker's was now two cartons of cigarettes richer and had been more than glad to tell

Crowley everything he wanted to know, especially if it meant negating the mark on his arm. Crowley left the mark there but did have the decency to stop it from working as a beacon. Anything that came looking for Anthony Marcuso would do so without any help from Crowley, despite the temptation to break his word. There were rules that had to be followed, even by him.

The problem was that most of the information Marcuso gave him was about as good as semaphore to a blind man. There were no full names, no addresses that hadn't been abandoned, and only marginal information regarding dates and times. Marcuso had been too wasted most of the time to keep anything like a record. It was really, really starting to get annoying.

But after his third night of barhopping and skull cracking, Crowley finally got a break. He learned the real name of the kid he'd assumed was Marcuso's brother. It was a fair assumption, as they had told several people that they were, in fact, brothers. That was a lie. They were cousins who had been raised by the same parents. Would have been easy enough to look into that, too, but the parents were both dead. Crowley guessed he was supposed to feel some sort of pity for the two lost waifs, but he didn't. It wasn't that he was completely heartless—though a few would have stated emphatically that he was worse than Hitler—it was merely that he didn't feel too much pity for anyone who spent a few years getting wasted and getting laid and using sorcery as a tool to accomplish those goals.

Marcuso and his cousin and a few loners had decided to form a cult for the sole purpose of scoring with the hottest chicks they could find. Added bonus: a few of the girls they scored with came with their own supplies of narcotics.

The problem with their little gig? Some dumb ass decided to add to the flavor of their cult by using legitimate books of sorcery. The bigger problem with that? They had no idea what they were doing. It was amazingly easy for the terminally stupid to make the damned books work out. It didn't matter what ingredients were called for or what the rituals entailed, because, frankly, the books were *supposed* to be easy to use. No one in their right mind with half an ounce of common sense would consider opening one of those books and performing any of the incantations. Most of the active practitioners who used them did so with extreme caution and followed the details to the letter, because changing the ingredients didn't stop a summoning, it just changed what was summoned and normally negated any protection incorporated into the spells at the same time.

"You don't switch the fucking toad's eyes for a frog's eyes if you want to make the thing work properly." Great. Just perfect. He was talking to himself again. Crowley sighed his disgust and looked at the address he'd recently beaten out of a very self-important moron with delusions of power. In this case it was a pimp who thought he had a group of people willing to fight for him. In truth they were willing to fight for free beers and nothing more than that.

It was a lesson the loser needed to learn, and Crowley was glad to be of assistance. All it cost the pimp was the use of his right hand until the bones knitted back together. Crowley didn't mind. He liked breaking a few bones, and he especially liked doing it to the sort of prick who beat on the women who served him just because he could.

This was the place. It was a dump, on the third story of a dump, which really wasn't very surprising. He didn't bother knocking. He just opened the door and looked around. The place had an air of serious neglect going. As in no one had been in the rooms for at least a week, and even the flies seemed hesitant to hang around.

There were dozens of fast-food wrappers shoved under the ratty old couch in the main room, and the kitchen looked like it was used for storage of porn mags instead of cooking. If anything like a dust rag had touched the place in the last year or so, it had probably been purely by accident. He didn't find much he could work with, but he found enough. There was a scrapbook under one of the sofa cushions. Inside it were several articles about the first girl who had disappeared, and in front of those articles were photos taken at a few of the Black Masses the group had been involved in. Multiple Polaroids of naked girls and several of a tall, thin kid with more acne than looks. As the photos all had inscriptions on the back, giving the names of the girls and several added the phrase "and me," Crowley had a strong suspicion he knew who he was looking for.

There were ways to find him now, too. All it really took was a decent picture and the right methods.

Crowley took several of the shots with him, shoved into his pocket.

He left the flophouse behind, but he also made certain to leave a few surprises there for the man in the pictures.

He made them specific. It wouldn't do to send a message to the wrong people. Especially if the wrong people were innocent.

Five minutes after he left the building, he was on the subway and headed for his final destination before he hunted down the acne-faced boy in the pictures. He wanted to make sure he had his facts straight before he finished the hunt.

The voices of the dead echoed in his skull, and he could feel their movements in the winds that blew through the area. The dead were everywhere, and most of them preferred to stay quiet. It was just his misfortune to be able to hear them anyway. Of course he was lucky there, too. He could make the sounds stop if he wanted to. There were plenty of people out there who weren't as fortunate. Most of them were in mental institutions or addicted to any substance that would make them numb to the sounds.

He was determined to help at least a handful of the dead to find their peace, but the last thing he ever wanted to do was make himself look as dense as the sort of people he normally wound up chasing down. They used sorcery with all the finesse of a five-year-old child with a pistol. They were at least twice as dangerous.

Somebody had to take care of the spankings.

Happily, Crowley liked his work.

CHAPTER 9

I

Simon MacGruder stared down at the artificial pond and wondered idly just how deep the waters there went. The quarry was as dead these days as the family that had owned it. Sad, really. The whole town had come close to death right along with the Blackwells. There wasn't a one of the lot he'd met that he hadn't liked at least a little, and he had met most of the family at one point or another.

The waters seemed still on the surface, and he stared at his reflection, marveling at how clear the image was and how old he was looking these days. It didn't matter that he saw his face in the mirror of his bathroom every morning. Sometimes the change of perspective was enough to make him notice the details he deliberately overlooked when he was shaving.

He watched his reflection for several minutes, barely

aware of the passage of time. Part of that was just because there was so damned much information filling his fool head these days. Most of what he was learning was still bouncing around inside his skull and trying to sort itself out. He couldn't have given statistics on a damned thing about the town if his life depended on it, because his mind hadn't worked out the numbers to even consider crunching. Besides, he wasn't an accountant. But the more he learned about Serenity Falls, the more he felt uneasy. He just couldn't grasp why he was getting so spooked.

Somewhere to his east, a little over a mile away, the center of the town he'd known all his life was filled with people he knew or at least knew of. They were the people who formed his entire world for all intents and purposes. They were good people, and they were by and large friendly. But thinking about them any more was starting to make him feel the need to pack his bags and run away, and he hated that. He never wanted to leave Serenity Falls. It was his home and had been for most of his life. Even when he was off in the military and doing his civic duty, he'd never seriously considered moving away from Serenity for another place.

But right now the idea was sounding like a fine notion, indeed.

Simon MacGruder spat and reached into his shirt for the cigar he'd purchased earlier. It was a luxury in which he seldom indulged, but today it just felt right. He struck a match after biting off the end of the stogie and rolled the cigar in his mouth as he stoked the flames touching the end. After half a minute and three matches, it was burning properly, and the thick, sweet smoke wafted lazily around his head.

"Sad state of affairs when a man gives himself the willies." He moved away from the edge of the cold, dark waters that hid most of the wounds caused by the quarry, and settled on a chunk of rough granite that worked just fine as a seat. Not all that far down the crude footpath, he could see Havenwood where it crouched. The night before he'd had a dream that the old place was moving, slowly sneaking up on his cabin. He fairly flew out of bed when the alarm clock went off, visions of the old place looming over his home like a mountain still sending ripples of fear through him, his pulse slamming through his body and his lips clenched against a scream. It wasn't a very comforting way to wake up.

He'd been on edge all day since then. His plans had involved asking questions of a few other prominent people in town and seeing if he couldn't get a little more information from the Glass family and the Pageants as well. Instead, he'd come out to Havenwood to make sure the place hadn't decided to sneak off and hide in the woods.

Somehow he found himself wandering back to the old quarry instead of going about his business. Returning to the scene of the crime, as it were. That was really what he was doing. He kept going over it in his head, the way his father had acted toward Erin Lockley, and the way she had always acted in return. They'd never once said a word about each other to him. The most he'd ever gotten from his father regarding Erin had been a noncommittal grunt, and from Erin about Dad there had never been a word. She always changed the subject, as if the notion of speaking about him was a subject she preferred not to think about.

And it bothered the hell out of him the more he thought about it. Bothered him as much as the way his father wouldn't look at him for a long time, as in months, after Erin's death. The thought wouldn't leave him alone, no matter how much he wanted it to.

He spent over twenty years of his life working at the quarry. There were memories on top of memories from working right in this very area, but all he could focus on when he thought about the place was his father and Erin.

"Enough to make a man wonder what the hell might have happened between them. That's what it is. And I don't want to think that way. Erin was a sweet girl, and my daddy, well, he was my dad. He couldn't have done anything with her and not had someone knowing about it. That's all."

The line of thought disgusted him, so he forced it out of his head. Instead, he looked at the quarry and tried to focus on other ideas, like when Fred Grant greased up the handles on every piece of equipment one April Fools' Day. That brought a smile to his face. Watching Buddy Hardwick trying to hold onto a hose after the pressure kicked in had been enough to get all of them laughing for about half a week. All of them except for Buddy. He hadn't laughed. Hell, seemed the only time a Hardwick ever laughed was when the joke was on someone else.

He finally gave up on getting anything accomplished for the day and decided to head for home. Of course that was a long walk, and he had a cigar to finish, so he walked to the edge of the quarry and looked down from the heights of the falls, down on the farmland and the town of Serenity Falls proper. From three hundred feet above and a mile or so away, the town looked about as pretty as a postcard. The roads were winding affairs, and fields of different crops crisscrossed the farmlands. He'd have to come back in the fall and take a few pictures. Maybe he'd even set them on a few blank pages at the right spots in the book he kept telling himself he was just writing for fun.

He ran across Mike Blake again on his way home. He was passed out in the woods, where, at least in theory, he could go mostly unmolested. The man just could not or would not stay sober. Most days Simon would have left him where he found him. There was a part of his character that said if a man wanted to drink himself to death, that was his right. He wasn't always proud of that philosophy, but it was there, and he dealt with it.

Today he was not in the mood. Simon reached down and pushed at the man's shoulder until he grunted and rolled over, looking up and squinting. Mike wasn't doing the happy drunk today. Instead, he was doing the I've-got-a-killer-hangover-and-want-to-be-left-alone drunk.

"Get up, Mike. We're gonna have us a talk." Mike sat up, looking irritated. There was a glint in his eyes, however, that was purely animal. That particular gleam said he thought there might be free booze in the bargain, and so Mike followed him all the way back to the cabin.

Simon entered his home after another half mile of walking and settled himself in the kitchen. He told Mike to clean up, and the man did. While the shower was running, Simon made a meal. He cooked up a couple of steaks and made some home fries with onions as a side dish. Nothing fancy, but it was filling. He also brewed a large pot of coffee and settled in to wait for Mike.

When the man came out of the shower he looked almost human again, and he smiled his thanks to Simon. Simon got them each a beer to wash down the food and watched Mike struggle not to drink it back in one deep gulp. One of Frannie's apple pies made dessert, heated in the microwave and topped with vanilla ice cream. The two men ate without words. The silence was both amiable and tense. Both of them knew that Simon was going to have a chat with Mike. But both of them seemed okay with that notion. For the moment at least. Food and booze would often work wonders for keeping a conversation civil.

Afterwards, Simon cleaned the dishes and put them in the rack next to the sink. By the time he was done, Mike had drifted into a light snooze. Simon cleared his throat three times before the younger man woke up enough to look at him.

"Mike. We've known each other for a long time. I wouldn't even have the roof over my head if you hadn't shown me how to invest my retirement money well, and for that I have always been grateful."

Mike sighed. "I hear a 'but' coming." He sounded almost sober. Mike was good at that.

Simon nodded and did his best to stay on track. He wasn't looking forward to the talk he was about to give, but he felt it had finally come around to time to get the whole thing settled once and for all.

He started off with an example. "Mike, what would you do if you saw a dog in the road with its back broken and half its belly torn out?" Mike got a disgusted look on his face. "Would you leave it to die?"

"I'd try to get it help, if I could."

"I know you would, son." Simon nodded. "That is in your nature, because you're a good man. It runs in your family, and it always has." Simon walked over to the credenza in his living room and opened the main doors above the set of drawers. He pulled out a bottle of scotch he hadn't bothered with in a couple of years and poured them each two fingers' worth.

He set the tumblers down in front of Mike and sat across from him at the table. "Go ahead. Have one." Mike nodded and reached for his drink. Simon set down a pistol on the table as Mike took a small sip.

"There's three bullets in that pistol, Mike. You go ahead and you take it."

"I don't need a gun, Simon. I've got no one I think needs killing." He was trying to joke, but he was a little out of practice.

Simon picked the weapon up and examined it carefully. He'd had it since Korea, and it was in perfect working order. "You sure about that, Mike?"

Blake looked at him closely. "What's on your mind, Simon?" When he didn't answer immediately, Mike pressed him. "Come on. Spill it."

"I'm working at it, Mike. Aside from maybe you, I'm the last person in this town who normally feels a need to have a serious conversation with someone. Hell, any conversation with anyone. I'm rusty at this."

Mike nodded and leaned back on the couch. Simon figured he'd have a snoring guest if he didn't talk soon, so he made himself say it. "Mike, Amy's dead. We both know that, and we both attended her funeral. It's a damned shame, Mike, because she was one of the finest women I've ever had the pleasure of knowing."

Mike said nothing, but he nodded, his face set like stone.

"I'm not trying to be a bastard here, Mike. I'm trying to do you a favor, okay?"

"Fair enough." Mike was looking about as happy as the victim of a sedative-free root canal.

"It's time, Mike. You've been in mourning for over two years now." When Mike leaned forward as if he wanted to say something, Simon held up a hand. "I know you don't want to hear this. I know you think about it from time to time already, but you're going to hear me out."

"All right, Simon. Let me have it." Mike was probably expecting a talk about sobriety. Well, he was in for a few small surprises at any rate.

"Here it is. Mike, Amy was a good woman, and I know she wouldn't approve of you pickling yourself every day. She'd want you sober. So you have two choices as far as I'm concerned. You can sober up and get on with your life and respect Amy's memory, or you can keep on drinking yourself stupid until your liver falls out. Way you're going, I figure that's about another three years of living like a stray dog off the generosity of others."

Mike stared at him long and hard. That was about what he'd expected.

"Listen. You know I think the world of you, Mike. But this is coming down to that question I asked you a while ago about the dog in the road. My answer to that same question comes down to how long I'd let it suffer. I don't think there's much can be done to patch up a dog in that condition. So do I let it suffer and howl and die by inches, or do I end its misery. Me? I'd end its suffering."

He stood up and walked around the table until he was facing Mike. The man on the couch had no choice but to look him in the eyes. Simon handed him the pistol. "Three bullets, Mike. Even if you're drunk, you should be able to end your suffering with three bullets. Either get sober, or get gone from the world. You're a disgrace to your family and to the memory of Amy. Fix it, or fix yourself." He walked over to the front door and held it open. "Now get the hell out of my house."

Mike stared at him for a few seconds, stunned. Finally he nodded and took the hint. He didn't say a word as he left the cabin, but Simon called out one last time as he went past, "I hope I see you alive when I see you next, Mike. But I also hope I see you living, you understand me?"

Mike Blake did not answer. He just kept walking.

A few minutes later, Simon MacGruder climbed into his bed and closed his eyes. He was awake for a long time, wondering if he'd just signed Mike's death warrant.

He hoped not. He really hoped not.

It was the last time he ever saw Mike Blake.

II

Serenity Falls Part Nine: Havenwood

When the Blackwell family decided to open the quarry, they knew they had a sure moneymaker on their hands. The quality of the stone was excellent, and the need for it was, as always, a constant thing. They had no idea just how quickly the money would come in, however. Their timing couldn't have been better. It was pure luck that one of the leading quarries of the time was having trouble meeting demands. It was luckier still that one of the men working for that quarry, Walter Blake, accepted a job with Blackwell only two weeks before the Silverston Quarry went belly-up. The granite deposits they'd always relied on at Silverston were simply not doing the job anymore. Everett Silverston was not as shrewd as his grandfather had been and had not paid enough attention to Blake's warnings that they needed to acquire a new source immediately if not sooner. For two generations the stone had always been there, and despite the numerous indications that the deposits were all but tapped out, the man never really believed it could happen.

Walt Blake took that to mean he should look for another job, and he made the leap to the Blackwells' part of the country as soon as the opportunity arose. He also took with him a copy of the client list for Silverston. Perhaps it wasn't the most honest thing he could have done, but he felt little guilt. He'd thrown out the life raft to Silverston and had it pushed away.

Blake brought the skill and experience to help Black-well make a name for himself. He also brought the best of the Silverston Quarry's men with him when he ar-rived. They'd known what he knew, and they took full advantage of the chance to settle down in security. Knowledge, manpower, and ambition were all present when the quarry opened. More importantly, so was a ready-made list of clients who suddenly found them-selves in almost desperate need of the materials to fin-ish all the projects that Silverston dropped the ball on.

Prosperity came quickly to the Blackwells and to Serenity. And if a few mistakes were made, that was all right. No one was hurt, and the nickname of "The Falls" was not meant in a harmful way. Hell, the fact that there was a source of water for the quarry was more of a boon than a bane anyway. Free water at the site meant not having to worry about expanding the water supplies to the area when the water drills were needed to carve through stone.

Of course, not everything was perfect for the Black-wells. One problem came around when their house caught fire. A bad storm took out a portion of the roof and spread to engulf the entire house in a matter of min-utes. They lost all of their possessions to the greedy flames. But no one was injured. They had insurance, their losses were only material, and while it was painful, they got over the worst of the experience in short order.

Within five years of opening the quarry, the Black-wells decided it was time to stop pinching pennies and have a little fun with the money they had coming in. They hired an architect and set up plans for building

Havenwood. It took two years to clear the land, lay out the electrical cables and water systems, and build, but it was two years' worth of waiting that they didn't mind in the least. The end result made up for the inconvenience of living in a smaller home than they were accustomed to.

Havenwood was big enough to hold four families with ease and comfort. But that wasn't why it had been built. All of the designs for the sprawling house were created with one simple goal: to allow the Blackwells to live in security and opulence. It was not a necessary home, but it was definitely noticeable. The master bedroom was bigger than most of the houses in the area. The bed designed for the room had to be brought in and assembled. They just didn't make beds that big. Herbert Blackwell worked hard throughout the day and decided if he wanted a bed big enough to give him a proper rest he would have it crafted and made. He could certainly afford it. The kitchen was large enough for anything smaller than cooking for an entire army and had a full walk-in refrigerator. It wasn't really needed, but as Blackwell intended to host parties from time to time, he felt it was best to have too much space for food preparation rather than too little. In truth, most of the parties he did host wound up being barbecues, so that was an extravagance that proved useful enough for storing the whole heifers he brought in for such events.

Most of the house was on a more realistic scale: it was only enormous rather than actually ludicrous. If the people in town thought Havenwood was a rather silly notion, none of them ever said anything to Herbert or his family. The simple fact of the matter was that without

Blackwell and his quarry, most of them would have been struggling to make ends meet. Serenity had never been a very well-planned community. It simply came into being and struggled along. From one industry to another—logging at one time, farming earlier than that, and for a short while a stint at canning foods and printing educational books had all helped keep the town going—they made do. It was the quarry that finally let the people of Serenity earn enough to make it all worthwhile.

If Herbert Blackwell was a bit of an oddball, he was an oddball who made money and seemed perfectly willing to share a bit of the profits. So Havenwood with its strange design—several people commented that it was a lovely house, just four sizes too big for its own britches—and large plot of land was easily accepted. Especially since Blackwell did indeed host parties, and normally they were for the families of everyone working for him. At Christmastime he hired caterers to come in and lay out a spread that would have done most of New England's wealthiest families proud. He footed the bill and paid bonuses to his workers that were handsome enough to allow a good holiday season straight across the board. Blackwell always set aside a portion of the yearly profits with bonuses in mind, and he always made sure it was a fair portion, as he knew the business could not thrive without loyal workers. "Treat your people right, and they'll return the favor," was one of his favorite sayings. For three generations his family kept to that motto, too. Even John Blackwell, officially the strangest bird to ever hold sway in the family business, never bent away from that rule. He may have been a recluse, but he was also a man who knew how to keep the workers happy.

The odds are good that the quarry would have kept going on forever if Joseph Blackwell had stayed sane. But Joe was not exactly a normal man from the first day he was born. He almost never cried when he was growing up, which his father Alexander took as a good sign. But after his father met an unfortunate end in his bathtub, Joe had more responsibilities thrust on him than he was really prepared for.

Angela Blackwell was a strong woman, and she'd managed the family business easily enough, but when Joe was finished with his time in school, she handed the reins over to him and told him to be strong. He was better at it than he imagined, but still often felt the need to go to his mother with questions about the way the company finances were handled. She helped him until she died, in her mid-eighties.

Some said her passing was a blessing for Joseph. He'd come back from his years at Harvard and brought with him a young bride. While there were few real displays of animosity between the two of them, it was common knowledge that Angela Blackwell was not overly fond of her new granddaughter-in-law. They were civil to one another, but they were not close, and they certainly were not friends. As with most of the ladies in the Blackwell house, Clarisse was a woman whose looks could make even a faithful husband look twice. She carried herself with the grace and confidence of a woman bred into money, and that, many believed, was the source of trouble between Angela and the younger Blackwell woman. Angela had been born poor, and there was the possibility that she resented the ease with which her only surviving grandson's wife grew accustomed to wealth.

Clarisse was also a devout woman, who believed that God should have a place in every house. The landscaping and interior of Havenwood took on a few signs of her faith as time went on, and this, too, might have been a part of the problem. Angela had always been quieter in her faith. She seemed to find Clarisse's need to advertise her religion moderately offensive.

Angela died in her sleep, in the enormous bed she'd shared with her husband. She and she alone had used that room since John died when Joseph was only seven. Within a month of the funeral, Joe and Clarisse moved into the master suite of the house and made it their own. From time to time Clarisse heard noises from behind the western wall of the room, but they were few and far between, and she opted not to tell her husband about them. Joe was just a little superstitious, and he might have wanted to leave the grand room for fear it was haunted. She liked the room too much to take that risk.

What a pity for her. The room didn't seem to feel the same way.

Clarisse bore her husband three fine, healthy children. Kristen was the oldest daughter, with light brown hair and green eyes. She was the sunshine in her father's heart, and likely to take over the family business when he decided it was time to retire. Allison was the second daughter, and while she was often rebellious, she was never so bad as to cause a scandal of any sort. Julia was the third daughter, and she was, sadly, rather sickly. She was given to fits, minor bouts of epilepsy that were treatable but always lingered like a threat. Julia was her mother's daughter in all ways, following her through the house as soon as she was old enough to walk, and enough like her mother that she could have been a miniature version of her.

They would have all been happy if Julia hadn't been quite a bit too much like her mother, and just a touch more curious than was good for her. Like her mother before her, little Julia thought she heard noises in the wall. Unlike her mother, she decided to investigate. The wall that Angela had placed in front of the room where she'd locked away the figures her husband had carved was well placed. Few would have noticed anything wrong with it at all, and even those few who heard the slight rustling sounds coming from the wall would have likely not paid careful enough attention to discover that there was a hidden room. Then again, few people have the same curiosity as a five-year-old girl who is bored almost to the point of tears.

Though she could not actually force the wall open, she could pry away the wooden trim with a little effort, and Julia, who had not yet learned that some things should not be seen, did just that. Beyond the barrier she removed, Julia could see a small portion of the room by resting her head against the floor and getting as close as she could to the small opening she'd created. What she saw was the sort of thing that, perhaps, all small children long to see: a room filled with dolls that moved and walked and seemed to live.

Julia was overjoyed. She wanted to tell her parents about the secret room as soon as she was finished looking. She might have even had the chance, if she hadn't been spotted by the miniature denizens dwelling in the room. One of the figures, a man who looked remarkably like her very own father, turned its small wooden head and looked in her direction, having heard her small gasp of pleased surprise.

The small wooden face moved into a silent scream, and even as Julia started rising from her prone position, she heard the scraping sound of not dozens but hundreds of the figures moving at one time. Before she could do more than rise to her feet, she was slapped down again by a violent seizure that left her writhing across the floor. Her head slammed into the hard wood paneling next to the hidden entrance, and she spun away from consciousness.

Her father found her on the floor almost an hour later. Her skin was pasty white, save where the blood from her injury had stained it in hues of rusty brown and fresh crimson. Joseph Blackwell loved is daughter dearly, more than he loved himself, to be sure. He picked her up in his hands and laid her carefully on the bed. His singular goal was to get her to the medical center and see to her every need.

He didn't pay any attention to the voices coming from the western wall of his bedroom until the phone he'd grabbed to make his call suddenly went dead. The voices were almost indiscernible. He could not consciously understand what they told him to do. That didn't stop him from obeying. He left his injured daughter where she lay and went down to the basement of the house his forefathers had built. He very calmly sorted through tools his father had used in his youth and that he himself had never touched in his life, until he found a proper weapon.

He spoke softly as he walked, but the words were not his own. They mimicked perfectly the hundreds of tiny voices that spoke to him of dark deeds and bloodshed.

Joseph Blackwell buried the hatchet he wielded deep in Allison's chest. She looked upon her father as she died and knew that the eyes looking back did not belong to him. He kissed her forehead when the deed was done, just as he did every night when he lay her down to sleep.

Julia was next, though she never saw his face or knew of the weapon that took her life. She was not aware of his tender kiss on her forehead or the time of day for that matter. Her mind was shattered long before he arrived, having been opened up to the desires that drove the wooden sculptures that had so delighted her.

Clarisse was watching the television with their oldest daughter, Kristen, when he found them. Clarisse died quickly, her throat hacked out by a vicious swing from the hatchet in his hand. Her blood covered him and made gripping his weapon difficult. He resorted to his bare hands with Kristen. His fingers tore flesh crudely, and unlike the others, she suffered greatly and screamed repeatedly before the mercy of oblivion was granted her. She alone begged for mercy, though she received none.

She breathed her last at the exact same time that the forces gripping Joseph Blackwell released him from their hold. He found himself above his daughter in a mockery of passion, his hands and face covered with blood, listening to her death rattle as he came to full awareness.

When he discovered what had happened to his family, Joseph Blackwell went a little insane. He charged from room to room, searching for a killer and stopping at the body of each murder victim, holding them in his arms and weeping anew. All that he loved in the world had been taken from him, and every shred of evidence pointed to him being the culprit behind the murders. Long before the search of the house was over, his voice was cracked and his vocal cords raw from his screams. He drew the only conclusion he could about what had happened to his family. The blood on his own hands and the way he found himself with Kristen were enough to make it clear to him that he'd killed them himself. He died the same way that his family died: by his own hand. He was just as cruel to himself as he had apparently been to Kristen.

The family was found almost five days later by Eric Blake, who in those days was the right-hand man of Joseph Blackwell, and Andrew Pageant. They called the constables as soon as they saw the bloodied remains of Kristen Blackwell. The sight haunted Eric for the rest of his days.

Andrew does not speak of such things. It has never been his way to exploit the losses of others or to tell tales out of school. Just as he never mentions the circus that once, long ago, came to stay on his father's farm and never left that place. Like so many people in Serenity, he knows how to keep a secret.

III

Information. As far as Jonathan Crowley was concerned, it was normally worth a great deal more than gold. Of course, it was easy for him to feel that way, as he was filthy stinking rich and didn't have to bother with things like whether or not he was going to eat a solid meal sometime during the week. There were perks to his work, and he was the first to admit it.

Information, that was the source of his current woes. Rather, it was the lack of information that was causing him troubles. He'd worked long and hard to get what he needed regarding the names of the—and it hurt him to think that somebody had actually come up with this title and thought it was somehow powerful and mysterious—Dark Light Cult.

There was only one easy way to handle the matter, and looking at the 47th Precinct in front of him, he decided he'd spent enough time investigating on his own. Time to let the guys who were actually good at looking in on crime scenes give him a hand.

Crowley walked through the glass doors at the front of the brick building and moved past a crowd of cops, witnesses, and criminals. A few people looked at him as he moved through the constantly changing chaos, but for the most part he was ignored. That was exactly what he wanted.

He moved back to where the detectives at the precinct did their work and scanned the desks until he saw the name plate for one Maria Argendelli. Maria was in charge of the murders he was looking into. She wasn't at her desk, and that suited his needs better than he'd expected. He sat down in her worn chair and turned on her computer. She was probably out and about, looking for a few more clues in one of her cases. If the cop shows had it right, she was also probably working on more investigations than she could ever actually handle.

All around him, the hectic police officers did their thing, never once bothering to look in his direction. He rifled her desk for files, and when that didn't work, he started searching the database of open cases. After almost two hours of hunting and pecking his way across the keyboard, he finally found the information he wanted. It was purely by accident. He sucked at using databases, especially when they were protected by a dozen different passwords. Getting past the security was easy enough, but it was also time consuming.

Whoever was doing the legwork on the cases wasn't really making the connections. The problem here was that every member of the Dark Light Cult he'd managed to track down, excepting only Anthony Marcuso, was missing or dead. A little dabbling in psychometry with a dash of necromancy had allowed him to wangle the names of the girls in the pictures. It had not, however, given him the name of the pimple-faced loser in the pictures with them. Now he was researching their whereabouts and learning that they were, in fact, as dead as he had expected. Looking at their track records, most of them had been busted for minor offenses on a few occasions. Nothing heavy, just possession for personal use and a few traffic tickets. Now they were dead. The real problem was that they were all dead from the same sort of causes and not really the kind that would red flag them in any other cases going on. Drug overdoses. Not exactly original or, for that matter, very bright. The best news was that whoever was working on their cases was also thorough enough to list known associates.

He was finally getting to the names of the surviving cultists—hopefully—when Detective Maria Argendelli cleared her throat and scowled down at him. She could have lost a few pounds. She also could have used a serious visit with a dentist, maybe a week or two of intensive study on how to apply makeup, and a new cologne because the crap she was wearing was almost enough to make his eyes water. He did not feel any immediate need to point these things out to her.

"What the hell are you doing at my desk?" Voice lessons would have helped, too. She wasn't actually screaming, but the shrill tone of her voice made it seem that way.

"Just passing the time." He looked at her and then clicked the Print Screen icon on the file he was looking over.

"Yeah? Well, unless you give me a goddamned good reason for you looking at private police files in the next ten seconds, I'm gonna make sure you have all the time you need, honey."

Simple magic. He reached into his shirt pocket and pulled out a blank business card. He smiled in her direction and watched the slight easing of her pissed-off facial features as she saw the badge she believed he was holding. "I'm Jonathan Crowley, Internal Affairs. I just needed to look at a few files on a case, and your desk was available. I've seen your record. I didn't think you'd have anything to hide, so I decided to go ahead and do what I needed to do. You have a problem with that?"

"No, sir. But next time I suggest you make good and damned sure you check with me before you go sitting your skinny little ass down where I do my work."

He nodded and stood up, reaching for the page that had just finished printing.

"Not a problem. Listen, since you're here, and since I noticed the trend, you might want to look over the files I've got pulled. I think there's a connection between all of the files I opened. Me? I investigate bad cops. You? You might find something you can use."

He folded the page without looking at it and walked away from her desk.

"Hey." He'd only known her for sixty seconds and already she was getting on is nerves.

"Yes, Detective?"

"Who you investigating?"

"Got a desk sergeant at the 62nd Precinct who's been taking sexual favors in exchange for get out of jail free cards."

"No shit?"

"I wouldn't lie about a thing like that."

She shook her head in disgust, and he waved a casual farewell, slipping back out the way he'd come. He figured by the time he hit the street she'd have told all the other detectives about his little investigation. Somebody at the 62nd wasn't going to like him very much. That thought put a smile on his face.

He looked at the paper when he was several blocks away from the police station. Best not to tempt fate. It was always possible that the good Maria Argendelli would decide to investigate whether or not there was a Jonathan Crowley in IAD, and he really didn't have the patience for being detained.

"I have you, boy." He spoke the words softly and smiled. There were only two names on the list that didn't have the word *Deceased* next to them. Marcuso was behind bars. That only left one member of the Dark Light Cult alive and able to commit the murders he'd been trying to stop.

Names have power, sometimes a little, sometimes a lot. In this case, it would be enough for him to track down the reason for his drive from California to New York.

There were three women he knew had been killed by the punk who was out and about searching for sacrifices. There were a total of four others he was almost certain were involved. That was good enough for Jonathan Crowley.

He'd been asked to help stop a murderer. That was exactly what he intended to do.

IV

It roared through the darkness, moving at speeds that would have shamed most aircraft. Where it went, the demon scattered nightmares and phobias to mark its passage. So far it had killed one town and seventeen people as payment for being brought back.

A small price to pay, really. But there were other things it had to do in order to gain its freedom. There were others who had to pay for the sins they had committed against its master and, of course, there was a small matter of revenge.

The Hunter had destroyed it, left it to suffer for all eternity in the special sort of hell designed solely to make failures regret their lack of success. That wasn't the sort of thing that could be forgiven without a little reciprocal bloodshed.

It was still aching from the tortures, and even after weeks away from its torments, it was till trying to remember all of the details of its previous incarnation. It would be nice to remember what its name had been.

Still, it was free now, ready to wreak destruction and misery upon the mortal world, even if there was someone else calling the shots.

Geography meant nothing to the demon, but it descended to the ground in a city in Pennsylvania. There, among the thousands who dwelled within the confines of the buildings with their lights, was a woman who had offended its master some years earlier. She looked to be in her early thirties, though it could sense the weight of centuries upon her.

Her building was protected against unwanted attentions. The demon didn't care. Recent feedings had left it swollen with power, and though the female human was strong, she was not strong enough to defend against its likes. The wards were easily shattered and with only minimal damage to the demon.

The woman was easily shattered, too, but because it had been given orders, it took its time and made her suffer as few ever had before. It stripped her of her clothing, her flesh, and her innocence all at once and then continued its degradations of her until the sun had risen. Still she did not die but tried to beg for mercy.

When the sun had set again, it finally tired of her and devoured her soul. And then, joy of joys, it once again caught the scent that had previously sent it into a frenzy. Closer now than before, it caught the spoor of the Hunter.

Its destination was to the north, a small place where the master had been greatly offended in the past. Happily, the Hunter lay in that direction as well. The master could make demands, but the demon had an agenda as well, and the Hunter was high on its list of priorities. It was time, at last, for revenge.

CHAPTER 10

I

Penelope Grey was a beautiful woman. She was still only half his age, but Simon MacGruder was never one to shy away from beauty where he saw it. She was also a delight to talk to.

Maybe it was a case of kindred spirits. With everything that had happened to her in the past, she never seemed to feel it necessary to spend a lot of time with the people in Serenity Falls. Probably she was just tired of the looks.

Penny's eyes were a nice, bright blue, and her face was more handsome than beautiful if you had to be picky, but her mouth practically begged to be kissed, and her thick auburn hair was exactly the right kind for a man to run his hands through. There was a scar on her face that marred her looks, and having spoken with her for a while now, he suspected that alone wasn't the reason she tended to be a bit standoffish. It probably had to do with her son, Lawrence. As far as he could tell, her world revolved around him.

They'd been talking for almost two hours, and the subject of Lawrence and of Daniel had finally come up. She'd asked him why he invited her to lunch, and he was honest enough to tell her.

"I want to know about what happened with Daniel. I know it's personal, and I know I can read all of the papers to find out, but the thing is, I'm trying to do a legitimate history of the town, and I want to know the facts from you, not from some reporter who read a police report. I've already talked a bit to Bill Karstens, but I wanted to know if you could figure out what happened with Daniel and why he went crazy." There, it was said, and there was no taking it back. He prepared himself to grovel an apology and be on his way. The problem with dealing with the nastier stuff was that, frankly, you sometimes had to deal with the tempers that remembering those things brought on.

Penny Grey looked at him for several seconds, a very faint smile playing around her lips. He wasn't sure if she was going to laugh or throw her coffee in his face.

"Simon, you and my father went back a long, long ways. Just about anyone else in this town I'd tell to go to hell. But you, just this one time, I'll answer your questions."

That was a relief. He hadn't been relishing the idea of second-degree burns. His face was homely enough.

"I appreciate that, Penny."

"You know you're the only person in town who still calls me that. Everyone else calls me Penelope."

She smiled with her eyes, and he changed his mind. She wasn't handsome. She was gorgeous. "Okay. Here's the answer to your question. Daniel went through his little fits a few times, as I'm sure you know."

He nodded.

"Well, when he got fixated it was all you could do to get him to change his mind. Remember his sister, Denise? She warned me once that he could be a bit . . . intense. That was just before we tied the knot. She wouldn't explain why she said it, but she made it clear to stay away from him when he was in a mood. I'd heard all the stories, of course. About how angry he could get. But he'd never shown me anything like that."

She stopped for a moment to collect her thoughts, and he took her hand in his paw. Her skin was soft and warm, and he maybe fell just a little bit in love with her. Happily, in his case at least, that feeling never lasted long enough to get him in too much trouble. Not since . . . well, he was trying not to think about that.

"He got some notion into his head that our son was evil." She shrugged. "I don't know how or why, but Daniel decided one day that Lawrence being born was going to cause no end of grief to this town, and to the whole world, the way he went on. He didn't say it to me, and he tried his best not to show it or let it come out, but it was there, Simon. He thought our baby boy was going to be the end of everything."

Lawrence Grey was a thin kid, underweight and sickly. He was shy to the point of being almost xenophobic, and on the rare occasions that anyone saw him outside of school or church, he was quiet and solemn. The only time he'd ever seen the boy smile was the one occasion when he'd been witness to the kid playing with a puppy. And had Penny had a fit over that? Yes. She had. She'd damn near had a coronary, because the puppy was a Saint Bernard that belonged to one of Lawrence's classmates and had probably already outweighed poor little Lawrence. She was overprotective of her only son, and Simon couldn't really blame her. Not after what they'd been through.

"That's crazy, Penny."

"That was the problem." She laughed, but the smile went away from her eyes. Ten years since Daniel had died, and she was still haunted by the fact that she loved him. Simon could understand that. "That was just exactly the problem, wasn't it? He couldn't get past the crazy part of his mind." She squeezed back on his hand, her fingers gripping hard. He let his free hand cover over her wrist and patted down a few times. When her father had died a few years back, Simon was just about the only person in town she would let comfort her. Hell, her dad was his fishing and hunting buddy back in the days when he was still spry enough to do both. There'd been a lot of holidays where he was just about an uncle to the woman sitting across the table from him. Of course back then she'd just been a little girl, not much older than her Lawrence was now.

"I feel like an ass, bringing all of this back on you. I'm sorry, Penny."

She waved his comment away and shook her head. "Don't be. Sometimes it's nice to have someone to talk to."

"You know you can call on me anytime. Just because

I'm not always calling on you doesn't mean you can't pick up the phone if you want to chew the fat."

"Well, the feeling's mutual. You were always so good to us, Simon."

"Well, hell, Penny. You're practically family; you know that."

"Still, if you hadn't stepped in to take care of all the insurance nonsense, I don't know what would have happened."

"You think your father would have wanted me to let things go wrong for you?" Damn it, he was getting misty eyed and he didn't want that. Men weren't supposed to cry. "I wasn't gonna let some Joe Blow at the insurance company take advantage of the things that were going wrong for you and yours."

She smiled again, wiping the excess moisture from her eyes. "I used to daydream that you and Mom would get together."

He almost choked. He'd just been sipping coffee when she said that. "Oh, that would have been a mess, now wouldn't it?" He was laughing when he spoke. Constance Merriweather Pageant—yes, of the Pageant clan, but from the black sheep side of the family—had not exactly approved of her husband running around with Simon MacGruder and had been politely vocal about that fact. She thought the older man was a bad influence on her husband.

"Oh, please, Simon. She didn't actually hate you, you know." It was her turn to laugh out loud. He liked the sound a lot.

"Nothing that she wouldn't have taken care of with a

frying pan to the side of my skull." It was water well under the bridge for Simon, and he had never held a grudge for the way the woman felt about him. He'd just accepted that they weren't going to see eye to eye.

"I think she had a crush on you and didn't like to admit it." He couldn't tell if Penny was serious or joking.

"I think she wanted me well away from your father and not taking him off on fishing trips once a month, is what I think."

"Well, I can tell you this much. It was her, not Dad, who always invited you over for the holidays."

He waved it aside. "That was just her being a good Christian."

"Don't you believe it. I was around to see the way she watched you when no one was looking."

"I thought we agreed that Daniel was the crazy one, not you." He spoke without thinking and expected a bad response. Instead, she laughed. He had never been good at understanding women. He figured that one mystery, more than any other, would remain a mystery.

"Trust me, Simon. My mother thought you were a handsome devil."

"If you say so, Penny."

She looked at her watch and smiled. "I know so. I agree with her."

Simon flushed a dark red and tried to laugh that off.

Twenty minutes later, they were back at Penny's house and making love. It was completely unexpected and one of the best experiences he ever had. The woman was passionate and loving and knew exactly what to do to make him feel like a young buck of twenty.

They spoke softly of different things for almost an

hour, and then Penny got herself dressed. Simon followed suit. They had one last long, lingering kiss, and Simon went out the back door of her house and into the deep woods behind it. Simon was old-fashioned, and the last thing he wanted was anyone seeing him and deciding to gossip about the dirty old man and the woman quite literally young enough to be his daughter and then some.

He thanked her when he left, and she, in turn, thanked him silently with a kiss on his lips that was chaste and loving. They never spoke of the matter again. They never had a meal together again, either, but it was a memory that both held onto for the rest of their lives.

II

Serenity Falls Part Ten: Necessary Evils

Daniel Grey was not exactly the nicest man who ever walked the streets of Serenity. He was not the meanest, but he would certainly have made the top ten list. But there were cases that would have proved a good argument against him actually being a bad person. He was charitable to those less fortunate, and on more than a few occasions in his life he actually instigated the quiet, dignified gathering of money or food for a family in need. He was not a cruel man nor a spiteful one. He was simply the sort who made those who knew him best wary of getting on his bad side.

It was his temper that caused the problems. At the age of fifteen, Daniel was still well liked and considered by the majority of the people in his life as a kind soul. He had never, to that date, lost his temper over anything. It's hard to say what changed that. Today the first suspect would probably be alcohol or drugs, by which so many people seem to find a valid way to escape the troubles of a hectic life.

Back then it was just as likely that rock and roll would take the blame, or even growing pains, that quaint euphemism for the insanity brought on by puberty and the tides of hormones that move through a body that is changing almost daily.

At sixteen, Daniel definitely changed. Had anyone bothered to ask him why, he would have pointed to the members of the opposite sex and explained that he could never really understand them. Girls didn't just confuse him; they left him stupefied. He'd seen and dated the same young lady for three months. A girl he'd known all his life, Margherita Sullivan. The problem, according to her, was that they should remain merely friends. That might have been easier if they hadn't actually been going beyond the kissing stage in their relationship. Still, he did his best to abide by her requests. It just left him in a foul mood.

That particular source of regret and bitterness left his life a few months after they became just friends. She moved to another state with her family, where they'd inherited a rather large plot of farmland.

He started getting his reputation as something of a

bastard around the same time. It might not have become
a truly bad thing, a nearly legendary sort of rep, if his sister had been left alone. His sister was, by the standards of
the time and by the standards of today, far too young to
be dating. In fact she herself, while often falling victim
to the desire to be swept away by a handsome man as
happened so often in the romance books she read, really
wasn't looking for a relationship. Not even for a boy
to hold hands with. She was being a good girl and saving
herself for Mister Right, who would doubtless make
himself known to her when the time came.

Robert DeMillio, not exactly a gem in the crown of
high society, must have felt that he was, in fact, her Mister Right. Perhaps that wouldn't have been a problem if
she'd found him remotely interesting. Even then, there
might never have been a serious issue. But Robert De-
Millio was not the sort to take no for an answer. He
wasn't even really the type who took the time to ask. At
forty years of age, he pretty much felt he could do what
he wanted, and never mind the consequences.

Denise Grey found out the hard way that Robert De-
Millio didn't much care whether or not she thought he
was Mister Right. He proved it to her when he dragged
her off the road she was walking down and covered her
face with his hand and her body with his own. He took
her innocence and very nearly her life. The only thing
that saved her was being discovered by Alden Waters, a
local hunter, who took her to the newly built medical
center. Waters was almost arrested for the crime himself, but he voluntarily gave up a blood sample and was
found to not be the same blood type as the man who'd
violated Daniel's little sister.

Denise was a very long time recovering from what had been done to her. Physically, she lay in a coma for almost a month. Mentally, she stayed lost to the world for the better part of a year. The people who knew Daniel saw what that year did to him. Saw him go from an easygoing, relatively calm young man and change into something just shy of rabid. He was still normally calm, mind you, but when his temper went off, it was volcanic. He spent two weeks in a foster home after beating Carl Bradford halfway into a coma for making comments to the other football players when he didn't realize that Daniel was nearby—though he likely would have made the very same comments if he had known. One second Carl was talking about how Denise was too young for him, but he could see where a guy would be tempted, especially with the way she shook her ass, and the next he was kissing the pavement as Daniel went bug shit crazy on him.

Daniel Grey rammed Carl Bradford's head into the ground seven times before the rest of the jocks there could come to their friend's rescue. Good old Carl had to have three of his teeth capped and spent several weeks looking like a few hundred miles of bad road. He was also the brunt of a few jokes, but those faded quickly after the next person to face Daniel came out of it looking much worse.

His second victim was a stranger in town who was a little too rude for his own good. When he bumped into Daniel and decided to scold the kid for bad manners, the kid whomped his ass for his troubles. Daniel went back to a foster home again, this time for almost two months. Something about having a fat salesman wagging a finger in his face just hadn't agreed with Daniel, and that pretty much was all it came down to.

He calmed down after that. Or maybe it was just that people stopped giving him reasons to go off. The latter seems more likely. It's possible that Daniel Grey could have gone the rest of his life without severe violence playing any part in his existence, but it was never very probable.

He was looking for someone, you see, and he found him.

In addition to being a less than subtle man, Robert DeMillio was also a less than bright one. He drank too much, and he bragged too much. And one night, while filled to the gills with Pabst Blue Ribbon beer, he made the mistake of bragging on the wrong subject to the wrong person. He told Elway Devereaux about getting himself a fine young virgin in the woods. He talked of how she'd screamed his name before he was finished, by God.

Devereaux was not the sort of man who went to the police when he heard bad news. No one in his family had ever been overly friendly with the law, though that is another story for another time. He was, however, the sort who believed in justice. It didn't take him much time to figure out what DeMillio was talking about. That made it a matter of telling the right person. Marcus Grey was a good man, but he was not a healthy one. Some people claimed he'd spent too much time around the cadavers he buried, but the truth was simpler than that. He was born sickly, and he'd never gotten better. As long as he left hard exertion to those better equipped to handle it, everything was fine. But when he got overly excited he was prone to fits—which had led to a few off-color comments about his sex life, but none that were actually meant in a nasty way—and when it came to fighting, he was about as capable as a toddler is of walking a high wire.

That left Daniel. Elway invited the boy to see him at his farm, and they spoke for a few hours. Elway urged caution, reminding him that his sister was likely to recover fully, and when she did, she'd be a mite sadder if her brother was behind bars or getting ready to ride the lightning.

He made Daniel understand that rage was a tool, like a saw, or like a hammer. It only worked right if it was used in the right way.

Elway even helped set the man up. They went out drinking again, at their usual watering hole, and when DeMillio was well on his way to pickled, Elway headed home. But not before giving his signal to Daniel in the darkness.

Daniel was patient. He let his rage grow and fester, felt the pressure of his need to hurt the twisted bastard who'd raped his sister become almost crystalline: a diamond pressed in the desire to avenge her.

He got his chance, too. Robert DeMillio stumbled out of the bar some time after one in the morning. He was drunk and feeling no pain. Daniel intended to rectify that. There are certain advantages to stalking a drunk. Among them is the simple fact that drunks are less likely to pay attention to who is following them around. DeMillio never even noticed the fact that he was being shadowed. He was too busy trying to remember his way home.

Daniel made sure he never got there. After his hours of scheming and planning, the actual capture of the piggish bastard was almost a letdown. He'd expected more of a struggle, possibly a few bruises he'd have to worry about after DeMillio disappeared from town.

It took one swing with the five-pound sledgehammer from his father's garage to drop the man like an anvil to the ground. DeMillio's scalp bled horribly, and for a moment Daniel thought he'd surely killed him. That in and of itself was the goal, of course, but he had plans on how to make the man pay for what he'd done. He had to suffer, just as Denise had suffered.

Payback wouldn't be done properly otherwise.

It took him over an hour to get the man positioned where he wanted him. Daniel spent twenty-five minutes carrying DeMillio over his shoulders in a fireman's carry before finally reaching the place where he wanted to be, deep in the woods, away from where anyone would hear or see anything. His shoulders were trembling from the exertion of bringing the man to his final resting place, and he felt almost nauseous from the effort. But it was worth it.

Deep in the woods near Serenity, several granite outcroppings rose from the ground. One of them was almost perfectly flat, and so well hidden by trees that the sun virtually never touched the ground. It was in that spot where Daniel set Robert down and secured him. He used the spikes from his old tent and the ropes that anchored the structure in place to leave DeMillio spread-eagled over the long, flat rock. He knew the stone was rough and uneven. He knew that lying across it would be about as comfortable as resting on a heap of bricks.

That, too, suited him. Daniel had spent almost an hour on that rock earlier, in almost the same position, while deciding if it was the right spot. Now he knew it was. Something about the area called to him, and the odd patterns in the granite—striations that almost looked like writing and were the color of ancient, dried blood—were almost mesmerizing.

He sensed he'd found the perfect spot.

DeMillio woke up to find himself naked on the ground, his body itching madly and his eyes half crossed from the earlier drinking and the severe concussion he suffered. The first thing he saw when he could focus was Daniel staring down at him grimly.

Oh, there were threats made by DeMillio. Promises of prison time, personal vengeance, and even death. Then came the begging and the crying. He had a family to take care of. He had children, a wife he loved, and a sickly old mother.

Through it all, Daniel sat silently. He listened to the words with a face that could just as easily have been a wooden mask for all the emotion he showed.

Robert DeMillio tried explaining himself. He talked of his deep loneliness, forgetting all about his loving wife at home. He spoke of his weakness, his need for alcohol and the way it made him do stupid things. He cried and moaned and wailed at the sad state of his life.

Daniel never said a word.

He merely pulled a photograph of his sister from his wallet and held it in DeMillio's face.

Then he pulled two beer bottles, the exact same brand that DeMillio himself favored, from a paper sack. After that he pulled a sock and masking tape from the bag and used them to make a very effective gag for the man he held captive.

The first beer bottle was shoved as deeply as it could be into Robert DeMillio's rectum. DeMillio screamed and did everything he could to get away. He was not successful in his endeavors. When that task was finished to Daniel's satisfaction—by which point Robert had passed out for several minutes and then come to—Daniel used the same hammer he'd employed on DeMillio's skull to shatter the glass.

He broke the second bottle on the granite next to Robert's bleeding body, listening to the sounds of the man's muffled agony and hearing only music. He used the jagged edges of his glass weapon to saw through the offending member of Robert's anatomy, ensuring that he would never hurt another girl with it, even if he managed to live.

Not that he had to worry. Robert died almost an hour later, blinded by pain and weak from blood loss. Daniel took back his tent pegs and ropes, his sock, and even the tape. He left the beer bottles and the corpse behind.

If he noticed the way the markings within the granite glowed when the blood touched them, he never gave it any thought. He was far too busy watching a man slither like a snake to pay attention to the moderately interesting glyphs.

Daniel waited patiently for the police to come to his door and take him away. He would have confessed the crime if confronted. They never showed themselves. He never volunteered the information to anyone save Denise, and she was in no condition to tell anyone anything.

Shortly after the murder, Denise began to recover. It

was still a slow process, but she began to climb back from whatever darkness had hidden her away, and she began to live a real life again.

In time, Daniel began to understand the concept of peace again. His temper calmed and was attributed to nothing more than growing pains. For Daniel at least, revenge was the best possible medicine.

III

He looked out over the skyline of New York and felt the same weird sense of loss he'd been feeling since he came into the Big Apple. Something was missing. It hadn't even been a year since religious freaks with delusions of being God's messengers had decided to take out the World Trade Center towers. He'd seen the news just like everyone else, but seeing the skyline without the two massive skyscrapers felt *wrong*. Well, then again, most things felt wrong to him. This was just a bigger wrong, and one he could do nothing about. After a moment, the sounds of the people on the rooftop below drew his attention again. Back to work.

Jonathan Crowley watched from the shadows, taking his time in assessing the situation. Two boys, probably in their late teens, and one girl around the same age. One of the young men was unconscious, or doing a good job of faking it. The other was doing his best to tie the girl onto his makeshift altar; a wooden contraption designed to look like an inverted crucifix. He'd gone all out and set it up to swivel, so the victims would actually be suspended upside down when he committed the deed. She was fighting back very vigorously and taking it personally that the punk was trying to take her clothes off her struggling form. Crowley couldn't blame her; it was barely in the fifties, and the air had a distinct nip.

Three weeks ago he'd received a phone call. Just the usual call from someone he hadn't seen or even much thought of in over a decade. A girl, Kristen Rainer, from Pennsylvania, quite pretty, as he recalled. He'd taught her when he was at NYU. She had never done anything wrong, but one of her sorority sisters had decided the best way to get good grades was to sell her soul. The sheer volume of stupid people he ran across never ceased to amaze him. It had been a minor affair, the démon riding her back was barely even dangerous to her, really, but he'd handled it just the same. Then, out of the blue, the girl had called, "just to shoot the breeze." She'd been thinking about him and tried the old number. What a surprise, it still worked. And then the conversation about the murders, seven of them so far, grisly affairs . . . After so many deaths already, she'd thought that maybe people would just be nice to each other for a change. Crowley could have told her it didn't work that way, but he chose not to. Instead, he'd ended the conversation with a promise to look into the matter, and that had been the start of the latest little mess.

Two days ago, after many, many patient days of research and walking through the crime scenes again and again, he'd finally made a connection. The boy down there was part of what had once been a fledgling satanic cult. Drugs and excesses had taken the cult apart bit by bit. Most of them had probably been in it for the free cocaine and sex, anyway. That was usually as far as most of them cared to go, and for that reason they were harmless. Naturally, there were always exceptions, like the moron on the other roof.

Crowley allowed himself a small grin as he watched the boy try to force the girl's legs into the proper place on his homemade altar. He hadn't designed the damned thing well at all. It was hardly conducive to getting her pretty legs locked down, and her struggles only made the matter worse. She was a fighter, which was why Crowley was taking his time. He liked a good fight. And, judging by the setup, the dork struggling with her was a rank amateur. The amateurs always got elaborate. *Probably,* he mused silently, *to make up for their lack of any really original ideas*.

The weather was cold and, being a young pervert, the kid had finally managed to strip her clothes away from her. Like as not he'd want to rape her before making her his latest sacrifice. Still, credit where it was due, he'd been smart enough to use condoms if that was the case. None of the other three obvious sacrifice victims had shown any evidence of semen, though all had been violated before they had their hearts cut out. The same could be said of the ones who hadn't been as blatantly exploited for use in calling up something nasty.

He watched on as the young lady—a cheerleader, if he was making out the clothes cast to the side properly—planted her foot on the side of her abductor's head and sent him reeling back, spitting profanities like a scalded cat. The geek's mouth was bleeding, and he looked a bit dazed, but not so stunned that he couldn't get inventive with his obscenities.

Crowley took a running start and cleared the distance between the two rooftops with ease. He landed on the tarpapered surface without gaining the moron's notice. He was good at not being heard when he set his mind to it.

As he moved closer, the heavy in the little play he was watching wiped the blood from his lip, staining his pimple-covered face. He couldn't decide which seemed angrier, the would-be killer or the rampaging acne that covered his skin from the chin all the way up to the forehead.

The boy shook his mop of greasy brown hair and made several promises as to what he was going to do to his victim. For her part, she kept mostly silent, the gag in her mouth preventing her from really getting into a verbal conflict at that time.

Crowley admired her body almost as much as he admired her feistiness. Still, she was a bit too young for his tastes, so he decided it was time to get down to business, even as she cut loose with a volley of kicks that kept the Pimple King of New York from managing to get her feet pinned in place.

She stopped kicking when she saw Crowley moving behind her captor, who was now panting heavily from the exertion of fighting her off. Her lovely brown eyes grew wide in a silent plea. Crowley winked at her and smiled broadly.

"Personally, I don't think she's in the mood to be sacrificed to any dark gods today." The kid almost wet himself as he spun around to face Crowley. "Maybe you ought to call it a night before she manages to get you a good one in your balls."

"Who are you?" He tried to sound tough, but the way his voice cracked took any possible threat from the scowl on his face. Still, Crowley gave him points for effort.

"I'm the good guy. The one who's here to stop you from killing the nice cheerleader." Crowley came closer, his smile growing wider as he approached. He added a little extra saccharine to his tone when he spoke again, just to get under the twerp's skin. "What's your name, sweet pea?"

The kid bristled. "None of your fucking business! Why don't you get the hell out of here, before I cut your heart out?" To make his words have some semblance of potential threat, he pulled a very long and very effective looking dagger from his belt.

Crowley's smile grew a little wider and a lot meaner. "Or instead, I could just shove that knife of yours right down your throat. Whattaya say?"

The kid moved forward, the ancient weapon held skillfully in his hand. Crowley sidestepped and planted his foot in the small of his assailant's back, sending him halfway across the roof before an air-conditioning unit stopped his forward motion. The dagger went flying and landed even farther away with a loud clatter.

"Clumsy, clumsy, clumsy. Who the hell taught you how to fight?"

The mocking tone in Crowley's voice only served to make the punk even angrier as he climbed back to his feet. Crowley let him get up without making any further attacks.

"I'll kill you!"

"Oh, that's an original threat. Try this one on for size. First, I'm going to break both of your kneecaps. Then, because I can, I'm going to hurt you. When I'm done and I grow bored, I'm going to snap your miserable little neck and send you straight to hell."

No words this time. Instead, the boy made a few quick gestures and smiled directly at Crowley. "I have friends you can't even begin to imagine." The punk walked forward confidently, his smile broad and sadistic. It rather reminded Jonathan Crowley of his own smile when he looked in the mirror. That would never do. He preferred being unique.

Crowley was about to speak when the hair on his neck rose, lifting as if touched by a heavy breeze. His eyes narrowed, and his heart thudded just a little faster. "What did you call, boy? What did you summon to do your dirty work?"

Zit-face smiled even wider, and behind him the girl screamed as best she could past the gag in her mouth. "A special friend. He takes care of me, and all I have to do is give him bitches like her." His gesture was casual, barely acknowledging that the girl he'd been attacking earlier was anything more than an object.

Crowley let his eyes slide over to the boy's victims again. The jock, who doubtless was with the cheerleader and on her side, was still out cold, possibly dead. The cheerleader was looking above her, struggling to get her arms free from their bonds. He let his own attention rise to meet whatever it was she found so fascinating.

There was nothing to see. No shadowy menace, no tentacled creature, not even a stereotypical imp. He hated when that happened. Because he knew *something* was there, and now he'd have to work for it.

The boy touched him. Actually put a hand on his shoulder, preparing to swing at his face. When it came to telegraphing his moves, the kid was a pro. Crowley turned to look at the twerp, looked at the hand on his shoulder, and looked at the kid again. Then he smiled. "Now that was a bad, bad mistake."

Apparently the kid felt the same way. He started backing up, his eyes growing wide as he looked at Crowley. "I-I have *Friends*! They'll help me!" His voice cracked on that last, and the boy looked around desperately for his elusive friends.

Something *Big* knocked Crowley off his feet; the impact felt like a luxury sedan slamming into him at high speed. He saw the fear fade from the boy's face, replaced by triumph, just before he was lifted from the ground by the impact.

Crowley felt the tarpapered roof smash into his face, and the hard, hot grip of something very strong holding the back of his head, pushing him across the roof. He was glad he'd taken off his glasses before coming here but less enthusiastic about the feel of his skin peeling back under the force of the attack. And the taste of the tarpaper and grit wasn't doing much for his mood either. He closed his eyes and pushed back with all of his might, struggling to free himself from the grip.

The Acne King's voice crowed cheerfully. "Oh, there she is . . ."

Whatever had him, had him good. It slammed Crowley's face into the ground a second time, pushing hard enough to make his nose creak and his teeth lose enamel. He closed his eyes and swung an arm awk-wardly behind him. His hands having to see for him as he reached for whatever it was that held him in place.

Braille for the terminally dense. He reached and touched the wet, scaly skin, his hand moving lower . . . that felt like a rib cage . . . that could just possibly be a hip . . . His hand slid lower, touching a muscular thigh as thick as a tree stump.

The thing hissed and pushed harder on his face, its strength much greater than he'd expected. He strug-gled, felt his lip pop open and start bleeding, and de-cided to end this quickly, before he really lost his temper. Crowley reached lower and found exactly what he'd hoped to find: male anatomy. That the penis was erect was not a promising aspect of the scenario, but he could live with it.

He found the testicles beneath the main body of the creature and looked up at the snot-nosed little punk who'd summoned the thing in the first place. Then he squeezed as hard as he could, while grinning savagely at the boy.

The pressure on his skull eased up, and Crowley looked to see what was attacking him. There was noth-ing there, just the massive weight on his body and the strange whimpering noise from where he figured a mouth would be. He whispered a few words and nodded with satisfaction as the illusion that hid the thing shat-tered like a porcelain plate dropped from the top of a house. It was a big thing, with little by way of flesh around its face. It rather looked like someone had stripped the skin away from a Mr. Universe contender and slapped snake-scale bandages over parts of its body. The shredded face looked down in shock, the glowing orbs where its eyes should have been going wider, and then it roared in pain.

The beast bucked and thrashed above him, trying to get away, but to no avail. Crowley's grip was like steel. The kid wasn't smiling anymore, and neither was the thing he was doing his best to make a eunuch. But Crowley was smiling a lot.

"You have absolutely no idea how badly I'm going to hurt you . . ." To emphasize his words, he twisted his handful of monster flesh and squeezed even harder. The thing squeaked this time, and Crowley finally managed to push it off of his body. His face felt raw and burned from pressing into the roof. But that didn't stop the smile. The taste of blood running into his mouth was hardly new and, as always, amused him.

He looked down at the raw mess on the ground, and his grin grew even larger. "I'll get back to you, cupcake . . ."

He looked at the boy. The boy looked back, terrified. "Y-You can't do that!"

"Why not? I didn't see that in the rules anywhere . . ." He stepped toward the nervous teen. "And I should know. I always play by the rules."

The kid backed up again, and Crowley came forward, his face getting nastier and nastier with the grin. Then he reached out for the frightened, cowering boy in front of him. There was no kindness on his face. "Rule number one: if you want to play with big, bad monsters from other planes of existence, expect me to take it personally. This is my world, and I expect a certain amount of order."

"K-Keep away from me," squeaked the nerd.

"No."

"I mean it! Keep away! That was just the warm-up!"

Jonathan Crowley laughed then. And the girl blanched right along with her would-be killer. Something about the way he laughed had that effect on people. Made them want to hide under the covers and stay hidden for a long, long time. It was something he dealt with.

"That was the best you had, sunshine. Now it's my turn."

Being of mostly sound mind and of limited courage, the boy turned and tried to bolt. Crowley let him get a whole two feet away before he made his move. One step, two, and then he reached out with his hand and wrapped his fingers into the bastard's greasy hair and pulled him backwards hard enough to lift him from the ground. The kid screamed very nicely.

"Come on, now, you're hurting my feelings. Here I go out of my way, I spend weeks looking you up, and all you want to do is run away." He added a little extra pout to his voice, a mocking noise that he knew would only make matters worse. "Is that any way to treat a guest in your fair town?"

He dragged his new friend closer before shoving him to the ground. When the kid tried to scramble away, Crowley brought his foot down on his kneecap and pressed until he heard something break. All the color drained from the ex-cultist's face, and he gasped faintly, the shock and pain taking away his ability to scream.

"Remember what I said I was going to do to you?" Crowley's voice was a purr, his smile almost serene. "That's one kneecap. Should I go for the other one, too?"

The kid started crying then, faint little hiccuping sounds breaking apart his words. "No. Oh, God, please, no."

Crowley leaned in closer. "Did the other ones beg you the same way? The ones you fed to your friend?" Crowley pulled back for a second, checking on the creature. It was still curled up and moaning. He nodded, satisfied for the moment. "You think about how you're going to answer that, sugar. I'll be back in a minute." He turned away, heading toward the thing on the ground. "Oh, and if you even think about moving, I'll cut your balls off." The boy froze in place as well as a statue would have.

Crowley walked past the girl, who was doing her best to get herself untied from the ropes that wound tightly around her wrists. "Stop that," he chided. "You'll only hurt yourself. I'll be there in a minute." The cheerleader stopped, her pretty face puzzled by the humor in his voice.

He looked down at his supernatural victim and smiled. "I don't think I've met you before; I would know. What, exactly, are you?"

It didn't respond, save to glare at him hatefully as it started to recover from his earlier assault.

"You *can* speak, can't you?" He walked a slow circuit around the thing as it started to rise, its face wrinkling with anger.

Its mouth opened, and it spoke in a guttural, barely understandable voice. "I'm the girl who's gonna rip your head off!"

Crowley blinked. *Girl?* Then he smiled. "You know something? I've met a lot of weird shit in my life, but never, not ever, a demon with a New York accent."

The creature's eyes bulged just a bit, and it made a hard swallowing motion that left Jonathan Crowley feeling good about himself. The musculature over its eyes coming down and back up as it tried to regain its composure was a display that was, frankly, disgusting to watch. "I *am* a demon . . . I am a *very powerful* demon . . ."

"From what I've seen, eight of the nine members of the Dark Light Cult—a *very* original name, I can assure you; I haven't run across it more than a dozen times, honest—died in the last year. Way I figure it, laughing boy over there decided to bring one of you back. Which one?"

The thing did its best to look puzzled, which, considering the lack of actual flesh over the body, was pretty damned impressive. "I-I don't know what you mean."

"Sure you do. You're not a demon. You just managed to hitch a ride here from wherever the hell you went when you died. So, let me ask you again. Who are you?"

"I'm Satan! Lord of the Underworld!" it roared as it rose to its full height of almost seven feet, the blaze of its eyes glowing more fiercely as it declared its name.

Crowley stood completely still for a good three heartbeats and then broke into laughter that left him nearly incapable of actually doing anything else. The sort of deep belly laugh that leaves a person aching afterwards. The skinned monster looked on, slack jawed by the shock of the laughing fit.

When he had himself under control, Crowley wiped his eyes with a finger, pushing the unexpected tears away. "Oh . . . thank you. I needed that." He chuckled. " 'I'm Satan, lord of the Underworld' . . . heh-heh-heh . . . That's rich."

"What are you laughing about!" He watched as the massive arms of the creature were planted on its hips in a decidedly feminine way.

"Toots, Satan wouldn't give you the time of day. Which one are you, Leslie Monroe, Noelle Dankins, Suzanne Comer, or Brandy Sinclaire?"

"Noelle Dankins," it confessed, its voice numbed by the discovery of its secret. "How did you know?"

"Trade secret. Let me see if I have this right. Zit boy over there wanted to bring you back from the dead, and you needed fresh kills to come back properly, only it didn't work out the way you'd planned. Am I right so far?"

The Noelle demon nodded.

"So you decided to find a new body. Only it hasn't been easy finding the right one, the one that could accept your energies?"

The creature stared at him blankly, its raw face expressionless. Crowley shrugged. "Close enough for me, I suppose." That said, he drove his thumbs into the monster's eyes. What had once been a young woman who fell in with the wrong crowd and did many stupid things before overdosing on bad heroin shrieked, falling backwards as he blinded her.

"You really are stupid, Noelle. You tried to deal with a devil. Devils lie. You never had a chance." He ducked a wild swing that lifted his hair with its passage. "You've been building a body, hoping to come back from the dead in a form that would be strong enough to withstand anything." Crowley talked on, even as he moved the few feet he needed in order to snatch up the dagger that the Acne Kid had lost in their earlier scuffle. "The thing is, even if you do make a good deal with a devil, they always end up shafting you. It's nothing personal; it's just what they do. The best you'd have gotten is what you are now." He shrugged. "Consider this a mercy killing, if that makes it any easier."

He threw the blade at the wretch's chest, burying it to the hilt in the exposed muscles. It screamed again—he really couldn't bring himself to think of the beast as a her, as the pretty, sad face he'd seen in her high school annual—and watched it twitch and falter, slumping to the ground before it breathed its last. The body decomposed in a matter of seconds, leaving behind only a thick black smoke that drifted away in the faint wind that picked up.

Crowley walked over and plucked the dagger from the ground where the creature had been, then walked back over to the boy who had started all of this insanity. The boy looked at him with wide, terrified eyes. "Your girlfriend won't be coming back. She shouldn't have come back in the first place." He leaned in close, his face inches from the shocky eyes of his prey. "That just leaves you and me, honeybee. And buddy, I don't think your chances are good."

The boy broke down. He closed his eyes and started crying quietly to himself. Crowley sneered in disgust. "Is this where I'm supposed to feel sorry for you? Where I realize that you were just a pawn in a game you didn't understand?" Instead of answering, the youth turned his face away. The tears kept coming.

Perhaps that would have bought mercy from some; he was, after all, a sad sight to behold. If Jonathan Crowley felt anything other than cold, sadistic pleasure from the boy's dilemma, he hid it very well indeed.

"I just can't do it, kid. I'd like to, but I keep thinking about the people you and your pet freak killed in order to bring her back. And every time I do that, you come out on the losing end of the scenario."

Crowley walked over to the cheerleader, who was looking at him much the same way a paraplegic might look at a train speeding toward the wheelchair he was bound to for movement. Her pretty brown eyes were as wide as saucers, and she looked ready to run, bound hands and all. He walked behind her and rested his hand on the ropes binding her wrists. As he untied her, he looked back to his new friend on the rooftop, the one with the shattered knee.

"I mean, how the hell am I supposed to feel sorry for you, when you were about to kill this girl for your own pleasure?" The girl moved her hands as the ropes fell away. She moaned softly at the pain of blood flowing into starved fingertips. "Am I supposed to look at your tears and think you've learned your lesson?"

The boy looked up and, through the tears in his eyes and the snot running down his face, he nodded. Crowley had seldom seen anyone looking so forlorn and genuinely pathetic. He reached behind him and handed the girl her clothes. Disheveled as they were, they were better than nothing.

Crowley looked at the girl and studied her face for a moment as she got dressed. "What do you think, sweetheart? Should I call the cops and let you deal with him that way?"

She looked from Crowley's face to the boy on the ground, her face a study in careful concentration and maybe just a touch of shock.

"I don't know . . ." she said.

"Really? Do you think he'll never try this again? Or something just as nasty? Anything he can in order to make his life a little better, even from behind bars?"

She looked at the quietly crying boy again, at the shabby clothes he wore, and the way his leg sat awkwardly from the knee down. He looked harmless enough. Then she thought about the words he's said when he was trying to strap her onto his altar.

"Keep your promise to him earlier." Her voice was as cold as the wind that crossed her flesh as she dressed. "Send him to hell."

Crowley smiled. "Not a problem."

It took a long, long time for Crowley to get bored.

Afterwards, the man who smiled far too often for the comfort of those around him got to the business of the last person on the rooftop. The young man who'd been lying unconscious since he first ran across his prey. He touched the teenager's form and felt that the skin was far too cold. He moved the man's head and felt and saw the wet redness welling up in a pool beneath the stranger's ruined skull. He was dead.

Jonathan Crowley turned away from him and looked at the cheerleader where she sat, facing the street far below. "If he was your friend, I'm very sorry. He's dead." His voice was soft, and as close to caring as he ever really managed. "For what it's worth, I don't think he suffered."

The girl turned toward him, her face looking more lost and distraught than even when her assailant was struggling to strap her to the altar. Her tears were genuine, and in his way, he felt for her. But he offered no comfort. He was not the sort who could make such gestures with ease. They always felt like a lie.

"Do you need a ride home?" The words were out of his mouth before he knew just what he was going to say. She looked at him with that same weird blend of relief and fear and sorrow that he should have been used to a long, long time ago but that still always made him feel just the least bit confused. The emotions she was feeling were at war, and Crowley very rarely had that problem. He always knew what it was he wanted. He seldom had enough doubt in his system to let the emotions go that crazy. "Or, if you prefer, I could just call you a cab."

Her expression switched over from fear to a touch of relief. He reached into his coat and pulled out his cellular phone. Despite what he'd been through, it still worked. He dialed quickly, and spoke into the mouthpiece even as his ruptured lip began healing itself. The process itched like mad but was very, very handy after fighting the occasional damned soul come back from the dead.

They spoke softly for a few minutes after he hung up the phone. He gave her his phone number and told her she should call if she ever needed help. Then he watched her go down the stairs, casting his little magic as she left. Jonathan Crowley waited on the rooftop until the cab came and picked the girl up. The fifty dollar bill he'd slipped her would cover the cost of the ride home. Seeing as he'd taken it from the ex–Pimple King of New York, he felt he could afford to let her have it.

She would, no doubt, be puzzled about exactly why she had bruises on her wrists, but her mind would make up a story before she got all the way home. Maybe an attempted mugging where her valiant boyfriend managed to save her but died in the process. Maybe something else that was just as plausible, but not the truth. She would forget about Crowley, and she would forget about the demon thing. At least for now. Later, if she needed to, she'd remember the number for contacting him. Just in case something a little past the mundane ever came into her life again.

It was a small magic, a little thing that hid the truth from her, and it was a mercy as far as he was concerned. Sometimes he could be merciful, but only ever with the people he suspected were truly innocent of any wrongdoings. They were few and far between.

Most of the time he left the memories intact as a warning not to ever do anything even remotely stupid again. Little offended Jonathan Crowley as much as stupid people. The only thing worse was monsters.

He made a call to the 911 emergency number from a pay phone nearby. "Yeah, I got a problem! Some stupid bastard is making too much noise on the roof, and I can't get any sleep! Would you maybe like to send a few cops over here? Before I have to do something everyone will regret later?" He gave the address for the building and hung up the phone. The bodies would be found; that was the important part.

Crowley had just started down the street when he heard the voice call out to him. He looked up to find the source and saw the dead jock looking down from the rooftop. He'd looked better. Whatever was trying to possess him—it wasn't Noelle, he knew that much at least—was too strong for the form to hold. "I see you, Hunter! I see you, and I know you!" The jock pointed with a hand that was rapidly blistering, smoldering from the strain of holding an uninvited guest.

Crowley smiled. Maybe this would get interesting after all. "Yeah? Well, big fat hairy deal, sports fan, I see you, too."

"You will be mine! Do you hear me? We have unfinished business!"

Before Crowley could respond, the jock's form slumped forward, plummeting down to the sidewalk below. Crowley watched until it hit the ground and broke. Terminal velocity was never pretty.

"Should have left me an address, sport. I'd have come looking for you." The body didn't respond, not that he'd expected it to. Crowley left the scene. He didn't really feel like putting up with the NYPD and any questions they might have. Besides, if they tried to restrain him, things would get ugly.

He always tried to save the really nasty business for the ones who honestly deserved it. In his own way, he could be merciful. Not that many others agreed with his personal definition of mercy.

CHAPTER 11

I

Bill Karstens was a dick. There was just no way around that simple fact. But he did like to hear himself talk, and for the cost of another meal at Frannie's, he told several stories to Simon MacGruder. He covered the attempted murder of Lawrence Grey, and he spilled the beans on Amy Blake's body. He wasn't the constable who found her, but he'd seen her and knew all of the goriest details.

It was a little shocking to think about how many people had been murdered in Serenity Falls. He almost had trouble wrapping his mind around it. Simon hadn't really given any thought to the sheer volume of violent crimes and murders in the small town until he sat with Karstens, but listening to the cop talk about some of his more significant cases made him realize that there was something very strange with the statistics.

He kept his mouth shut about it through the meal,

despite wanting to ask the constable if he thought the numbers were odd. Asking Bill Karstens something like that would be unwise at best. Karstens was a good and upstanding member of the community and a respectable law enforcement officer, but Simon didn't trust him in the least. There was something about the man that practically made his hair stand on end when he was dealing with him. Nothing concrete, mind you, just a sort of feeling that said it wouldn't be wise to ask too many questions.

Karstens might well take the curiosity the wrong way, and there was a little voice bouncing around inside his head that said getting on the wrong side of Karstens might be a very, very bad idea.

But he pushed that thought out of his head as quickly and quietly as he could. Bill Karstens had two children and a loving wife. He knew they were a happy family the same way he knew Mike Blake was a drunk. It was obvious to anyone who saw them. He had no reason to even begin suspecting Karstens did anything like beat his wife or even spank his kids too hard. The one thing Simon knew he was good at was reading people, and there was just no way in hell that a family unit could act happy all the time unless they were happy. Maureen Karstens was also a lovely woman and about as capable of keeping a secret as Simon was of successfully performing open-heart surgery on himself.

After lunch and thanking Kartens for his help, Simon decided to walk off the heavy steak and fries he'd eaten. Too many more interviews over lunch, and he'd lose his girlish figure.

He hadn't gone but a couple of blocks before he ran into Sam Hardwick. Sam was a potbellied man with dark hair, dark eyes, and a reputation for being a little on the rough side. He always managed to find work, because he was a damned fine worker, but he also managed to find time in his busy schedule to get himself into a brawl or two a week.

That was a proud family tradition with the Hardwick clan. Near as he could figure, they never went too rough into the violent crimes, just enough to get their wrists slapped. Simon sometimes wanted to ask Sam if it was genetic, this predisposition to carnage. Happily, he'd always remembered that he didn't have a death wish before actually opening his mouth.

Sam was in a good mood. He had his boys with him, Walt his son and his grandsons Hank aged ten and Marty aged sixteen. The scariest thing about them was that they were so obviously related. Even the tyke was big.

They were leaving Darnell's grocery store and carrying enough food to handle a small army. As they were a small army, it worked for them.

Sam lifted one bushy eyebrow as he nodded. Simon nodded back. Walt, on the other hand, looked at Simon MacGruder as if he'd just spotted a particularly nasty and unidentifiable lump stuck to the bottom of his shoe. "I heard you're writing a history of the town."

Simon looked at the man. "Yeah, Walt. At least thinking about it."

"Why?" The man looked at him as if he'd committed some horrid sin.

"Well, mostly because I think people should know

about our town, but also because I want to know about it."

Walt shook his head. "Ain't nothing needs to be known except it's a fine place to live."

There are moments in almost every life that beg for a chance to take back something said aloud. Simon MacGruder had one of those moments right then and there. He turned his back and started toward his home, never imagining that his mouth could so quickly become a traitor. "Yeah, well, not all of us want to remain ignorant."

He froze the second he realized what he'd said. It was meant to be a thought, he knew that. It was his damned tongue that disagreed.

"What did you say to me, old man?" He heard a shuffling of bags, heard the youngest boy grunt as he was handed the bags his father had been holding, and thought about turning around. Walt was nice enough to help him along with a hand on his shoulder and a rough tug that half pulled Simon off his feet.

"I didn't mean—"

Walt wasn't in the mood to listen. He just liked to hear people try to explain themselves while he was rattling them.

His big beefy hands pulled on Simon's shirt hard enough to lift Simon off the ground. It had been a lot of years since anyone had manhandled him, and he wasn't at all prepared for it.

"You best watch your mouth around me, old man. My daddy might take a shine to letting you get away with calling him ignorant, but I don't much like it, and I'm not as forgiving."

Sam Hardwick ignored the activities of his son. Just

went about loading the back of the family's battered old station wagon as if there wasn't anything at all going on. The two younger boys both had smiles on their faces. They didn't speak, but they watched their father like gamblers watch the horses running down the track.

From down the road, past even the sounds of Walt's voice and the thundering of his own aged heart, Simon heard the roar of a motorcycle engine coming in their direction. There was no one else on the street, and if anyone inside Darnell's was looking in their direction, they didn't bother to step outside to put a stop to the whole thing.

"You ever think no one in this town wants the likes of you looking in to our business? You ever think about that, MacGruder?"

"What the hell is wrong with you, Walt? Put me down!" He was doing his best to sound calm and cool and failing miserably. It was something of a miracle in his eyes that he hadn't wet himself.

Walter Hardwick didn't bother to listen. Instead, he moved around so he could push Simon into the side of the station wagon. "You need to leave well enough alone, Simon. Don't go snooping where you don't need to. I can just imagine the shit you're making up about my family."

"Walt. I can and will press charges if you don't put me down right now."

Walt was a reasonable man from time to time, but this wasn't one of them. His kids were watching, and his father, too. In his case, impressing the family unit seemed to take precedence over not getting his ass thrown in jail for a week or so.

"I don't much like threats, asshole."

The motorcycle noises stopped, and Simon Mac-Gruder craned his head around, hoping beyond hope that it was a state trooper or someone else that could come to his aid. Instead, he saw a giant of a man climbing off the bike. He was enormous and looked more likely to join in on bashing an old man than to come to his aid.

Walt was too busy preparing to cave his face in to notice. The rest of the Hardwicks were too busy watching Walt and Simon to much care. The man climbed off of his bike, and the shocks sighed their relief. It was a damned big Harley, but looked like a moped next to him.

"Hey!" The man's voice boomed when he called out. "Get your hands off him before I bust your ass!"

Simon quietly thanked God for the save, and Walt looked over at the Goliath moving in his direction and paled slightly. Walt was a big boy, but the red-haired giant heading in his direction made him look like a schoolgirl. The man had the thickest arms Simon had ever seen, and next to him, Walter Hardwick just wasn't even remotely threatening. A bull would have been hard pressed to look intimidating next to the red-bearded man.

It was Walt's turn to stammer. He tried to speak, but nothing came out. The man spoke for him. "You get off beating up old men? You think that makes you tough shit?"

He loomed over Hardwick, his massive paws clenching into fists. "Get the hell out of here before I beat your ass down."

Hardwick didn't have to be told twice. The entire clan got into their car, moving faster than Simon would have thought possible. He would have laughed, but he was a little terrified himself. The man had to weigh in well over three hundred pounds, and there might have been a little flab under the black leather jacket, but Simon didn't feel like checking.

"Thanks, mister." He managed to squeak the words out as he watched the Hardwicks beat their retreat.

"You didn't owe him money or anything, did you?"

"Hunh? Oh, no. I don't owe him a damned thing."

"Good. I'd hate to think I helped the guy get ripped off." He waved amiably and started walking. Simon watched him go, still not quite sure what had just happened.

He stood there for a few more minutes, gathering his wits from where they had fallen all over the place, and then he walked home, doing his best to avoid being seen by anyone.

He had no idea why he'd gotten lucky in avoiding the ass kicking he'd stepped into, but Simon MacGruder called it a day earlier than usual by several hours.

II

Serenity Falls Part Eleven: Growing Pains

Serenity Falls was not always the place it is today. In the very early years the area was forested by trees and hidden away in the shadows cast by those very same monoliths. Though the area was not exactly avoided by the native peoples, it was also not favored by them. Accidents tended to happen more often there than almost anywhere else in the near vicinity. The old-growth forests were treacherous, and many of the root systems were bared to the air, hidden only by a thick layer of dried leaves and mulch.

As is often the case, nature took care of that problem all by itself. A particularly nasty forest fire cleared a lot of the oldest trees from the area and left little by way of usable wood. Only a year after the fire had destroyed most of the vast forest, when saplings were starting anew and the elements had scrubbed most of the ashes into the soil or away from the area, newcomers moved into the valley. Unlike the stories that can be told of many areas where European settlers decided to make themselves known, there were no great conflicts with the indigenous Indians. The fire had left the area devoid of much by way of possible enemies.

So when the first families settled in and staked their claims, they did so without much grief. There were hardships, certainly, but not many that involved the loss of life or limb. The ground was fertile, the saplings were easily removed from the area, and the remaining wood from the older growth, while often burned through for several inches, worked well for producing good lumber.

The founder of the settlement was Niles Wilcox, a Puritan of devout faith and a low tolerance for nonsense. Wilcox was not a large man physically, but he was fearsome in his presence and more than capable of intimidating most of the people around him when the mood struck. Still, for all of his temper and reputation, he calmed almost immediately when the settlers reached their destination. Local legend has it that he proclaimed he had found in the area that which he had always sought throughout his life. When asked what that was, he smiled and responded, "Serenity."

The name stuck, and as time passed, the township of Serenity became a reality. The hills around Serenity were made mostly of granite, though enough topsoil covered most of it to hide that fact for quite a while from the settlers and their descendants. It wasn't until the Blackwell family came along that anyone gave much credence to the idea of actually starting a quarry in the area. And that very quarry was the reason for the change in the name of the town from Serenity to Serenity Falls. Within a month of the quarry's opening, the underground stream that had remained hidden for as long as recorded history and even longer became a known fact. As soon as the water started running off from the quarry, spilling from the hills down toward the edge of the town, the locals started calling the area where the stream cut through Blackwell Falls, more as a jest than as a deliberate landmark. Again, the name stuck and later was shortened down to merely The Falls.

The Falls was devoured by the township of Serenity as time went on, becoming merely another part of the prospering area. Along the way, people started calling the town Serenity or The Falls or even Serenity Falls. The name just sort of happened. Serenity Falls was made the formal name of the town in 1976, during the nation's bicentennial celebration. Agnes Dandridge suggested the new name as a symbol of the changes that had occurred within the township over the last two hundred years. Agnes was aggressive in her campaign and managed to get enough votes to make the name change official. Agnes Dandridge had that effect on people, not because she was popular or beautiful—though she was both, despite a name that made most people think of an elderly aunt, Agnes was a stunning example of womanhood—but because when she decided to make something happen, she was twice as savage and determined as a rabid terrier on cocaine.

There were plenty of voices raised in opposition to the name change. More than anyone had expected, in all honesty. One of the most vocal was David Wilcox, who claimed to be a direct descendant of Niles Wilcox. The very idea of changing what the founding father of the town had decided on was offensive to the man, and he made his point well known to any and all who cared to listen—as well as to most who did not.

Wilcox might have had a chance if he'd been as good at the political game as his opponent. Simply put, however, he was as lousy at politics as he was at being civil to those around him. David Wilcox was never one to ignore the fact that he was a descendant of the town founder. He was, truth be told, far more likely to rub it in people's faces. Nobody in town liked him, and he in turn felt that he was better than everyone else. Politics just wasn't meant to be his forte.

David Wilcox lost badly to Agnes Dandridge, and he took it with his usual grace and style, which is to say he took it very poorly indeed.

Three days after his protests to the name change for the town were voted into oblivion—after much hollering and screaming on both sides most everyone was glad to just have it over one way or the other—David Wilcox burned down the family home of Agnes Dandridge, killing her and her entire family. Her mother, father, and two younger brothers died with her. He was caught near the scene of the crime by the local constables, and his guilt was immediately established by the scorch marks on his own clothing and his fingerprints found on the can of gasoline he left behind.

Wilcox never denied his blame in the murders, but he remained dazed about the entire affair. He claimed, though no one believed him, that he had no recollection of the incident. Wilcox was sentenced to life in prison for his actions. He lasted three weeks before managing to get himself stabbed four times in the back and kidneys. It seemed that several of the prisoners took offense to his attitudes about his long family history.

David Wilcox left behind an estranged wife and three children, Maria, his oldest, Phillip, his second child, and lastly, Oliver who was only four when his father went to prison. David's wife, Elizabeth Foster Wilcox, inherited a great deal of money when her husband passed away. Unfortunately, she also inherited several of his enemies. Despite doing her best to be her own person, she was forced to bear the mantle of having married a man who was genuinely disliked by many.

Money did not help her situation. If anything, the inheritance she was granted and the life insurance she received only made matters worse. Where before she was almost viewed as a victim of her husband's idiosyncrasies, many now simply directed their resentment toward him on his remaining family. Perhaps that would have been tolerable, but the murder of four people was among the sins that were transferred to Elizabeth and her children.

There were a few who felt that David Wilcox had died too easily and not suffered enough. And unfortunately for his family, some felt the child should pay for the sins of the father. Four months after her husband died in prison, Elizabeth Wilcox lost her children as well. In their place, she received a ransom notice demanding one million dollars for each of them. The note also told her to remain absolutely silent regarding their disappearance if she wanted to see them alive ever again.

Elizabeth was frantic. She spent three days doing all she could to arrange a proper loan against the estate her husband had left for her. Despite having money enough to live very comfortably, she did not have three million dollars to her name. The loan came through, but barely.

At the appointed time and place, Elizabeth left the money and went home and waited with nerves stretched to the breaking point.

Seven days later Marcus Grey—father to Daniel and grandfather to Lawrence—found the bodies of all three children in the Dumpster behind his funeral home.

Elizabeth endured the grief of her children's' murders as best she could. Chief Constable Walter Crenan informed her of their being found and questioned her extensively about everything that had occurred. She answered his questions as best she could, while fighting hard against the deep grief that threatened to engulf her. She killed herself the same night.

There are a few old-timers who like to tell the story

of how Serenity Falls got its name. None of them ever mention Elizabeth Wilcox or her children when they tell the story, though most mention her late husband and the family of Agnes Dandridge. Perhaps most have never made the connection between the two crimes. And perhaps those who understand the ties that bind a simple change of name to the atrocities committed upon Elizabeth and her children simply find the story too grim to think about, let alone to tell.

III

Interlude: Camden, New Jersey

He felt both of the tires on the right side of his Lamborghini blow in quick succession and cursed under his breath. The car handled beautifully, of course, just as it was designed to, but he would hardly be able to drive with only two tires, and he had only one spare.

It should have been a nice, comfortable ride, but it hadn't turned out that way. Just a quick shot down Federal Street and then to Route 130 and over to the Benjamin Franklin Bridge. Next stop Philadelphia. No problem. But instead, there had been road construction, and he'd found himself driving on down Federal Street away from the nice homes in Merchantville and straight into the sort of area that gave New Jersey a bad reputation. Now he was on a road he'd never even heard of, and driving into the worst sort of slum he'd ever imagined.

He cursed under his breath, feeling the start of a nasty headache. Served him right. He knew what sort of place Camden was, that every negative thing in its reputation had been earned. But he never knew how much could change in a short time. Last time he'd been through this way, the Airport Circle had still been a circle, and he'd been too confident about the route he wanted to take.

John Crowley pulled to the side of the road in the ruins of what had once been a prosperous town. Camden, New Jersey, had seen better days and was now little more than a nest for the sort of people who had long since forgotten how to actually do anything but exist. Most of the buildings that were still standing had long since been condemned, and those that weren't probably should have been. Crowley remembered hearing about the state's plans to level most of the older buildings in the hopes of making the area livable. He saluted their decision. A proper nostalgic appreciation of history was a wonderful notion but failed to keep its glamour when the only people left were either homeless because of bad fortune or homeless because they were spending all of their money on drugs.

Everything that had once been good and clean and decent about the area was gone, replaced by the worst sort of human debris. Crowley felt nothing but disgust driving onto the area. It was the sort of thing that grated on his nerves and made him want to scream in anger. Chaos and poison, disease and filth spreading like a cancer. Everything that he worked so hard to eradicate from his world, and here it festered like a leprous sore.

Still, the people in the area—those that mattered in his mind, the clean ones who at least had the decency to hide their mental aberrations—were trying to make it a better place. It hadn't slid into a local version of hell overnight, and it couldn't climb back any faster. Still, just looking around made him wish for a few cans of gasoline and a blowtorch.

Crowley climbed from the car and inspected the damage to the tires. Both were flat and looked like they intended to stay that way. He shook his head and walked around the side of the car toward the trunk, then stopped himself when he saw the people moving in his direction.

They were not exactly healthy-looking individuals. Most of them were unbathed and wore clothes that had surely last been washed several months earlier. They were of all races, and they looked hungry, desperate.

More importantly, they looked mean and ready to take out their frustrations on him. He looked down at his clothes—nothing too extravagant, but his shoes probably cost more than any of these people had seen in the last year. He looked back at the crowd—twelve, thirteen, a group moving in from the side that held at least another five—the numbers were definitely not in his favor.

Crowley smiled.

"Hi there. Nothing to see, just a man with too few tires on his car." He broadened the smile as they looked at him, their expressions showing shock that he would sound so casual about the situation. They didn't have to know that his stomach was twisting itself into knots of apprehension. "I don't suppose any of you folks would happen to have the number of a reliable towing service . . ."

One of the smaller ones darted toward him, teeth bared in a feral snarl. Something metallic gleamed in the filthy right hand of his attacker, and John Crowley ducked away as the shining object whipped past where his head had been a second before. Without a second's thought, he kicked out with his left foot and connected with his attacker's head. The scream that came out of the mouth was feminine; not that he much cared. The bundled form staggered backwards, dropping a small knife from its hand.

Jonathan Crowley eyed the crowd warily, sliding his glasses off his face and slipping them into his shirt pocket. The crowd acted like it was a signal and began moving in en masse. Crowley smiled again. He loved a good fight.

Crowley drew first blood; planting his hand on the face of another short one, he lifted himself into the air and executed a flawless side kick into the chest of one of the taller members of the pack. He felt the nose of Shorty crack and slide under his unexpected weight and heard the sound of ribs breaking in the one he kicked. It maybe would have worked better if he hadn't slipped when he landed, sliding in a puddle of something it was probably best not to dwell on. He managed to keep his balance but dropped his guard in the process.

Three fists hit him simultaneously. One of them was wrapped inside a set of brass knuckles. Crowley felt his arm go numb from the impact on his shoulder and grunted as someone's foot landed squarely in his solar plexus. He shot his elbow backwards as someone tried to wrap an arm around his neck, and felt teeth give out under the force of the blow.

All of this, he thought, *because I wanted a* real *Philly cheese steak sandwich.* Someone in the crowd knew how to fight, and how to fight dirty at that. He felt his knees swept from behind and dropped like a sack of potatoes.

Before he could even regain his sense of place, a very heavy foot stomped down on his stomach, knocking what little air he had left completely out of his system. He tried to breathe, tried to remember how to take in air without hot pain in his gut, and failed miserably.

Too damned many of them. Crowley grunted again as he felt one of his attackers pulling his wallet away. Another was working hard on his left wrist, trying to get his watch. His smile came back as he brought his right leg up and caught the watch thief on the back of his head. There was another faint moan of pain, and then the one at his wrist went off to la-la land. Bigfoot stomped down again, planting that massive, scuffed boot of his on Jonathan's stomach with all of his weight behind it. It felt like someone had driven a spike through his belly and into the concrete beneath him. Crowley didn't even manage a groan this time; the pain was too intense. He watched the boot lift upward and saw blood trailing from the blade along the side of it. Bigfoot had a nasty little sticker on a sheath of some kind. Very handy in a fight, but not really very sporting.

A small army of human cockroaches crawled over him, pulling at his clothes and taking everything they could get their hands on. Try as he might, he couldn't get his body to respond to his orders. He hurt everywhere. Suddenly, he wasn't smiling anymore.

One of the ragged folk stepped away from him, waving his car keys triumphantly. Another took one look at the prize and charged, intent only on getting the shiny keys for himself. Judging by the size of the mostly ruined hiking boots on his feet, Crowley guessed that one was Bigfoot. The prize changed hands quickly, and the shaggy black beard on the victor's dark face parted to reveal his four remaining teeth in a smile. A girl who might have been pretty if she wasn't so damned thin and covered with sores squealed excitedly as she slipped Crowley's glasses on her face.

Crowley watched as the herd of thieves stood around, examining their prizes. One of them—he thought it was male but couldn't tell under the clothes and dirt—waved a wad of bills. "We're rich! That bastard was loaded!" They gathered around him, not fighting this time but looking on in awe at the thin stack of money. "Seven Ben Franklins and twice that many Andy Jacksons! Let's get some food!" There was moderate cheering at the notion, and Crowley watched them mill around excitedly at the prospect. Here was a group of people he could almost have sympathy for. And for John Crowley even getting close to the idea of sympathy was a rarity.

He watched as they helped their fallen and wounded stand, and lay where he was, all but forgotten. Every square inch of his body hurt.

Damn stupid and careless! How the hell did I get so sloppy? He must have made a noise as he chastised himself, because they turned back to look at him almost as if one puppet master was directing all of them at the same time. The girl with his glasses moved closer but remained out of his reach. "What about him? What do we do about him, Cecil?"

Bigfoot came closer, looking at Crowley through squinted eyes. Crowley looked back and saw the sudden change come over the face of the de facto leader of the pack. His eyes went from slightly stoned to clear and sharp in an instant. That in and of itself might not have surprised him, but the odd tinting that spilled into his irises caught Crowley off guard. Something was happening to the man right in front of him.

Something or someone, he corrected himself, *just hopped inside of Bigfoot.*

Cecil's face split into a smile again, showing his remaining teeth and the fact that they desperately needed a good cleaning. "You guys go on ahead . . ." He moved a little closer to Crowley, and the stench from his unwashed body was almost enough to make him gag. "I'll take care of him."

The others looked at Cecil for a moment, and finally they started moving. The girl with the glasses was the one who stayed long enough to ask another question. "Where should we eat? Where can you find us?"

"Go over to the diner on Cherry Street, Tricia. I'll be along in a few."

Tricia nodded, then ran to catch up with the rest of the crowd, leaving Bigfoot and Crowley staring at each other. Crowley tried moving and realized for the first time that he'd been hurt in a bad way. As soon as he shifted, he felt warmth run down from his stomach and trickle down his side.

Bigfoot slapped his stomach hard enough to make

him wince. "Bet that hurts, doesn't it?" The voice was completely wrong. It didn't sound at all like the man who'd just told one of his friends where he would meet the gang after he'd taken care of the dirty work. For that matter, Cecil wasn't looking much like himself anymore, either. "This one, Hunter, this body is better than the last one. It has been touched and tainted before, it has felt the darkness in its cells and known more than it should of pain and suffering. It has been strengthened."

Crowley's eyes widened. He knew the voice. It had spoken to him before, in New York a few nights earlier.

Despite the nausea he had blooming in his stomach, just under the red-hot pain from where the man before him had stomped down with a blade, Crowley did his best to sound nonplussed by the changing creature before him. "I'm sorry, but you have me at a disadvantage. Have we met?"

Bigfoot leaned back and laughed, taking the time to slap him on the stomach again, splattering the blood from his open wound. Crowley winced and felt the world go a little gray. "Oh yes, Hunter," he replied, his voice filled with good cheer. "We've met." He looked down into Crowley's eyes and leaned down until their faces were only inches apart. The tint in his eyes grew darker, and the pupils actually changed shape while the two looked at each other. "I promised the last time that I would be back, and that I'd kill you slowly."

Crowley smiled through the burning pain in his stomach. There was nothing familiar about the changing face in front of him, not in the eyes or elsewhere, but that didn't mean he hadn't met whatever presence was warping Bigfoot. It just meant he'd have to work a little harder when the time came to discover who or what was playing games. "Yeah? That makes you and damned near every other freak I've ever met." Crowley's smile grew even broader as he felt the itchy fire start under his skin. He was healing, and the proximity to a threat made the process hurt more and work faster than it usually did. "Are you going to actually do something? Or am I going to die of boredom?"

Cecil's face bloated and warped as he threw his head back and roared. The dark brown skin on Bigfoot seethed and moved as if an army of bugs was crawling inside an inflatable doll. His skin paled, fading to a light gray, and the hair on his head and face fell out in clumps. His remaining teeth fell out, pushed out of their positions by the daggerlike teeth that erupted from his gums in a spray of black ichor. The shape of his face warped from human into something vaguely fishlike, and his voice ground from a throat that was rapidly developing a bulge like a frog calling for potential mates.

Cecil's body didn't want to accept its uninvited guest anymore, and something, some genetic factor from its heritage, was activating. John Crowley looked on as the arms elongated and the body changed in a hundred subtle ways. Webs stretched between the fingers of the man who'd been laughing at him a second ago, the yellowed nails on his hands thickened and blackened until they were more the claws of a predator than the nails of a junkie who was past his prime.

Bigfoot/Cecil clutched at the sides of his head, screaming in pain and thrashing his skull in denial of the pain he was feeling. "Too soon! Not yet, damn it all to hell, I'm not finished with you yet, Hunter!"

The beast in front of him had been seen in the past by
people, long ago, before humans had settled into cities
of any size. From time to time they were reported over
the centuries, and in the last century they had inhabited
a town in New England and been found out by the U.S.
government. They had many, many names, but the one
most commonly used since a writer of pulp fiction stories had heard about them was "Deep Ones." Crowley
had never seen one before and doubted he would again.
They were hard to find.

Almost a shame to have to kill it, but only almost.

Crowley's grin stretched across his face as he reached
forward and slapped both of his hands into the sides of
the misshapen head. The skin he touched was cold and
sweaty and felt all too much like the belly of a rotting
fish. He felt bones that had not yet finished their transformation break under his grip and squeezed all the
harder.

The thing bucked and croaked, lashing out with a foot
that had grown too large to be restrained by the boot it
had been wearing only moments before. Long, agile
claws scraped down his thigh and shin, tearing through
the denim that covered his legs and cutting through skin
like it was butter.

Crowley hissed and continued squeezing. Every
muscle in his arms corded outward and vibrated as he
continued to apply pressure, crushing the head he held
with as much strength as he could muster, even as the
freak of nature before him clawed frantically at him, its
eyes growing wide from both surprise and pain. The
Hunter's teeth showed clearly in the darkness of Kaign
Avenue, and his breathing was a rapid, frantic bellows.

The head in his hands broke, and the cold, gelid mass of Cecil's altered brain rushed between his fingers in a thick wash of viscera.

Crowley dropped his prize and felt as much as saw the trail of energy that leaped away from the remains of his enemy and tore through the night sky like a dark comet. It moved to the north on a deliberate trail.

He shook his hands to remove the worst of the mess. Anyone walking past at that time would surely have run screaming from him. With the broad smile on his face and the bloated ruins of a thing from the past at his feet, he looked like madness waiting to claim a victim.

Crowley reached into Cecil's jeans and fished around for his car keys. He half dragged himself over to the Lamborghini, the blood from his torn legs flowing freely. When he opened the trunk, he pulled out his suitcase and a container of Handi Wipes. He washed himself quickly and then he changed his shirt. Going into a diner, even in a place as miserable and lawless as Camden seemed, would be much easier if he wasn't covered in the remains of something else's blood.

He removed his pants and watched the flesh on his legs scab over. Damn but he'd have paid good money to get the itching to stop. *On the other hand*, he mused, *no itch might mean no healing, and I'd rather be able to walk with what comes next.*

Crowley traded out his ruined jeans for a nice, comfortable set of slacks. Then he looked at his car and shook his head. "Well, get on with it. I'm not wasting my time changing one tire and driving on a flat, and I could well decide you're not worth the effort."

The car shifted, a slow laborious transformation from

a Lamborghini into a 1963 Ford Thunderbird. The two flat tires reinflated as he watched. Crowley grinned. "Yeah, I know, it's cheating not to do it the old-fashioned way, but what the hell, I've earned a break." His smile changed then, growing darker and more menacing. "Besides, I can't have our new friends seeing you outside the diner when I pull up. They might try to get away, and I still have a few things to say to them." He reached for his glasses and then remembered that someone else was wearing them just then. "Oh my, yes, I have things to say . . ."

Crowley patted the car affectionately and then slid into the driver's seat. It took him only a few minutes to find the crowded diner and all of the scum sitting inside. They were laughing, eating, and having a wonderful time. If they thought about what was taking Cecil so long to get there, they didn't let it show in their faces. The girl with his glasses was chewing on a rare hamburger when he walked through the door.

Jonathan Crowley let a slow, easy smile stretch across his face and watched as the patrons of the diner recognized him. The waitress serving them took one look at him and very carefully backed away until she'd reached the entrance of the kitchen. "Hey, kiddies!" He moved with a grace that was absolutely predatory and scanned the eyes of every person sitting at the three tables they'd pushed together. "I expect all of my things to be set on the end of your table right now." His dark eyes pinned the girl wearing his glasses in place, and he relished the way the color drained from her face. "And if there's even a thumbprint on the lenses, cupcake, I'm going to take extra time in beating the shit out of you."

Every person in the diner looked at Crowley and thought very hard about his words. One by one, they set his possessions on the table. He reached over and picked them all up, sliding his watch back onto his wrist and tucking his wallet away after doing a quick count of the bills inside. He held his hand out to the one that had taken the wallet earlier. "My money." The kid looked ready to argue about that part. Crowley hoped he would. He dearly, truly hoped the little shit decided to make a stand.

Fear and greed warred on the acne-scarred face in front of him. Greed won out. The kid took a swing that was as wild as the winds in a hurricane, and John Crowley grabbed his arm even as he ducked, helping him across the room and through the plate glass window. The window felt obligated to shatter and take several bites at the brave little thief in the process. Crowley followed after the freshly wounded punk and performed a flawless drop kick into the face of his newest adversary. While the kid spat blood and teeth and tried to remember what his name was, Crowley slid the money out of his pockets. He counted quickly and nodded his satisfaction.

Several of the group that had attacked him earlier tried their luck again, and Crowley's smile widened even more. He'd been caught soft footed before, completely unprepared for a fight when the only thing on his mind was changing a tire. This time he was ready, willing, and able. Years of training came into play and made it look easy for him. He was hit, kicked, and bitten a few times, but while he was taking a few lumps he was also breaking a few of their bones. It was turning out to be a good night after all. Their screams were like a symphony to his ears.

As he punched his fist into the throat of his last opponent, Crowley considered the thing that apparently wanted him to go somewhere and have a proper fight. Twice in one week it had made itself known to him and called him a title he seldom answered to. It was a puzzle he was looking forward to solving.

He took enough time to count out three hundred dollars, which he handed to the owner of the diner. He'd helped break the window, and fair was fair, after all—and to get directions back to the interstate before he left Camden. He drove to the north, following the trail he'd seen his unknown enemy take earlier. His cheese steak sandwich could wait a while, he reckoned.

With a few twists of the dial, he found a station playing classic rock and roll on the radio. That was good, better than almost anything he could think of for getting into a happy mood. Crowley liked being happy. It made the times when he was alone far more tolerable. And Crowley, though he didn't like to dwell on it, was almost always alone.

He wanted desperately to find and destroy the thing that had come after him, but he knew that he couldn't. Not yet. First, he had to find it. That would probably be fairly easy as whatever it was seemed intent on finding him, and that made the job much simpler. Second, even if he did find it, he wouldn't be able to do anything about it unless he was asked to. That was one of the rules he had to play by, and as much as he sometimes hated it, he had to follow the rules.

Eric Clapton started singing about a woman named Layla on the radio, and Crowley sang along with him, though without anywhere near the same talent. He never could sing worth a spit, but what he lacked in ability he more than made up for with enthusiasm.

The road before him was wide open, and the few cars that were driving the same way he was seemed to move off to the sides without any argument. Maybe it was the car, maybe it was just that the people in New Jersey were polite, but most likely it was the smile they saw on his face as he drove through the night. Something about his smile just did that to people. Not that he minded all that much. At least they got out of his way when he was in a hurry, and he was most definitely in a hurry. He had places to go and things to kill.

Crowley liked to stay busy. It helped him sleep at night.

CHAPTER 12

I

When Simon MacGruder woke the next day, he made a quick breakfast of oatmeal and coffee. Both sat near him as he wrote out his notes from the day before.

Then he settled in for the real writing. He was barely conscious of time flowing past as his fingers hunted and pecked away at the history he'd been thinking about for months and only recently started researching. He stopped once for a pee break and otherwise spent the entire day hammering away at his work.

When he went to sleep that night, it was only because his eyes were crossing. The next day, he did the same thing again, writing faster than he would have imagined he could, searching his mind for most of the notes he needed and only stopping from time to time to double-check his dates.

Most of a week passed before he stopped typing

away like his life depended on it. But even when he was done, he knew that the story hadn't been told completely. There were a few more details he had to look into, whether he wanted to or not, apparently.

He needed to find out what he could about how Amy Blake died. There had been rumors, of course, and there was a long list of suppositions, but almost nothing was really known.

He wanted to find out, because he knew it meant something to Mike Blake. The town drunk had been drinking for far too long now, and it was important to Simon that he put a stop to that insanity. Damned near every person in Serenity Falls could look back and find a time where Mike had saved their asses, but these days, most seemed to want to forget about that. He was guilty of it himself, had done nothing at all to help the man until the other night. Instead, he'd slid Mike a few bucks from time to time, knowing full well that the money would be used for nothing more than another bottle of hundred-proof anesthesia.

It was time for Mike to stop being numb. Maybe he could help with that. He didn't know for sure, but he suspected finding out the truth about what had really happened to Amy might make a difference.

And there was only one person he could think of who might be able to give him the answers. Constable Tom Norris was the one who found her. If Simon remembered properly, the man had been doing his regular drive down the roads of Serenity Falls and run across her car pulled off to the side, the engine still running.

A hundred yards away, he'd found what was left of Amy Blake. He knew she'd been raped, and he knew she had been murdered, but there were always rumors that what was done to her was not exactly the normal sort of tortures. Simon wanted to know the truth, and that meant he had to deal with Tom Norris.

He found Tom at home, kicked back on his recliner and watching reruns of *Three's Company*. Tom was a good kid, all of thirty-five, if he remembered correctly, and he was honest almost to a fault. He also had a tendency to leave his police work where it belonged, at the office.

That could be a problem. But Simon thought he knew a way around that particular difficulty. The truth, as they say, shall set you free.

Simon knocked politely and asked Tom if he was interested in having a decent meal for a change. Most of what the sad-faced man normally ate came out of a can or in a brown bag from home. Due to the nature of their discussion, Simon proposed a meal out of town, at a restaurant called The King's Highway up in Beldam Woods. Since a meal at the five-star restaurant started in the low sixties and rose quickly from there, Tom was more than glad to join Simon once he made it clear that he would be paying.

They had a good meal and talked about trivialities all the way through the main course and into desert. When the time came to ask Tom for his help, Simon was as honest as he could be.

"Listen, Tom. I'm sure you know there was an ulterior motive to calling on you for dinner . . ."

Tom lifted one eyebrow and lowered his chin to his chest. "I'm not stupid, Simon. Of course there was something beyond my company on your mind. I've heard all about your little history project. Tell me what you want."

"I want to know what you saw when you found Amy Blake."

"Shit." Norris looked away from him and studied the reflections on the window to Simon's left.

"It's confidential, Tom. I need to know, and it will not go into my history of Serenity, but I need to know."

"Why?" Tom Norris, who was so damned mild mannered that it was easy to forget he was a constable, turned suddenly hawkish eyes on Simon and pinned him with a hard glance. The intensity of his gaze was the only change in his face, but it was enough to make Simon blink. "Tell me why you 'need' to know about what happened to that poor woman, and then I'll think about it."

"Because I think it might have happened before, Tom. Not recently, but a long time ago. Like before I was born . . ."

"Gedoudda town."

"I'm completely serious. You have to look at the town history, but there have been some . . . unusual deaths in Serenity Falls."

Norris nodded his head slowly and then looked around to make sure no one was watching him. "You swear to me, Simon, that this goes no farther than this table?"

"On my mother's grave."

Norris leaned forward and spoke softly. The words he uttered sent shivers of repulsion through Simon Mac-Gruder. He was right. It had happened before.

II

Serenity Falls Part Twelve: A Family Reunion

Daniel Grey was not a happy youth, but as he grew older, he learned how to at least fake it properly. He remained unhappy until the day he met and fell in love with the woman he eventually married. Her name was Penny Pageant, and she was beautiful. He married her fourteen years before his son would change the face of Serenity for all time.

If he'd been asked exactly what it was that he loved about her, he wouldn't have been able to tell a single, solitary soul. To be sure, she was a stunning woman. Her face was flawless, her eyes easy to lose oneself in, and her lips were full and sensuous without being too blatant. She was an amazing kisser, to boot, and that didn't hurt. She had a beautiful body, and she was genuinely attractive.

But that wasn't enough for him to fall in love.

Maybe it was the fact that he didn't find her so damned confusing. Most women left him wondering exactly what was wrong with him, and some even gave him a headache.

Whatever the case, he decided he was in love, and Penny seemed to feel the same way. They were married and lived happily ever after.

For about one year. Then Penny got pregnant. They'd been trying to have a baby almost since the very first day. Long before they were married, they'd agreed that they both wanted a large family. It was one of the many things about his wife that he loved.

Daniel was overjoyed about her pregnancy at first. He told his coworkers at the quarry about the good news and celebrated with his friends. He treated Penny like a queen, never letting her out of his sight for long if he could avoid it, and all but taking over the housework in an effort to avoid her straining herself too much. Despite the temptation, Penny did not take advantage of the situation. It just wasn't in her nature.

For three months Daniel seemed like the happiest man in the world, and for possibly the first time since his younger sister had been viciously raped eight years earlier, it wasn't just an act.

And then the dreams started. In his sleep, Daniel saw and heard horrible things. He heard the screams of his hometown, saw the faces of his wife and his family torn apart and broken like bloody china dolls. And always, always, he heard the sounds of a baby cooing and laughing. When he awoke from his almost constant nightmares of death and suffering, he always turned to look at Penny, and saw the small child growing deep within her in his mind's eye.

Four weeks after the dreams started, he realized that he was looking at her growing belly with fear. She barely showed at all; the infant growing within Penny was scarcely more than a small collection of cells, but the thought of what those cells might mean sent slow shivers through his body.

Daniel didn't like the things he was thinking. Didn't like the idea that it might be for the best if he took a coat hanger and rectified the growing problem within his wife's womb. While it was true enough that he'd occasionally gotten violent, he did not consider himself a violent man. And while he had once delivered his own form of justice on a man who richly deserved it, he was not a murderer. Especially, he was not a murderer of unborn children.

He did the only thing he felt he could do in that desperate situation. He ran like hell, fleeing Serenity Falls and his wife and unborn child before he could do something he knew he would regret for the rest of his life. He knew he would never be able to forgive himself if he did something to hurt Penny, and he knew that she would never be able to forgive him if he took from her the child she'd wanted since they first met. The idea of Penny hating him was not one that sat well.

He had a painful choice to make, and he made it. He left one night with only a small collection of clothes shoved into the back of his car. His note to Penny simply said that he loved her and was sorry.

It wasn't really too surprising that he ran from the woman he loved to the woman he'd loved in the past. He made his way from upstate New York to the rural farm country in Pennsylvania. He ran from Penny to Margherita Sullivan, who was, in his heartfelt opinion, the only person who could make him see how foolish he was being. Maggie had always been able to persuade him to avoid being foolish, which he was the first to admit was a state he normally managed to either stay in or gravitate toward with remarkable ease.

He needed to get away from the damned images and dreams. He needed to find something or someone to help him stop being foolish. He needed the first girl he'd ever kissed and the best friend he'd ever had to make him see the light of reason. Those were the reasons he went to Pennsylvania. They were not the only reasons he stayed.

Margherita was even more beautiful than he'd remembered, hard though that was for him to actually believe. The first two days they spent near each other they talked about the past. He told her everything that had happened in his life, even trusting her with the fact that he'd committed a murder to avenge the rape of his sister. She did not condone what he had done, but she understood it. That was more than he'd dared hope for.

Maggie had room to spare at the family place. Her parents lived in the main house, and she lived in a smaller cottage by herself. He stayed in the spare bedroom, despite a few cold glances from her father, a man he both admired and feared: he was very, very large, and not known for his gentle ways with anyone who might hurt his daughter. There might have been troubles if her younger brother had not been there to make sure things stayed platonic. Like his father, he was almost a walking mountain. Unlike his father, however, he was a bit of a hellion.

Put another way, he couldn't have cared less if his sister was getting laid. He was far too busy working on achieving that same goal himself.

Nothing happened at first. Both of them behaved themselves properly. But the attraction that had led to their earlier sexual encounters years before was still there, and though she had said long ago that they should remain only friends, their relationship became physical.

Despite, or perhaps because of, their passions getting the better of them, Daniel eventually came to realize that he had, indeed, been a fool to abandon Penny. Margherita was wonderful to him, and the times when they were together were some of the best times he'd ever had.

But he did not love her. Not the way he loved Penny. He'd made a mistake and allowed himself to be driven off by irrational fears. He didn't come to that conclusion on his own. Maggie helped him see the error of his ways and convinced him to go back to his wife, back to his unborn child, and to beg for forgiveness. The odds were good that he'd never have managed to build up the nerve to risk it on his own.

He left Pennsylvania reluctantly, part of him wishing desperately to stay with Maggie, even if that feeling was wrong. She was good to him, and he'd been right when he thought before that she was the only person who could make him see he was being foolish. He'd miss her when he left, and he doubted he'd ever see her again, though he couldn't have said exactly why. They shared a last kiss that was far sweeter for the bitterness it left within him, and Daniel went back to face his fears.

Penny didn't seem overly thrilled by his unexpected reappearance, and he honestly couldn't blame her. But she was a loving woman and far more tolerant than he deserved. It only took two weeks of begging for her to finally let him back into the house.

There was tension between them, and he'd expected that. But he was determined to make it work this time. He would not, he swore, allow his feelings and strange fears get in the way of his being with Penny. He would, he promised himself, be a good provider and a loving mate. He would love his child, male or female, and he would get over his silly fears.

It would have worked, too, if the dreams hadn't come back. Death, mayhem, and suffering that made what his sister Denise had endured seem mild: these things haunted his sleeping nights and kept him in a growing state of paranoia. When he was awake he could imagine that it was all his imagination, but in his dreams he knew, knew that his child would be responsible for it somehow. The more he tried to deny the images in the light of day and reason, the more convinced he became that the visions haunting him were not merely dreams but premonitions.

On a night three weeks before the baby was due, Daniel decided it was time to do something about the images he kept seeing. He searched through the attic of the house he and Penny lived in and found what he hoped would answer his questions in a derelict box in the corner. He hadn't played with the Ouija board in years, had seldom taken any of the responses seriously, but had kept the old battered game for the sake of nostalgia.

And because there was a small part of him that remembered the few times when something he and his sister had asked the board had been accurately answered.

He set up the board, placing his hands on the planchette and trying to relax his mind. "What will happen if my child is born?" was the one question he asked.

The pointing device his fingertips touched leaped across the board. Though his fingers only grazed the cheap plastic lightly, Daniel felt as if his skin had been bonded to the surface on a molecular level. He watched as the pointer slid from letter to letter, the pressure from the planchette on the cardboard leaving deep grooves in the surface. Five times he received the answer to his single question. The letters spelled out the same phrase again and again, sending waves of dread through his body.

The words were direct and simple: *EVERYSOUL-WILLSCREAMEVERYSOULWILLSCREAMEERYSOUL WILLSCREAMEVERYSOULWILLSCREAMEVERYSOUL WILLSCREAM.*

Before the phrase started again, the plastic under his fingers cracked, shattered by the weight of whatever force might have driven the planchette, be it his own mind or something far more powerful. That might not have been enough to convince him that the words had meaning. It could still have only been his mind making up the words, and Daniel was just the sort who would have rationalized the whole thing.

It was when the Ouija board combusted that he decided to take heed of the words. The cardboard didn't just smolder and smoke. It exploded with a sickly green burst of flame that singed the hairs from his hands and arms and left a smell like rotting eggs in the air. The planchette itself did not burn, but rather melted in the sudden flash of heat. His flesh should surely have been blistered away by any flame strong enough to slag the plastic, but was only lightly singed.

Daniel stared at the remaining ashes for several minutes, barely able to breathe, barely able to think. The thoughts he could manage were jumbled and crazy. He wanted nothing more than to flee a second time and never to return. Instead, he thought of Penny and his family and decided to take care of the problem once and for all. His wife might never forgive him, but at least she would be alive to hate him for the rest of her days.

He crept down from the attic and into the kitchen on the floor below, intent on finding some tool that would let him kill his unborn child and leave his wife alive. He found a long, thin knife that he felt might do the job if he could find the child's skull within her womb.

Daniel Grey had committed one murder in the past. For the sake of his wife and everyone he knew, he hoped he'd be strong enough to commit a second. If thinking about committing the murder of an innocent was bad for him, actually attempting the deed was far, far worse. He crept up on his sleeping wife and stared down at her, his mind railing at him to stop himself before it was too late. He'd done enough to make her life miserable. The very idea of doing anything more to hurt her was enough to make him almost sick. And even as he thought it, he had to leave the room, There was nothing almost about it. He barely made it to the bathroom and the toilet before vomiting violently. It felt like everything he'd eaten in the last week poured out of him in an instant, and the dry heaves lasted a few eternities to make up for the short run of productive spewing. When he was finished, he sat in the bathroom and thought long and hard about what he had to do.

Killing Robert DeMillio had been a necessary evil. The man had deserved to die for what he'd done to Denise. But a baby, and his own child at that?

He slowly stood up, finally realizing that there was no way he could manage the task. He'd take his chances with things the way they were. Maybe, later, if it became necessary, he could manage the problem.

He took the knife back downstairs and settled it back into the drawer, making as little noise as possible. And when he turned around to go back upstairs, he saw Penny looking at him. She had tears in her eyes, and the look on her face broke his heart.

"You were going to kill our baby, weren't you?"

He had no answer.

She pushed past him, her belly before her, swollen with child. She reached into the drawer and pulled the exact same knife back out, flipping it over in her hand and cutting deep into her palm. She thrust the handle at him, her entire body rigid.

"If you've ever loved me, you'll leave now and never return. If you want to kill the baby, you do it now and make sure you get me, too."

Daniel backed away from her, horrified by his options. He tried his best to explain what he'd gone through, but she had no desire to listen to his ravings any longer. She'd taken all she could, and pushed the knife against him again and again as she screamed at him, her face red from crying, her eyes blurred by tears.

Daniel took the knife from her. Not because he feared for his life and not because he wanted to end hers or their child's, but because every time she pushed against his chest, she cut her hand more deeply. He feared she'd cripple herself if she wasn't careful.

Perhaps she merely slipped, her eyes so bleary from crying that she could no longer see clearly. Perhaps she meant to do it. Whatever the case, Penny fell forward, her face running into the sharpened blade, flesh peeling away from her cheek like the rind of an orange. He called the ambulance himself while he did what he could to stanch the heavy flow of blood from the gash that ran from just under her eye back to her ear. It took thirty-eight stitches to fix the injury, and Daniel went to jail without hope of any form of bail to set him free until the trial.

He pled guilty to the charges of assault with a deadly weapon and received two years in prison for his trouble. Penny did not visit him. But the dreams did, getting profoundly worse as time went on.

When he finally got out of the maximum security facility in Utica, he was a changed man. For two years he endured the abuses of his fellow inmates and a few guards who felt he was the worst sort of scum—aside, of course, from the type who would rape or murder a child—and he did it without fighting back in all but the two occasions when the prisoners decided to make him a sex slave. On those occasions he fought back hard; once he was even successful in stopping the sexual assault. The first time he failed. The second time he almost castrated Billy "Hammer" Hampton. He didn't have any weapons. He used his teeth. After that, he got the privilege of staying in solitary confinement for the rest of his time in the prison. Just him, alone with his thoughts and his dreams.

And his nightmares. The last eighteen months of his time in prison were not merely hellish; they were unholy. He was visited again and again by nightmares of his wife and family dying. Through all of the dreams of slow mutilation and screaming agonies that left him in a cold sweat, he continued to hear a child's laughter and knew with the same icy certainty as always that the young, happy voice belonged to his own progeny.

And then one day he was free. Two years is a long time, not necessarily in the grander span of a person's life, but a long time nonetheless. Daniel changed in that time and almost expected the world to have changed with him. He did not go back to Serenity, not at first. Instead, he stayed in Utica, looking for work and failing in his endeavors.

He thought of seeing Margherita but decided he could not. He didn't want to bring his own grief and troubles back to her again. It simply wouldn't be fair to her.

But he could go back home, even if he wasn't welcome. He went to see Denise, his sister for whom he'd committed murder years before. She'd married since then, and she was happy. He stayed for one day, rapidly realizing that his presence was not a comfort for her, and that her presence did nothing to soothe his own pains.

Lost and bewildered, uncertain just what he should do with his life, he finally made up his mind to see Penny again. Though they had not spoken, though she had never responded to any of the many love letters he sent her from prison, he knew where he would find her and where he would find his own child by her. A child he'd never met, never seen before.

He realized as he approached the house that he didn't even know if she'd given birth to a girl or a boy.

With the same sort of dread he'd had over two years earlier, he walked to the front of the house, prepared to have her tell him to go away before she had to call the police. Miserable and depressed as he was, he would leave if she asked him.

She did not ask.

She did not answer the door. And as he continued pounding on the oak door with the locks that had been changed, he grew angrier. Everything he'd endured had been for her sake, for his family's sake. None of that mattered anymore, not if he couldn't at least see the woman who'd been his wife in name if not in actions for the last four years. The same cold hatred that had allowed him to murder Robert DeMillio years before became a white-hot fury within his soul, and even those who knew him best would have never believed him capable of the sorts of actions he tried to commit.

When the door would not yield to his fury, he broke through a window in the living room, cutting and scraping his skin away from his arms and his knees as he climbed through the frame encrusted with glass fragments. He would not, he yelled to his wife, by God, be denied the right to see her, to see his child.

Penny had other ideas. While he ranted and raved, she called the constables and begged for help. She had not been informed of his release, and her busy schedule of work at the Havenwood estate—something that had to be done if she intended to raise a son on her own—college, and child rearing had left her frazzled enough that she never even thought about his immanent freedom.

Penny didn't hide herself away when her husband broke in. She was far too busy trying to make certain her son would be safe. Daniel saw her and screamed, barely recognizing himself in the voice that demanded to know where his child was.

Somewhere between the time he reached the house and the time he broke in, Daniel had decided that he must surely meet the source of his nightmares and face the little demon if he wanted to keep his sanity. It wasn't really a conscious thought on his part, but it was an imperative. It was almost an instinctive need.

He reached for Penny, part of his mind wanting to make everything right again, but that part was small. Most of his consciousness wanted to make sure that the child he should have been helping to raise never got the chance to reach maturity. It was, he felt in the core of his being, essential that his child never grow up.

He grabbed Penny, the woman he loved and had sworn to honor and protect, and tried beating the information from her. She managed to avoid his blows long enough to grab a pair of scissors.

The first cut she made on him hurt. It was a deep gash that ran across his right hand and let the bones of that hand see the light of day for the first time. The second cut was much, much worse, and drove him into a blind rage. He remembered nothing at all about what happened after that until he found himself in a strange house, a screaming, wailing child in his hands.

The toddler looked at him with wild, fearful eyes—the eyes of the woman he'd married. On a table in the living room of a house he'd never in his life entered, he saw his son for the first and last time. He had just long enough to see the heavy blade in his hand and look upon the wailing face of Lawrence Grey before the door leading to the room was broken open.

The man who looked at him from the opened door did not take the time to speak to Daniel. He did not take the time to try reasoning with the madman who threatened an infant with death. He merely pulled the trigger on his pistol four times and ended the threat.

The last face Daniel Grey ever saw belonged to a man he'd gone to school with. Constable William Karstens saw his duty and performed it to the best of his ability. In that moment he sealed both of their fates.

Daniel Grey died quickly with the knowledge that he had failed his loved ones foremost in his mind.

III

"Is there any chance I can get a different seat?"

The waitress was cute enough, despite her cigarette breath and the fact that most of her hair refused to stay in the ponytail she'd vainly tried to pull it back in. She was even friendly, but that didn't stop him from having trouble enjoying his meal.

The problem was the two kids in the booth behind him. They were in constant motion, in a bad mood, and ready to let the world know it. Loudly.

Jonathan Crowley couldn't say that he actually hated kids, but he certainly had no patience for them. They made noise and they whined. The really small ones he could forgive, but these two were getting on his last nerve. Mommy and Daddy Tourist were just sitting there, like the noise and angry shrieks of the their precious little waifs were perfectly normal. Maybe they were to them, but he personally had just about reached his limit.

One of the little darlings was pulling the hair of the other one, and calling his sister a "booger head." The little girl, understandably, was protesting this treatment by slapping at his hands. Crowley looked at the reflected family in the window as he felt the two kids slam against their side of the shared backrest for the thousandth time in the last twenty minutes. The parents looked only at their food—which they had gotten before him, despite the fact that he'd been waiting a good ten minutes before they arrived—as if afraid to catch the eyes of someone who might recognize them or in any way make the connection that they and the demon spawn in the seat facing theirs were related.

Jonathan Crowley looked over at the waitress expectantly, hoping beyond any hope that she might be able to move him to another table before things got ugly. She looked at him and shook her head sadly. "I'm sorry. We're full up. I could maybe get your food to go, if you wanted."

Crowley closed his eyes, reached calmly for his coffee, and took a sip before answering. "Maybe that would be for the best."

The coffee was an unexpected delight, just strong and warm enough to be pleasant. He drank another mouthful, or at least he tried to. Whatever the hell her brother was doing to her finally set the little girl off, and she went ballistic. Crowley heard the sound of the little girl screaming bloody murder and then the sound of tiny little hands slapping a tiny little face. This was immediately followed by the noises of the little boy at the table behind him changing from playful teasing to a squeal of pain, and Crowley felt something hit the back of his head. Hot coffee flowed past the place where his lips met the cup, washed up in a wave that filled his nostrils and spilled down his chin before splashing across his dress shirt and his jeans.

Crowley coughed as the brown ambrosia violated his sinuses and kicked past his gag reflex. He set the coffee down on the table and covered his mouth and nose with one hand while he automatically reached for his napkin. He closed his eyes against the tears that came with his fit of coughing and used the napkin to clear most of what he'd just spilled off his face.

The waitress looked horrified. The people at the closest tables looked surprised. The little darlings at the table behind him laughed, apparently very amused by the idea of him choking to death as a result of their escapades. Crowley opened his eyes and looked at the reflected angelic faces in the window beside him. Both of them were smiling and happy, all personal wars stopped for the moment. Their parents' reflected faces still looked down at their plates, still focused on the food in front of them with a passion most people normally reserved for their lovers.

Crowley set down his napkin and smiled at the waitress.

She flinched.

"Excuse me for a moment, won't you?"

She nodded vigorously in reply to his question, and he rose from his seat. Jonathan Crowley walked the foot and a half over to the booth behind his and looked at the two little darlings who were watching him with that same happily entertained expression on their round little faces. The girl had grape jelly in her hair, and the boy had enough spaghetti sauce around his mouth to make him look like an extra in a *Living Dead* movie. Their mother stopped feeding her face long enough to look in his direction skeptically.

Crowley looked at the little darlings and felt his smile grow even broader. "SIT DOWN AND SHUT UP!" His roar made half the people in the diner freeze where they were, but a few brave souls actually applauded, even as the man who seemingly couldn't stop eating finally managed to look his way. Both kids dropped like rocks, sitting on their asses and staying quiet.

Then Mom opened her mouth. "How dare you talk to my children that way?" She glared at him with an outraged expression on her flabby face.

"Are they yours?" Crowley's voice was soft and smooth, almost a purr.

"Yes, they are. Now why don't you go back to minding your own business."

Crowley leaned over the table, his hands moving carefully between spills of catsup and cola to find clean spots. His smile was back, and suddenly he was in a better mood. Confronting the terminally stupid always did that for him. The woman looked at him and continued to throw angry expressions in his direction. "They became my business the second they made enough noise to ruin my relaxing meal. I just didn't do anything about it until their disgusting behavior made me wear my coffee. Now, why don't you learn how to make the little darlings behave themselves, before I have to get nasty about it?"

"What do you mean?" Still she managed to sound offended, as if he was the one who had started this entire mess.

"I mean I'm trying to eat my meal in peace, and I don't need your brats kicking against the goddamn table to help me along in my meal."

The little girl covered her hands with her mouth, shocked by him. The little boy smiled and pointed. "Daddy! He said a dirty word."

Showing an amazing ability to not get involved on more than a perfunctory level, the father of the two youngsters sighed mightily and looked to his son. "Shut up, Arnie."

Arnie looked at his father as if he had grown a second head. "But Daddeeee. . . . !"

Crowley looked over at the kid and smiled. "Didn't I tell you to sit down and shut up already?" The kid looked at him and paled slightly. He looked down at his plate in a perfect imitation of his father.

Well, that was about as much as Mother was going to take. She threw her napkin from her lap and stood up to face Crowley. Her face couldn't have been redder if she'd actually chosen to paint it with the overly glossy lipstick she wore. "How *dare* you!"

"It's frighteningly easy, just at this moment, cupcake!"

The woman made no noise, but her mouth opened and closed repeatedly as she shook and trembled with suppressed fury. Crowley just smiled sweetly at her. "You probably don't even have children, do you?" Her voice sounded mildly triumphant, as if this logic had somehow managed to score a vicious blow to his side of the argument.

"No, I do not. But if I did, you may rest assured that they would be far better behaved than your little whelps."

Once again, the woman made fish faces, shocked beyond belief, apparently, by his sheer audacity. And once again, the idea simply made him smile. She was a rare one, too angry to be frightened by him. He rather liked the change of pace.

"You need to watch your mouth, mister." Her voice was low and threatening, her face a storm just ready to break. "You need to learn how to behave yourself."

"I'll take that under consideration. In the meantime, try teaching the same notion to your children, and you can avoid having any more conversations like this with other people who are trying to ignore them."

Well, that was pretty much the straw that broke the camel's back. The woman was not a fighter, had absolutely no finesse whatsoever, but she made up for it with the power of her swing. Had he still been standing in the same spot when her fist and all the weight behind it passed through the area where his head had been, Crowley had little doubt he'd have been spitting teeth. But Crowley had the good sense to step to the side, and that left the woman swinging at nothing and throwing herself off balance. Despite all her fury, she had all the grace of a drunken sailor in a stormy sea. She spun in a half circle and wound up managing to stand only because she caught herself on the edge of the table, where she promptly set her hands into the food her youngsters had used to refinish the linoleum.

Crowley laughed, finding the exhibit absolutely hilarious.

The woman's whole body heaved with a sigh of nearly biblical proportions. In the glass he saw her reflected face grow angrier and then almost serene.

"Bernie, if you don't teach this . . . this *animal* some manners, I swear you'll never have another night's peace as long as you live." Her reflected eyes glared darkly at the reflected face of the man who would not stop eating, and his reflected head shook sadly.

"Mister, why don't you apologize to my wife, before I have to get nasty about things?"

Crowley almost felt for the poor wretch. He was fairly certain that what he'd originally taken for embarrassment on Bernie's part was actually simple exhaustion, or perhaps even the loss of life force that was being drained by the woman turning slowly to gloat in his general direction.

"Gosh, Bernie," he said, his voice fairly dripping with sarcasm. "Much as I'd like to accommodate you on this one, I just can't. Here's a counteroffer: you take your lovely wife and your darling children and leave here, now, and I'll do my best to forget about this whole thing before it gets even more unpleasant." He put on his best rational-man-trying-to-keep-things-cool smile, but it didn't seem to have any effect.

Bernie stood up, and Mrs. Bernie smiled triumphantly, certain that the bad man who offended her children was going to get his ass kicked. Crowley backed up a step to give Bernie a fair chance. Behind him the manager of the diner was making nervous noises, and the waitress had joined him in the decidedly interesting sounds. Crowley couldn't decide if they were imitating sheep or speaking at seventy-two rpms in a thirty-three rpm world.

Crowley watched Bernie heave his considerable weight out of the booth, looking for all the world like a man who just desperately wanted to sleep for a few hours. They eyed each other—Bernie trying to decide the best way to handle the matter, and Crowley wondering if the other man's body was fat or meat under his road-weathered clothes—then Bernie stepped forward, his hands at his side and swung halfheartedly at Crowley's head with a hand the size of a ham hock.

Crowley ducked easily, very conscious of all the people watching them and the potential pitfalls of moving the wrong way. He could hook his foot on a chair, trip over someone's leg, or even inadvertently hurt one of the other diners whose meals had now been ruined.

"Bernie, don't make me do this. Think of how bad it's gonna look to your kids if I have to take you down."

"Mister, nothin' personal, but you don't look like you could handle a fight with a Chihuahua."

Crowley shook his head again, the smile broadening on his face as he ducked another slow, casual swing from Bernie. The man might be trouble if he was in a mood, but it was obvious he just wanted to finish his meal and be on his way. Bernie's wife started screaming for him to "Take that bastid down," and Bernie started getting a little more energetic in his efforts.

Crowley was doing fine until he saw the damned kids and their damned little faces. He was just having a ball right until he noticed both of them looking at their father with saucer-round eyes and trembling lips. He just knew they were going to start with the waterworks the second he laid into Bernie, and even though they both desperately needed a few lessons in etiquette, he didn't want to be the one to shatter their illusions about their father.

He just knew he was getting soft.

And then, to prove him right, Bernie socked him square in the jaw with a fist that proved the old boy still had plenty of meat under his cellulite. Crowley's head snapped back, and he felt the world tilt wildly on a brand-new axis. Then his knees went watery, and he landed on his rump on the tiled floor of the diner.

Even then he would have been willing to stop, but Bernie apparently liked the feeling of winning for a change of pace, and decided to punt John's head into the next county. He moved enough that he only saw stars instead of constellations when the man's boot connected with his skull.

John looked up and watched the three Bernies become one again. It was rather unsettling, all told.

Bernie towered over him, his face looking meaner than before. "You need to apologize to my wife and kids, mister."

"Not in this lifetime, Bernie. Nothing personal."

Bernie swung his foot in a wide, predictable arc that would likely have broken Crowley's jaw, and Crowley blocked it with both hands. Then he pushed hard and watched Bernie do a one-legged jig across the floor before it was his turn to fall down and go boom. In Bernie's case, falling down meant taking a table with him. Mrs. Bernie screamed bloody murder as her husband fell to the ground, and the small herd of people eating at the table he landed on added to the noise.

Crowley stood back up as Bernie grunted and rolled over, rising slowly to his feet. Any chance of a simple ending to the matter was destroyed by the creamed chipped beef dripping down from the back of Bernie's head. The man looked about ready to fight a rabid bear.

Crowley looked over at Bernie's wife and smiled. "If you love your husband, you'll make him stop now."

"You go to hell!"

The rational approach was not working, so Crowley did a spinning roundhouse kick into Bernie's jaw. Just before his foot would have disconnected said jaw from its natural resting place, he applied the brakes, leaving less than an inch between his penny loafer and Bernie's flesh. Bernie's eyes grew wide, and he looked at that foot where it stopped, feeling the wind from the aborted strike on his stubbled cheek. He watched it all the way back to the ground, and he felt his bladder fill up a bit more.

"This is your last warning, Bernie, me lad." Crowley smiled viciously, his eyes almost seeming to light up with their own devilish glare. "You got one free shot and a bonus kick to my head, and that's all you get. Make any more moves on me, and I'll hang your ass as a trophy."

Bernie looked at his wife and told her to shut her trap. She made fish faces again as he threw money on the table and all but dragged his kids from the diner.

Jonathan Crowley watched them climb into a Winnebago that had seen better days a decade in the past and then he sat down to wait for his meal. He ate with great enthusiasm and even flirted with the waitress before he'd finished eating. The day was looking just a little bit better, and he was glad of it. The end of his visit with Bernie's family almost made up for the throbbing in the back of his head.

Despite the wait, the food was worth devouring. He ate, he rested until his head was feeling more like a

head and less like a tree stump being assaulted by
woodpeckers, and then he got back on the narrow two-
lane road running between a seemingly endless stretch
of trees. Somewhere up north, and likely on the very
road he was driving, something unnatural with an attitude kept sending him messages and making threats. In
and of itself that would have been enough to make
Crowley head in that general direction. But whatever it
was claimed that they'd clashed in the past, and that
meant it was unfinished business as far as he was concerned. Little bothered Jonathan Crowley as much as
leaving matters unresolved. Every time he did, they
came back to bite him.

He was switching the stations on the radio—the one
decent station he'd found refused to stay clear, and the
white noise of the static was starting to annoy him—
when the Winnebago hit his car on the right rear quarter
panel. The Lamborghini almost screamed as the impact
crushed the smaller car and rocked the RV.

Crowley hissed and cursed and gripped the wheel
tightly, fighting to stay on the narrow road. Timing was
everything, and the bastard had struck well and hard just
as the road grew thinner and reached for the bridge over
one of the endless rivers in the region. Why they insisted
on making bridges narrower than the roads they met
with was one of the many things he knew he'd never
truly understand. He managed to actually get onto the
bridge without going over the side, but it was an effort.

Just to add insult to injury, the radio was playing a
disco song he'd deliberately pushed out of his memory
and bringing back hellish fashion statements that he'd
have sooner left in the deepest recesses of his mind.

He looked into the rearview mirror and saw—*Well, surprise, surprise*—his good friend Bernie behind the wheel of the massive camper heading his way again. Crowley scowled and gunned the engine of his car. It was like watching a rabbit on amphetamines blast passed a sloth on Quaaludes.

It would have all been over then and there, if not for the damned school bus.

There it was, big as day and twice as solid as an oak tree. A school bus. And what was climbing off of the school bus? Why, that would be little kids, around the ages of seven or eight. Five of them so far and more still climbing down from the interior of the dull orange behemoth. Off to the side of the road, he could see the parents standing around with looks ranging from boredom to anticipation.

Oh, but isn't that just too damned clichéd? It couldn't be a bus full of prisoners, oh no, that would be an easy choice. Instead it had to be kids . . .

Crowley slammed on the brakes. Traffic from the other direction was too heavy to slip through—they had all stopped for the bus, naturally—and there was no way to slip around the vehicles. To make matters worse, even if he cleared the bus itself, the little kids were all milling around and waiting for their parents to pick them up. Parents and children alike, each moving at a speed that made snails seem hyperactive. So Crowley slammed on the brakes and looked back again as the RV came toward him. Damn, it was big. Through eyes made wide by fear and a strong sense of self-preservation, he saw Bernie's face. Bernie had a look of gloating triumph scrawled across his features. Said features were beginning to smolder and blacken, leaving little doubt as to the source of Bernie's sudden need to turn his car into a pancake. Beside the possessed driver, Mrs. Bernie had her mouth opened in a wide, panicky scream that couldn't be heard through the barriers between them.

Crowley opened the door to his car and dove toward the asphalt. His landing was less than graceful, leaving him with a torn and bloodied palm and knocking his glasses away from his long face. Just beside him, the RV and his own vehicle collided with a sound not unlike thunder might make as it struck someone in the head. He saw Bernie's wife screaming still as the gas tank of his Lamborghini crumpled, sparked, and exploded just below her.

And then the shock wave kicked in as the fireball grew larger. Jonathan Crowley screamed loud and long as he was lifted by the explosion and thrown high into the air. His clothes were burning, his hair was aflame. He felt the skin on his own face blacken and catch fire. He felt his lungs begin to burn as he drew in a fiery breath to scream again, his mind giving way to pain and panic.

And then he felt nothing at all. The world went black as Jonathan Crowley's burning body struck the edge of the bridge's railing and bounced once before hitting the river below.

CHAPTER 13

I

Simon took three days off for good behavior. He walked around the cabin, cleaned, cooked, ate, and watched a lot of mindless television shows. He did anything and everything he could except work on the damned history of the town, because, frankly, he was trying to avoid what he had to write next.

When he was done making excuses, he sat down and wrote the story of what had happened to Amy Blake. He didn't check his notes; he didn't look over any paperwork. He just wrote. The worst part was that he wrote the complete truth about what had happened to her, and to the best of his knowledge he wrote it without ever having really learned the facts. He looked the papers over several times when he was finished and even threw them out and started from scratch. But the second time around he wrote the same words again.

"Damn it. That's just not possible. It can't be right."

He talked only to himself. He was used to that. He'd been the only person to respond to most of his comments ever since he decided to try his luck with being a recluse.

He settled down at one point and decided to read everything he'd written down. His eyes scanned the pages of manuscript, and his hands broke a sweat that marred the writing. In the end he realized that there was no way around it.

The words weren't the ones he remembered writing. No one else had been in his house, he was sure of that. Most of what he'd written had been facts and statistics, with a few suppositions thrown in. The first chapter of what he'd typed out was almost exactly what he remembered, but the rest of it? There was a lot there that he couldn't have possibly put down, because he hadn't found that sort of information in notes.

Somehow or another, he'd been writing somebody else's words. Worse still, there were indications in the writings that something was going to happen to Serenity Falls. Something big and dire and probably deadly.

Unless he'd suddenly developed psychic powers, the words he'd written about what was to come had to be somebody's idea of a joke. He didn't have ESP, and he even double-checked that notion by trying to see the future. He closed his eyes and thought hard about what might come to pass, but got nothing for his troubles except an achy brain. At no point did the winning numbers for the lottery appear in his head and likewise, he saw no visions of what the future would bring to his hometown.

Instead, he got a knock at the front door of his cabin. The noise was so unexpected that he almost pissed himself. One more incident like that, and he decided he'd have to invest in some *Depends*. He stood on slightly shaky legs and walked over to the door, opening it slowly and peering outside. The sun was up, and the day was nearly perfect. The man who stood on the other side of the door was a complete stranger to him.

He had a thin build, a dour face, and short hair that gleamed like tarnished silver. He looked more like a revivalist minister should than anything else.

"Can I help you?" Simon's tone was brusque, but considering the way he was feeling, it was the best he could do.

"Are you Simon MacGruder?"

"Yeah. I am. You have me at a disadvantage. Who are you?"

"My name is Albert Miles, and you have something that belongs to me."

He knew the name but couldn't for the life of him remember where he knew it from. It was familiar, to be sure, but there was no association coming with that knowledge.

"What do I have of yours, Mr. Miles?" Whatever the case, he knew he didn't like the man standing just outside of his front door.

"A history of this town." A very brief smile flashed across the man's lean face, replaced almost immediately by his previous glum expression. "Your hands did the writing, but the words were mine."

"I don't know what you're talking about." He spoke

the words but felt the lining of his stomach freeze. There was a certain element of truth to what Albert Miles told him; he could sense it.

"Nonsense. You've just finished reading the history of Serenity Falls. It is, I believe, exactly what you wanted to read. I felt I owed you at least that much."

Simon MacGruder looked at the stranger and felt that frost growing through the rest of his innards. He wanted to run, but his legs seemed to have forgotten how to move. "Mister, I think you better be leaving here, before I have to call the police."

"I can't do that. We have unfinished business, you and I." The cold gray eyes of the stranger looked into his own, and Simon MacGruder felt his bladder let go.

"Albert Miles . . . That isn't possible." Warmth ran down his thighs, and his heart was stuttering along fast enough to make him worry about a possible coronary incident.

"Oh, but it is. I assure you, Mr. MacGruder, that I am as real as you and likely to be in this world a good deal longer."

The man claiming to be Albert Miles walked past him and into his cabin as if he owned the place. "I used to have a house in this very spot, Simon. It wasn't as elaborate as yours, of course, but it was home."

"I'm going to call the police."

"No." The man looked around the room, barely even acknowledging Simon. "No, you most certainly are not. I have already planned today's activities, and dealing with the local law enforcement is not slated among them."

"What activities?"

Albert Miles looked over his shoulder, his eyes focusing on Simon again. "Well, for starters, there's your sacrifice."

"Excuse me?" His voice was a squeak.

"Your sacrifice, Simon. You are going to help me destroy this town."

"Mister, you're out of your fucking head."

"Probably. I've been known to go a little crazy from time to time."

Simon tried to move, tried to get his hands, his feet, even his damned head to shift or move or even just shake. Nothing happened.

Simon MacGruder was alive when Albert Miles came for him. His lips were pressed tightly together, and his body trembled as the sour-looking man pulled out a wickedly long blade and cut his clothes away. Simon tried to move, to scream, to do anything at all that might have saved him from death.

He failed.

Even his screams were muffled by the paralysis that sank deeply into his muscles and sealed his lips against most of the sounds that tried to escape him. Simon thought about what he'd written regarding Amy Blake—or what Albert Miles had written through him—and whimpered. He was conscious throughout the process.

God help him, he was even conscious for what happened to his body after he died. He felt every last bit of it. And in his mind, he screamed. But that was the only mercy Albert Miles afforded him.

II

Serenity Falls Part Thirteen: Amy

There are virtually no towns that exist in the United States where violent crime hasn't taken place. Serenity Falls differs from some but has much in common with others. Wherever there are people there is inevitably violence. One man looks at another's wife and feels that she should be his. How does he handle it? Sometimes with violence. One woman takes a beating at the hands of her husband and accepts it as just punishment for some previous sin, real or imagined, that she has done. It is only later that she tires of paying for that ethical breach again and again. It is only later that she puts an end to it. Not all that long ago it was considered virtually impossible for a man to rape his wife. What he took was his just reward for supporting her and protecting her. That he might be worse than what he allegedly defended against wasn't really an issue. That was simply the way it was.

There are endless shades to alter the perception of truths like these. Some are subtle, and some are bold. All of them are valid, and all of them are lies. The truth, it seems, is too often in the eyes of the beholder, and most of those who view these truths see something different.

Amanda Watson was born in Serenity and lived there her entire life. She was, by virtually all accounts, a good woman. She was also mostly happy. There were a few things that went wrong in her world and really, who among us can claim with complete honesty that every day we remember was without some small grievance? The important thing here is that she was mostly happy.

She was also patient with the man she decided to let into her world. A man she'd known only distantly for most of her life who suddenly caught her eye in a favorable way. In time and with patience, she managed to shape him into a better person than he had been, and even he would admit it was true. She took the often temperamental Michael Alan Blake and soothed the worst of the pains life had dealt to him. She calmed him and helped him refocus his energies into something a bit more creative than being a ruffian and a part-time bully. It wasn't the easiest task in the world, but she managed, and the rewards made it all worthwhile for her.

Eventually she and Mike married. She became Mike's Amy, rather than Amanda. And that, too, was good.

There were troubles, of course. Nothing major, but a few arguments now and then that kept the two newly-weds on their toes and avoided that illness capable of killing all but the strongest relationships: complacency. Mike referred to their disagreements as "just the right level of spice to keep everything new." Amy's terms were less colorful but along the same lines.

In a perfect world they would have been happy forever. In a perfect world there would never have been a situation that could make everything go wrong.

It has never been a perfect world.

There was an argument. A small thing, really. In the grander scheme of things, it was the sort of debate that would be easily forgiven later. But when she left the house she was angry, and she was hurt. Words had been said that left her feeling deeply wounded; never mind

what those words were, that is best left between a man
and his wife.

The roads in Serenity are not exactly dangerous.
They're well paved and well tended, and most of the time
they are litter free. But on that particular night, there
was debris on the road. One could almost guess that it
had been put there deliberately. Whatever the case, the
tires on Amy's little Protege were chopped into so much
confetti by the scrap metal on the asphalt, and though
she was a decent driver, she was not exactly a demoli-
tion derby driver. The car rolled over twice, and when it
stopped, she was only barely conscious. She wasn't in
any shape to make out the details of the man who pulled
her from the car, nor was she capable at that time of
fighting back.

Her attacker was deliberately brutal. There was no
part of her he did not misuse, and when he ran out of
ways to brutalize her with his own body, he resorted to a
knife. But he was very careful not to kill her. She would
have made for a boring palette if she were dead, and he
had much to say. The tools he used had been crafted
by his own hands from the bones of four young children
he'd murdered shortly after siring. They had been carefully protected over the years, because they were not
only the beginning of the curse but also the method by
which it could be brought to its conclusion.

With meticulous attention to every detail, he gently
pulled back layers of her skin and wrote what he had to,
making certain that each character was dried before he
moved on to the next. And through his work, Amy did
her best to scream. Keeping her quiet was easy in com-
parison to keeping her conscious, but he managed well

enough. He'd had years and years of practice. The ink he used to mark her flesh was precious indeed, having been made from the very metal that had once bound his wife as she burned. His own blood and that of his wife had served as the first sacrifice to the curse he placed. His four bastard children had been the second. The woman he used so brutally served as the final ingredient to make his revenge complete. It should be noted, however, that the man who actually did the deeds did not use his own body. He used the body of another, while he was physically in a different part of the world, planning and meticulously executing his plans for that place with the same sort of care he used in Serenity Falls. Arranging the debris was a small thing and easily accomplished.

Finding a body to use was even easier. Michael Blake was well into his fourth beer when Albert Miles possessed him. He found a certain humor in having the man kill his own wife, whether or not he was truly aware of what he did. When it was all said and done, he sent Mike back home to attend to his own affairs. He was careful to clean the man's body of all evidence of the crime. Mike became a sort of pet experiment. He wanted to watch how another man acted when faced with the same sort of dilemma he'd faced himself once upon a time in the same town.

After that, all he had to do was wait.

Curses could be fickle things.

Almost two years later to the day, the death of Amy Blake finally served its purpose.

And before the night was through, Serenity Falls learned what vengeance was all about.

III

Dr. Arnold Warrington walked through the intensive care unit with his eyes on his files and his mind on dealing with the flock of student doctors under his charge. It was a duty he enjoyed, going over rounds with the young doctors, but now and then he almost wished it wasn't so damned mundane. Frankly, though he felt for the patients, there was little about them that he found interesting aside from their injuries. Most of them remained unconscious either from their traumas or from the painkillers they received.

He really did prefer the excitement of the emergency room and the trauma ward, but these days he didn't always feel up to the long, grueling hours that the areas demanded. At fifty-seven years of age, he needed his sleep now and then. Sad but true, he was getting older.

The third room on the left was the closest thing he had to an exciting case these days. John Doe was definitely not the common patient. For one thing, they could find absolutely nothing about the man. His fingers were too badly burned for fingerprint identification, and all of the other leads the police claimed to have were absolutely useless.

The man was a mystery, and he rather liked that aspect of the case. For another thing, the man in the bed shouldn't have been alive at all. He'd suffered too many traumas to his system, enough so that there had been a great deal of debate as to whether or not they were doing him a favor keeping him alive. Between the burns, the lacerations, the head trauma, and the ruptured organs, most of the doctors had their doubts.

Still, he was a challenge, and Arnold Warrington had always loved a challenge. He wasn't conscious of the fact that his patient might not see things the same way or even that his reasons for keeping such a close eye on John Doe had to do with his fascination with medical anomalies. But they were factors just the same. The doctor smiled as he entered the room. He was looking forward to explaining about John Doe to his interns.

Still, he wished something would happen to spice the day up a bit. He looked at the mass of bandages and tubes that hid John Doe away and entered the room, setting his voice into the proper lecture mode.

John Doe watched in silence as the doctors came into the room. There was Dr. Ellis, Dr. Warrington, and three interns. He could see them even through the veil of cotton gauze that covered his face. Beside him, the heart monitor reminded the world that he was alive. Warrington came over to him and looked at the chart next to his bed.

Through the haze of painkillers pumping through his system, he heard the doctor talking to the group of younger doctors. He listened and did nothing else. He hurt too much to do anything else.

"This is John Doe number four. John came in after a rather nasty car wreck. An RV struck his car from behind, and he was the only survivor of the accident. A few people were there and saw the entire incident, and if they hadn't been around, John would very likely be dead."

He looked at the doctor and breathed heavily.

"John was actually out of his car when it happened. The witnesses say he was actually running from the car and would likely have been killed instantly if he'd stayed where he was. The patient has second- and third-degree burns over seventy-five percent of his body. His eyes were burned, and despite the best efforts of our surgeons, they couldn't be saved. All of his clothes were burned off him, leaving us with no identification to try to learn more about him. Unfortunately, the patient is also suffering from severe damage to the right front cranium. When he first came in, he was posturing, his limbs pulling hard to the right without his conscious effort. That's abated to a certain extent. His motor reflexes are almost nonexistent, and there is very little hope of him ever making a full recovery."

He listened to the words and tried to make sense of them. His eyes were burned? If that was the case, how was it he could see? His head ached, true enough, but he had felt up there earlier with his left hand and had felt no sort of cavity or bump under the bandages. How had they fixed his skull?

The doctor droned on about the damage he'd suffered. Broken wrist, shattered patella, damage to the lumbar and sacral portions of his vertebrae, ruptured left kidney, torn liver and ascending colon, and severe bruising to most of his remaining internal organs—most of which couldn't be worked on at the present time because the patient was considered too badly injured to risk surgery until he'd had a chance to stabilize. The man's voice was cold and efficient, reflecting what little he knew of the doctor.

The other doctors listened to every word, as if they

were hearing the most exciting news of their lives. He looked at each of them and wondered how long they'd been at the hospital. How long he'd been here. His thoughts were fuzzy, diffused by the endless drip of the chemicals going into his veins. Or maybe by the brain damage he'd allegedly suffered.

He tried to remember his name, and nothing came to him. It was annoying, and if he'd had the strength, he would have asked the doctor to shut the fuck up and let him concentrate.

". . . And so for the present time John Doe is effectively a ward of the state, meaning that your taxes and mine will go to paying his bills, and all we can do is hope that the man is strong enough to recover from his injuries . . ."

He just kept going; like the Energizer Bunny, the man would not shut up. It was really very frustrating. Just for a change of pace one of the younger doctors asked a question, but he couldn't quite make it out. His skin was itching madly, and the feeling was starting to go deeper into muscle and bone.

Warrington, the doctor standing next to him, made some sort of witty comment that got the rest of them laughing, and he could have screamed if the damned itching wasn't trying to drive him completely insane. God! Even his damn brain was itching now, an endlessly frustrating pain that kept going deeper and deeper like a wave of ravenous termites into wood, burrowing so far inside of him that he thought for sure his head would explode.

He was vaguely aware of voices calling out, the sounds of people talking in urgent tones. He felt his body moved and repositioned carefully as the heart monitor next to him went into overdrive and started beeping faster and faster.

He closed his eyes, wanting it all to go away. *No eyes . . . The damned fool doesn't know what he's talking about. I just closed them, didn't I?*

The itching got worse, and finally he screamed, the pain enough to make him move. His hands moved up, one grabbing at the suffocating bandages over his face, the other pulling the tube from his arm. The IV stand crashed on its side, the plastic bags that had been feeding into him spilling their contents on the floor as the tube fell from his grip. He rose from his bed on legs that felt about as firm as overcooked spaghetti noodles and pulled harder at the mesh of gauze over his head.

As the gauze peeled away from his face, taking a thick coat of burn ointment with it, he sucked in air greedily. There was another tube stopping him from breathing by forcing cold oxygen into his lungs. He pulled, ripping the obstacle away as he felt hands trying to force him back onto the bed.

Without giving any consideration to his actions, he lashed out, pushing one of the doctors away from him and then hitting the meaty orderly who'd apparently come in to restrain him.

The itching was starting to fade away, and as it muted into nonexistence, he felt his memories washing back to him, flotsam and jetsam for him to gather and study. He wasn't really sure, but he thought he'd been in this situation before. There was a serious feeling of déjà vu messing with his mind.

Jonathan Crowley grinned at the people around him,

his eyes moving from one to the next as he shook out the stiffness from two days in an ICU bed.

"I'm feeling much better now."

Dr. Warrington looked at him with eyes that refused to believe what they were seeing. "You . . ." He looked Crowley over, uncertain as to exactly when the lean man in front of him had managed to sneak in and take the place of the dying wreck he'd seen only a few hours ago. "Who are you?"

"John Doe number four." Crowley stepped forward, grinning widely, his eyes looking from one person to the next. Somebody in the room—or at least in the nearby vicinity was brimming over with unnatural influences. Without that, he'd likely have been lying in the bed behind him for the rest of his life. Without the trigger of the supernatural, he was just a normal man. Or at least that was what he liked to tell himself.

Just at that moment, he wasn't really sure exactly who or what he was beyond the name Crowley. He was still healing, and a lot of the past seemed fuzzier than he was used to. Bits and pieces of his life were there, floating around for him to examine, and he knew he'd piece them together again in the near future. But not just yet. He was about to be a little too busy for that.

His eyes settled on Dr. Ellis, and the man stepped back from him. Ellis's eyes were wide behind his glasses, and the skin on his forehead was sweating from nerves, all the way to the crown of his head where the hair had receded. "Listen, it's not that I don't appreciate the hospitality, but can you tell me where the hell I am?"

"Y-You're in the Northgate Memorial Hospital, Utica,

New York." The man got a sort of fuzzy look in his eyes, and Crowley knew he was telling the truth.

"And can you tell me how long I've been here?"

"Two days."

Crowley reached out and straightened the lapels on the man's coat. The good doctor looked up at him and flinched. "That's just swell, Doc. Thanks. Now, can you tell me where my clothes are?"

The orderly on the ground moaned, regaining consciousness slowly and painfully. Crowley looked away from the doctor long enough to determine that the man on the linoleum floor was not an immediate threat.

"Um, your clothes were burned away." He looked at Crowley and shook his head, having absolutely no desire to give the man anything that resembled bad information. "What wasn't burned was cut off of your body when you came in."

"I see." Crowley looked around at the other people in the room. "So . . . which one of you wants to loan me some pants and shoes?" No one volunteered, so he pointed to the one who was closest in size. "Tell you what, just the pants will be enough, but I have things to do and people to see. What say we work something out."

"I, I have surgical scrubs . . ."

"That'd be great, really." Crowley smiled and nodded his head. The man looked back, his eyes locked on the patient who shouldn't have been up and about, and he nodded in unison. "Why don't you go get them on, and then you can give me your clothes, okay?"

The man continued nodding as he left the room, and Crowley watched him go with an amused expression on his long face. "Well, that's settled. So, can one of you folks tell me where my car is?"

Dr. Warrington swallowed hard and looked at him. "I believe it's being held at the junkyard on Willow Way Avenue."

"Really?" Crowley frowned. "Not looking its best these days?"

"They couldn't tell where your car ended and the RV began."

"Well, I can't say that I'm thrilled with that notion, but there it is." He scanned the small crowd of doctors and looked at a woman who was frumpy and tired, but pretty in her own way. "Can I bother you for a lift to the junkyard?" His smile was warmer than usual, but he knew from past experience was just as intimidating to the people around him. The reaction to his smile was one of those little things he'd never quite understood. Still, as he looked into the woman's eyes, she nodded and said she'd give him a ride.

Fifteen minutes later, he thanked her for the lift and wished her a nice day. She returned the sentiment and started back toward the hospital, her face clouding over briefly as she seemed to wonder exactly why she was out near a part of town she likely never frequented under normal circumstances. Crowley smiled as she drove away. He could have told her that he was responsible for her sudden loss of memory, but that would have ruined the point of his taking her memories in the first place.

Whatever it was that had been with her had decided to stay around with him instead, and that was just fine. If it hadn't been snooping around, he wouldn't be up and moving. He could sense the thing, the energy of it as it moved near him, watching him and doing little else. He was better equipped to handle it than she was, and like as not it had been after him anyway. He focused more carefully on the entity and felt its malignance. It wanted him hurt and suffering and dying. The thought amused him. If it had left well enough alone, it would have had its way.

He looked at the hurricane fencing around the junk-yard and grimaced. Jonathan Crowley had never been a man who liked to get dirty, and if the rusted exterior of the dump was any indication of what he had to look forward to on the inside, he was going to hate the search for his car.

Still, he had to do what he had to do, and he was something of a sentimentalist in his own way. He entered what the locals euphemistically called a "Waste Reclamation Center" with his shoulders squared and a sour look on his face. In addition to the certain knowledge that something unnatural was moving in on him at its own speed, he had to contend with the stench of the place. *Not more than twenty or so years worth of soiled diapers in this dump, I'm sure,* he thought to himself. *And with my luck, I'll find the most disgusting of the lot in no time.*

If what he stepped in wasn't the worst of the lot, he didn't want to know. Despite the odors and funky piles of things best not identified, he eventually made it to what passed as an office in the landfill. The small mobile home was set on cinder blocks and had several cables running up to the telephone pole at the edge of the property. He seriously doubted the connections were legal, or if they were, the safety standards in the area were abysmal.

Crowley approached the front of the building and heard the sound of laughter from inside. It sounded like several people, all male, and rowdy. He allowed himself a very brief grin before he made himself sober up and walked through the door. The laughter stopped the moment he was in their view.

There were five men in the small room, crowded around the desk that was the centerpiece for the organized chaos inside. None of the five looked like they weighed in at less than 250 pounds, and he figured at least a third of that was flab. They were situated around a table, playing poker by the looks of it, and he understood immediately that these were not exactly hard-working men of means.

One of the men, the one behind the desk, looked at him and scowled. "Can I help you with somethin', buddy?"

"Hi there. I was in a car accident the other day. I understand you have my car here . . ." He kept his face calm and his voice light. He didn't really want any trouble, though he had little doubt he could handle it if it came his way.

The man scratched his chins for a second—there were at least three that Crowley could see, and he had no doubt a few more were hidden where the man's neck should have been. "We get a lot of cars here, buddy. What kind was it?"

"Lamborghini."

The man laughed phlegmily and so did his friends. "Oh yeah, buddy, I got your car. It's over in section nineteen, behind the crusher."

Crowley blinked slowly. "Behind the crusher? As in behind the thing that makes cars into cubes for recycling?" His voice was slightly less pleasant, but none of the idiots in the office seemed to notice.

The leader of the fat pack nodded, his face reddening from his laughter and pointed with one sausagelike finger toward the general area Crowley wanted. "Yeah, buddy . . . That's the very place. Your car got crushed yesterday."

"And was there a reason for your crushing my car?" Crowley's voice became a purr, and he allowed a slow smile to spread across his face.

And still none of them noticed. The empty bottles from Jim Beam and Jack Daniel's might have had something to do with their easygoing attitude, but Crowley suspected most of it came from the simple fact that the manager of the place was comfortable in the knowledge that he was king of the shit heap.

"Hey, I get 'em, and I crush 'em. There wasn't enough left to do anything else, buddy. The paperwork is all in place, and your insurance company owes you a car. What can I say?"

Crowley shook his head and made himself count to fifteen. Ten just wasn't going to cut it, and he was already in a bad mood. When he was done counting, he sighed. "Mind if I take a look-see?"

"You do your thing, pal. You go on and do your thing."

Crowley nodded his thanks and left the area before he felt the urge to act on the things he was already tempted to do to the man and his friends. He muttered under his breath, feeling more foul than he had in a long time. His mood changed for the worse when he saw what was left of his car and got darker still when he saw the remains of the RV. His car was, just as he'd expected, a cube. The RV was still in one piece, relatively speaking, but it was not any prettier to look at.

It would be a lie to say he'd liked the people in that RV. Jonathan Crowley rarely found anyone he liked. But, despite himself, he cared about them. The family that had been in the massive land yacht had been obnoxious, the mother rude and the father weak-willed, the kids spoiled to a degree he found reprehensible, but he'd never wished them any harm. Manners, yes, but not a flaming death or possession by a hostile spirit. He squinted against the glare from the sun as he looked at the ruins of the vehicle's front end and remembered all too clearly the look of terror on the mother's face as their worlds collided in a ball of fire and debris.

And he remembered the kids from the diner. Spoiled, yes, but also far too young to die the way they did. He didn't like kids, and he doubted he ever would, but still, they'd barely had a chance to live.

And whatever had killed them had been gunning for him. For one brief second he felt a flash of guilt. It was small, but it was there, and he hated it. He hadn't asked for any of this, had never wanted any part of it. But he was stuck with it just the same.

In the back of his mind he kept track of the thing that had followed him from the hospital. He still had no idea what it was or what it wanted. All he knew was that it hadn't done anything yet. That was fine. He wasn't much

in the mood for arguing with disembodied entities. He
had places to go, even if he didn't know exactly where
those places were as yet.

Crowley looked at the cube that had been his car for a
long, long time and grimaced. "Well? Are you planning
on sitting there all day? Or were you thinking you might
actually do something about your current condition?"

Not surprisingly, the crushed lump of metal made no
response.

"Fine. Be that way."

Crowley sulked for a few seconds, then turned and
started walking. It didn't take him long to reach the
trailer and office of the king of the shit heap. He opened
the door and slipped inside as the man behind the desk
started dealing cards again. The man started laughing
again when he saw Crowley, shaking his head apologet-
ically all the while.

"I salute your efficiency." Crowley moved in closer,
until he was standing between two of the chairs. "Now,
on to business. There were two suitcases in the car.
Would you have any idea what happened to them?"

"No, can't say as I recall."

Crowley leaned in closer, his face almost aching
from the smile that spread there. "That's not exactly the
answer I was hoping for. I'm a long ways from home,
and I need those suitcases. So I want you to think very,
very hard about this. Both of them are made of stainless
steel, and have big, fat locks on them. They're made for
withstanding bad things, like, say, my car being crushed
against a Winnebago. Now, have you seen them?"

The man leaned back in his seat, the liquor in his

system finally wearing off enough for him to really see Crowley and think about what was being asked. A few of the boys hanging in the office made grumbling sounds. Crowley ignored them.

"Yeah, I've seen 'em."

"And where would they be now?"

The man was sweating, his eyes locked on Crowley with a defiance that was almost amusing. It probably would have been funny in most cases, but right then Crowley wasn't feeling very humorous. His memories were still too fuzzy, and he was wearing someone else's clothes. These were not things that made him happy. "In my back room, locked up nice and tight."

"Well, sunshine, why don't we go get them?"

One of the boys sitting next to him rose from his seat, pushing the chair back across the floor as he stood. "Mikey. You want me to get rid of this loser?"

Crowley kept staring, looking deep into Mikey's eyes. Mikey shook his head. "No, Lou, that's all right. I'm just gonna get his suitcases for him. I'll be right back." If anyone noticed that Crowley's lips moved softly at the same time, in perfect sync with the manager of the dump, they didn't say anything.

Lou sat back down with a sigh that said he would have preferred a yes answer to his question. Mikey stood up and shifted his bulk around the desk, moving almost gracefully around the rest of his friends and heading into the back half of the trailer. Crowley followed him. They found the suitcases in a matter of minutes. Both were still sealed, but it wasn't for lack of trying on someone's part. Crowley unlocked them with ease, despite the lack of a key, and pulled out a spare pair of glasses, fresh clothes, and a second wallet.

Sometimes it paid to be prepared. He ignored Mikey completely while he changed into his own familiar threads. Mikey returned the favor, looking for all the world like a fat, sloppy mannequin. Despite the temptation, Crowley didn't change anything about the man while he had him in his grasp. He left the room and then the trailer five minutes later, burdened with his two suitcases.

Once in the junkyard proper, he set down his luggage, carefully avoiding diaper bombs.

"Now, what to do about money . . ." He looked around the junkyard for a moment, then back at the trailer where a fat man had screwed up his car in ways he hadn't thought possible. Slowly a grin spread across his plain face, and his eyes fairly shone with humor. "There's an idea."

When he'd taken care of business, he left the five men far more broke than when he entered. He had no idea where he was going, but he knew it was likely to take a good long while to get there at his current rate of speed.

He got lucky. Not five miles later, he found someone willing to give him a lift.

Jonathan Crowley settled into the passenger's seat and smiled as pleasantly as he could. The portly, half-bald man in the driver's seat nodded back a little nervously. "Where you headed?"

"North." He let his senses go and sought the trail he'd been following before he became flambé. "Yes. To the north, if you could."

"No particular town?"

Crowley smiled as he buckled himself into his seat. "I'll know it when I get there. After that, who can say?"

The man drove slowly and carefully. That was all right with Crowley. He'd had enough car accidents of late.